C0-DVR-940

LOCKED IN

THE LOCK AND KEY SOCIETY BOOK 2

LORI MATTHEWS

ABOUT THE BOOK

In the quaint town of Cedar Bluff Maine lies a mystery that even the most secure locks can't contain.

Flynn O'Connor, a top-tier operative from the Lock and Key Society, is dispatched to the enigmatic Everlasting Manor—a property whispered to be haunted. Guests report unsettling voices and inexplicable disappearances. While he's quick to dismiss ghostly tales as mere pranks, the grim discovery of a girl's body jolts him into action.

Harper Edwards, the town's fiery Deputy Mayor is convinced that the mansion hides more than just echoes of the past. She believes the manor holds clues to the girl's fate and she's determined to find out the truth.

Drawn together by a web of intrigue, Flynn and Harper must decrypt the manor's darkest secrets while fighting their own dangerous attraction. But as they dig deeper, they're about to realize that some doors, once opened, can never be closed again... Just how far will they go before the manor claims its next victim?

Locked In
Copyright © 2023 Lori Matthews
eBook License Notes:

You may not use, reproduce or transmit in any manner, any part of this book without written permission, except in the case of brief quotations used in critical articles and reviews, or in accordance with federal Fair Use laws. All rights are reserved.

This eBook is licensed for your personal enjoyment only; it may not be resold or given away to other people. If you would like to share this book with another person, please purchase an additional copy for each recipient. If you're reading this book and did not purchase it, or it was not purchased for your use only, please return to your eBook retailer and purchase your own copy. Thank you for respecting the hard work of this author.

Disclaimer: This is a work of fiction. Names, characters, places, and incidents are products of the author's imagination, or the author has used them fictitiously.

*For Paula Fiske Martel and
all my other fans out there.
I can't thank you enough.*

ACKNOWLEDGMENTS

A huge thank you to my editor and sister from another mister, Heidi Senesac. You are amazing. Another fantastic individual is my assistant, Sara Mallion. She makes everything so much easier, and I would be lost without her.

My fellow writers, Janna MacGregor, Stacey Wilk, Kimberley Ash and Tiara Inserto, are all truly amazing authors but even more, they're the friends who keep me grounded. Thank you, ladies, for always being there. My super supportive family also deserves a big thanks. They keep me laughing and make every day better.

And last but not least, to you the reader. Your emails and posts mean so much. Thank you.

CHAPTER ONE

Astrid Windsor wiped her sweaty palms on the skirt of her little black dress as she looked around the room. All her life she'd heard rumors that this house was haunted. But every year people came and stayed there. Grand parties were thrown with all kinds of celebrities attending. Even some of the TikTok Influencers she followed had stayed there. Now she was one of the insiders. No longer just a townie but an invited guest.

Heavy brocade curtains muted the howling wind, but rain lashed against the windows and there was a puddle growing at the base of one. Old houses were like that. Leaks and quirks came with the ghosts. That's what her father had said. He said they were lucky they didn't live in one of the old mansions on the beach. The upkeep would be astronomical.

But she wasn't glad. She'd always wanted to live in one. And now she was realizing her dream. A smile crept across her face, and she hugged herself. If only Audrey could see her now. Her best friend wouldn't believe it. They were due to go off to college this fall, but Astrid was going to have the best summer of her life here in Everlasting Manor.

She just knew it.

Wandering over to the bookshelves, she trailed her fingers along the dusty spines. She touched title after title about the historical witch trials of the area which was. not surprising with Salem located just down the interstate. The room, a library of sorts, was only lit by a single lamp in the far corner. Dark paneling on the wall made it hard to see, even for her teenaged eyes. She looked around for another floor lamp but there didn't seem to be one. A fact she found odd in a room this size.

In front of a fireplace, a leather sofa was flanked by two matching chairs. A rustic coffee table and matching end tables completed the seating area. In another corner, she spied a desk with a small lamp on top. She went over to it but hesitated before turning it on. He'd said to make herself at home. Surely turning on a lamp would be okay. After all, he'd promised her she would feel at home here for the summer.

Her stomach fluttered. Suddenly she didn't feel so good. The howl of the wind escalated and the light in the corner flickered. Her heart thudded in tempo with the rain lashing the windows. *What if the power went out?* She didn't have her cell phone. He'd taken it, quoting some regulation about them being forbidden in the mansion, but hadn't influencers posted pictures on TikTok of the interior of the house?

Her palms were sweaty once again, only this time it wasn't nervous excitement. Her breath quickened. *I wish Audrey was here.* She was the brave one. *She* wouldn't be scared. A loud banging sound came from the window, startling her and making her heartbeat surge. *Calm down. It's probably just a loose shutter.* Suddenly, she wished she was anywhere but here. She wanted to go home. It didn't matter what Audrey or anyone else would think. She longed for the familiar safety of her bedroom.

Her skin-tight dress and sky-high heels made it difficult to move quickly across the floor, but she reached the door and turned the knob. It wouldn't budge. Hand trembling, she tried again but it wouldn't give. Was it stuck? She rattled it. *God, she'd been locked in.*

Her breath shallowed as fright built at the base of her skull. *What was going on?* He'd said he'd be right back and now she was, for lack of a better word, a prisoner in the room.

She kicked the door and pounded on the wood, yelling for someone to help her. She stopped hitting the barrier and listened. No approaching footsteps, or shouted reassurances that someone would be there soon. Just the rain lashing the windows, and the boom of thunder. She tried again but still…nothing.

Tears rolled down her cheeks. What had she done? She went to the leaking window and tried to lift it, but it resisted her efforts. *Unlock it.* She flicked the lock, but it still wouldn't go up. Frustrated panic gnawed at her throat. She shuffled to the next one and tried again but it wouldn't budge either. Her teeth started chattering and her hands shook as she skimmed them along the window frames. Were they painted shut? How was she going to get out?

Looking around once again, she noticed the lamp on the desk. Hurrying across the room, she bent down and unplugged the small but weighty light and picked it up. She'd throw it through the window, clear out the glass and jump. She was only on the second floor. Surely, she would survive that fall.

She lifted the lamp, and someone grabbed her from behind.

"Where do you think you're going?"

Before she could scream a hand clamped around her throat cutting off her oxygen. "No, honey. I promised you fun and you shall have it. You wanted to belong and now you do."

Astrid tried to fight but the world shrunk to two small pin holes and the darkness closed. *This was all one big mistake.*

CHAPTER TWO

Harper Edwards stood off to the side, staring down into the hole where Astrid Windsor's body was partially uncovered. The teen's hair was still intact, but the rest of her body was badly decomposed. Despite the advanced decay, there was little doubt about the victim. The dress she was wearing the night she disappeared was in tatters around the corpse and then there was the necklace. A small gold heart locket that her parents had given her for high school graduation.

Harper wanted to scream at the injustice of it all. How would this have happened? Her heart broke for Astrid's family. For the whole town. This would rock everyone to their core. But mostly it broke for her niece Audrey, Astrid's best friend since kindergarten.

"Ms. Deputy Mayor," Detective Jason Merritt said as he came to a stop beside her on the bluff.

"What the hell happened?" she demanded.

He shrugged. "We don't know. A jogger running with her dog found her early this morning. She'd been following along the path on top of the bluff when the dog, a Jack Rat took off down here and started digging. He dug up her hand and ran off with a couple of the fingers. When his owner, Mrs. Barstow, caught up with him, she immediately called 911."

Harper wrapped her arms over her chest. A biting wind came off the Atlantic Ocean, but she was glad for it at the moment because if she was too cold she couldn't be ill. "What is a Jack Rat?

"Cross between a Jack Russell and a Rat Terrier. Goes by the name of Brutus"

She cocked an eyebrow. "Brutus?"

He grinned. "Apparently he's got quite the personality."

Oh, Lord. "Did they…" She shuddered to a stop. Never in her life did she think she'd have to ask if someone's body parts had been recovered.

"Yes, we got the fingers back. But it took a bit of doing," he admitted.

Her stomach rolled at the image that came to mind. "Any idea what killed her?"

The smile slid off his face. "Not yet. The medical examiner is on her way." He ran a hand through his sandy blond hair. "This is a tough one."

"Yes," she agreed. "The whole town is going to be upset. Tempers will flare for sure."

He turned toward her. "I know the chief is counting on her Honor the mayor to help diffuse the situation."

She made a non-committal noise. To put it mildly, Susan Duggan, the Mayor of Cedar Bluff, Maine, did not like Alvin Clark, the current police chief. The two fought like cats and dogs. No, Harper had seen cats and dogs get on way better than the mayor and police chief. "I'll do my best…But you know how she can be."

"Yeah, I know. But Harper, we need everyone on the same side on this one. Throwing stones at each other will not help all of us get through this."

He was not wrong. Cedar Bluff had a population of about ten thousand souls. Every one of them would closely follow this situation. Throwing the police under the bus wasn't going to help matters. It wasn't their fault they hadn't found Astrid.

Of course, suggesting Astrid had just run away had been stupid. Anyone who knew Astrid would have, and did, tell them that. Even Harper had known in her heart of hearts that Astrid must be dead when she hadn't shown up in the first twenty-four hours. It was too late for the police to do anything but search for her body, but the police had maintained it as a missing persons case. With no proof of foul play, they had to continue the motions of searching for her.

Astrid's disappearance had bothered everyone in Cedar Bluff. It was just so unlike her. The grim reality was that someone had killed one of their own. Harper cursed silently.

"Detective Merritt," a young guy in a suit called. He gestured toward the sky. "Do you think we should?"

Jason looked over at him. "Go ahead," and then turned back to Harper. "There's a storm coming in. We're gonna put a tent over the burial site to try and protect it."

"I didn't know you guys had tents for this type of thing." God only knew her boss would go ballistic when she found out. She complained bitterly about the police department budget on a regular basis. Emergency services ate up a huge percentage of the budget and Susan resented it.

"We don't. The tent belongs to me. I bought it for my sister Carly's wedding a few years ago. It's been sitting in my garage. With the storm coming I thought it might help."

"Good thinking," she agreed. She nodded toward the guy in the suit. "How's Lazlo working out?"

Jason sighed. "Good kid, but a little excitable."

Billy Lazlo was an overgrown Labrador retriever puppy. He was all flailing limbs and goofy grins. At six feet, five inches, he should have been great at sports, basketball, or football but he was also clumsy and, sadly, he seemed to lack a competitive nature. He must have felt Harper's eyes on him because he turned and gave her a wave and a smile. Not the most appropriate reaction while standing over a murder victim. His red hair flapped in the growing breeze while his big brown eyes focused on the mystery of how the tent pole worked.

"Lazlo is smarter than you think. Look, we're going to do everything we can on this, Harper." Jason's soft blue eyes were sad. "I just wanted you to know that. Please try and get your boss to see that. Her tendency to throw up roadblocks won't help anything."

Harper's phone vibrated and she looked at the screen. "I know, Jason. I've got to take this." She moved further down the path away from the commotion. "Hello?"

"Harper, what's going on out there? Do they know anything yet?" the mayor demanded.

"Other than it's obviously foul play, no. It is Astrid, though. I recognize the necklace." Bile rose and she swallowed to force it down.

"Are the press there yet?"

Harper turned back and studied the scene. She was standing on a bluff next to the ocean about a mile and a half down a local jogging path that followed the cliff. Around her were empty fields and a few stands of trees. It was hard to believe that her condo was about two miles down in the other direction. At the moment it seemed a world away.

She craned her neck but couldn't see the parking lot at the beginning of the path from where she was standing so she had no idea if the press had arrived yet, but they would. In droves, she had no doubt.

"I don't see them yet, but I'm sure they'll be here soon."

"I'm heading your way. We need to look like we're on top of this. The people of Cedar Bluff deserve the truth."

"Yes, but we need to be rational about this," she reminded her boss. "We can't go blaming the police department."

"Why not? They should have stopped this. They should have found Astrid before this happened."

Harper clamped her jaws together and drew in a deep breath. If her boss made that stupid of a statement in front of the cameras, she'd look like a hysterical female. "Susan," she started, "you can't say that on camera. No police department on earth could have found Astrid before she was officially missing. Just take a beat. I know you're stressed and there's a lot going on, but throwing Chief Clark under the bus will not help. We need the police to help keep people calm. They need to find out who did this so Astrid's family gets justice. Claiming the cops are idiots will just make it harder on Astrid's parents."

Susan didn't respond for a moment, but in the end, she acquiesced. "Fine. I can see what you're saying but Clark better not fuck this up or I'll have his head on a platter." She hung up.

Harper let out a long breath. Susan was a pain in her ass every day, all day, but she was also a damn good mayor. She'd brought new jobs and businesses to Cedar Bluff. New people were moving in every day. The plans Susan had put into place were revitalizing the town.

By the end of Harper's first week on the job, she realized her duties were more about keeping Susan in line than anything else. The mayor bulldozed everyone else, including her press secretary, so it was always up to Harper to keep the train moving in the right direction. Two years into Susan's four-year term and Harper was already running out of steam.

This was not going to be good for her, for the town and most especially, for Astrid's family.

As she watched Lazlo figure out the tent, she tried to marshal her thoughts. Jason Merritt was a good cop, and she knew he'd do his best to find whoever killed Astrid. She looked over at him. His sandy hair fluttered in the breeze. They'd gone out in a group a couple times after work. She knew he was interested but kept him at arm's length. Dating the top detective in the department would complicate her work life even more than it currently was.

Still, Jason was attractive and smart, always a winning combination, in her mind. Cedar Bluff was still small enough that there weren't a ton of options in the dating pool either. She could do a whole hell of a lot worse. Currently, however, he had to be freezing his ass off. His navy sports jacket and a light blue button-down with a pair of khakis were likely not useful in keeping warm. At least she had a black wrap over her suit jacket and she'd thought to put on tights under her slacks this morning.

Winter wasn't far off. The air had a bitter edge to it for the last week or so. Fair enough. It was late October. The cold, and this murder, were going to put a damper on Halloween. They were going to have to figure out something to make sure people came to the annual Halloween extravaganza in the square. She needed Chief Clark on her side on this one. He had to make people feel safe if the event was going to be the success she wanted it to be. The mayor had started it a few years ago and needed an easy win. Maybe if they billed it as an event to bring the town together?

"Her Honor?" Jason asked, gesturing to her phone.

She dropped the cell phone into her purse with a sigh. "Yes. I think she's on her way."

"So is Clark. Fingers crossed they keep their shit together."

Harper frowned. "Where's Detective Crawley?" She hadn't seen his bulky form at the crime scene anywhere.

Jason grimaced. "George is on a leave. He had to get a hernia operation last week. He'll be out for a little while longer."

"Oh no. Will you be on this all by yourself? With Lazlo too, but well you know what I mean." Harper could see trouble brewing a mile off. Susan would have a field day if Jason was the only one working the case.

"It's just me and Laz for now. If the chief thinks we need more help he'll bring in George." At Harper's glum expression, Jason sighed. "Don't worry. Lazlo is good. He's new but he will be a solid detective one day."

"One day..." Harper tried not to let the idea of Jason being the sole detective on the case get to her. She wanted this solved as quickly as possible.

"Besides, you know what George is like. The investigation will move faster with him out of commission."

She bit back a snort as she acknowledged the truth of Jason's statement. George Crawley had one speed; glacial. His plodding pace was known far and wide. Nothing seemed urgent when George was working a case. Jason was likely right; this would be better.

He looked over and nodded hello to the medical examiner as she arrived. "Hey, Mandy."

"Hey, Merritt."

He gestured to Harper. "This is Deputy Mayor Harper Edwards. Harper, this is Mandy Paulson."

The two women shook hands. "Sorry to meet you under these circumstances," Harper said. Then they all turned to watch as two uniformed officers put up the tent.

Mandy turned to Jason, "Who told them to do that?"

"I did. Storm is coming in."

"Good thinking. Let me get to it then. Hopefully, I will

be able to get something for you in the next day or two. The morgue is busy these days."

"I'm sorry to hear that," Harper said. The thought of all those people out there mourning someone made her heart heavy.

Mandy turned and studied her for a second before saying. "Thank you for saying that. In my job, it's easy to forget that more work means more loss to others."

Harper's cell buzzed again. She withdrew the device from her pocket and glanced at the screen. *Susan.* "It was nice to meet you, Mandy. Please keep me informed if you can. Astrid," she gestured toward the tent, "was a beloved member of the community." With that, she stepped away, answered the call, and moved down the bluff toward the parking lot, dread building in her stomach with every step.

CHAPTER THREE

"Maine? Why do I get all the best assignments?" Flynn O'Connor sighed as he took a sip of his beer. He hated small towns. And a small town in Maine was not somewhere he'd ever wanted to go. Growing up in Woodside Queens was just like a small town. The close-knit Irish community might be in the heart of bustling New York City, but that didn't stop everyone from always getting up in everyone else's business.

Not his thing. Not at all. He liked his anonymity.

"It could be worse," Sterling pointed out. "You could have to go to Lancaster, Pennsylvania with the Amish."

Flynn shot his team leader a dirty look.

"Does the Society even have a place there?" Cash Walker asked.

Ryker smiled. "We do. Flynn, you'd have to ride a horse."

Cash started to laugh. "Oh, I'd pay to see Flynn on a horse. He's such a city slicker, he wouldn't last an hour."

Flynn said, "And you would fit right in. All those animals." He let a wolfish smile loose on his face.

Rush snorted and almost spilled his beer. "Don't give Cash any ideas."

They were sitting at a table next to the pool at the Jasmine Door Resort in Miami. It was their catch-up meeting, as Ryker called it. The top operators of the security team for the Lock and Key Society. Ryker was their defacto boss mostly because no one else in their right mind wanted to deal directly with Archer Gray.

"Maine could be interesting." Cash grinned. "I hear the Society's house there is haunted."

Flynn cocked an eyebrow. "Seriously?"

"Yup. That's the word on the street," Cash said as he checked out a blonde who walked by wearing a tiny string bikini.

"It's true," Ryker agreed. "Some of the members have been complaining that they hear things at night. Voices when no one is there. Things have gone missing. Someone needs to go up and investigate." He pointed to Flynn. "You drew the short straw."

"I don't remember drawing any straw," he growled.

Ryker sighed. "Okay, I'm assigning you. Rush is busy in New York. Cash is looking after a few things in Italy. I'm flying out to Hong Kong."

"Maine isn't so bad," Rush added. "Get it sorted quickly and then come to New York. I could use your help."

Flynn took another sip of his beer. There were very few things about this job he did not like. It gave him purpose, money, and kept him busy. Every once in a while, though, he had to go somewhere he'd rather not be. Ryker was right. It could be worse, although it was freaking winter in Maine. "Fine. I'll get it done and then go to New York with Rush."

"Good." Ryker saluted him with his tumbler of bourbon.

"Anything I should know about the Maine gig? Other

than I'm there to investigate a haunting?" He sipped his own drink to keep from snorting.

"Eli Fisher is there."

"Jesus," Cash breathed.

Rush's beer bottle *clunked* on the table. "Fucking animal."

"Agreed," Ryker said. "But he's still a member. He's in Maine and rumor has it he's up to his old tricks. Archer instructed me to ask you to keep an eye on him. A close eye."

Ask him? More like *I'm telling you to do it. No fucking questions allowed.*

Flynn focused on what he knew about Eli Fisher. The scumbag was the lowest of the low. Human trafficker and rapist. "I'll be sure to keep on him," Flynn agreed.

Rush leaned forward, keeping his voice low. "If he breaks any rule, any single one, you take him out. Call if you want help. I'd love to be in on that."

"So would I," Cash added.

Ryker nodded. "We all would. Just make sure it's justified if you're going to go for it. He has to break a Society rule with the most severe consequence attached. Archer can't back you if you don't work within the rules."

"I think killing Fisher would be worth it," Rush growled.

Flynn clinked his beer bottle against Rush's. He was in full agreement. Taking out Eli Fisher was high on his bucket list. "Anything else, besides that lowlife?"

"Just the ghosts. Get it sorted and then get down to New York. You leave in an hour. The jet is waiting for you."

Flynn finished his beer. "You boys enjoy the sunshine. Think of me freezing my ass off in Maine." He stood.

"We're all leaving in the next couple of hours. You're not missing anything. Lots going on these days, and I don't see it stopping anytime soon." Ryker stood. "Watch your six," he said as they clasped hands and bumped shoulders.

"Always," Flynn replied and gave the rest of the guys a lax

salute. He admired the sights as he walked back toward the lobby. He liked Miami. The need for so little clothing mixed with all the pretty women made for great people-watching. Too bad Maine was so damn cold. The layers of clothing would make it hard to study the female form.

The landing was rough. Captain Griffey immediately apologized. "Sorry for the bumpy landing. Tough crosswind out there today. Storm's due to hit this evening. As you can see it's already started raining."

Shit. "No problem Captain. Thanks for getting me here so quickly." He stood and shook the man's hand. Then he walked down the stairs and immediately regretted not wearing a heavier jacket. He was going to have to do some shopping while he was here.

A Society SUV waited on the tarmac. A black BMW X5 was parked at the base of the stairs. Flynn got in and then hit the button for home on the GPS. The nav would take him to Everlasting Manor.

The manor was a recent addition to the Society's stable of retreats, resorts, and recreational facilities. The newly added residence might be the only one with ghosts.

He snorted. Ghosts. Seriously. He supposed he should look at it as a nice break from dealing with the growing criminal element within the Society.

Okay, that wasn't true. The criminal members were smart enough to not draw too much attention to their activities, and usually held true to the rules. The politicians and the businessmen were the major offenders. He'd found them all to be lowlife assholes. Abusive both mentally and often physically to those around them. Some of them were also rapists. Not to mention murderers, thieves, and the run-of-the-mill cheats. He enjoyed enforcing the rules when it came to these types. Rapists, in particular, were a scourge he had no trouble getting rid of. He knew the rest of the team felt the same way.

Eli Fisher was on the top of all their lists on that score. They all wanted a piece of him. Someday he'd screw up while they were watching. They all knew it. The only thing they could do until then was keep close tabs on him. The fact that he was here in Maine was a bonus. As far as Flynn was concerned. Maybe he'd have a reason to put him down. That brought a smile to his face. He could only hope.

He checked the GPS as he cruised up to the entrance. A realtor's sign had been jabbed into the grass at a fork in the driveway. For sale? That was odd. No one mentioned that. Pulling up to the gate, he showed his ID to the guard. Flynn hadn't met this man before, but he did work for the Society and technically they worked for the same department, albeit on different types of tasks. Flynn always made sure to acknowledge anyone who worked in security and treat them with respect. Never know when he'd need backup. Of course, he wasn't sure what kind of backup one needed when ghost hunting.

"Mr. O'Connor." The guard had emerged from the small, stone gatehouse. After studying the ID Flynn had presented, he stepped back until he was partially under an awning. "I was told to expect you. Welcome to Everlasting Manor."

Flynn glanced at the man's name tag over his left pocket. "Thank you, Mr. Wallford."

"Karl, please," the man said as he wiped rain out of his eyes. The small overhang on the guard shack wasn't doing much to protect him.

His close-cropped white hair wasn't stopping any of the rain from streaming down his craggy face. He looked like he'd spent a lot of time outside and his expanding middle said he was past his prime, but his blue eyes were bright and there was an intelligence behind them that Flynn didn't often see in a security guard.

"Flynn," he said offering his hand through the open window. "You look like this isn't your first rodeo. Military? Law enforcement?"

"Both. Was in the army and then spent thirty years with the Sheriff's department. This is my retirement. I just couldn't sit home and do nothing."

"I hear that," Flynn said. "I'm not much for sitting around myself. What's with the For Sale sign? No one mentioned the place is on the market." What a nightmare that could be. People would want to walk through it, which meant corralling all the members and making sure they were behaving themselves. Or temporarily closing the doors to members.

"That's for the property next door. We share a driveway at the bottom but it winds behind the Manor and then goes to the far side of it. The property is about forty acres. Been for sale for a while."

"Huh. No takers? How come?"

Karl took another step back until he was in the doorway to the gatehouse. He slicked water away from his shoulders as he explained, "Zoned for residential. Also, some sort of bird habitat so potential buyers can't do much with the shoreline. Cost a ton to put in any kind of jetty. People around here want ocean frontage they can use."

Made sense. He'd want to use it too. Staring out at the ocean wasn't his thing. He'd want to be in it. "So, know anything about ghosts?" he asked with a grin. "Apparently I'm here to investigate a haunting."

Karl didn't return his smile. "I've lived here my whole life and heard stories about the Manor that would curl your hair. My advice; take the rumors seriously."

Flynn studied the other man for a moment. "Thanks. I'll come find you if I need help. Sorry for getting you wet."

"Yes, sir. Not a problem," Karl stepped into the small building and hit a button. The gates slowly swung open. "Good luck."

Flynn waved as he rolled up his window and proceeded through. That was not the warmest of welcomes and it wasn't what he'd thought he'd hear from someone like Karl. Maybe Karl was right and he needed to take this much more seriously.

He drove along the paved driveway that wound through the trees and climbed slightly up hill. Eventually, the trees gave way to rolling lawns with Everlasting Manor perched at the very top of the bluff overlooking the Atlantic Ocean.

The house itself was huge but butt-ugly. It looked to Flynn like it started off in one style and somewhere along the way, another owner added on a wing in a completely different style. The end result was three stories tall, with lots of windows reflecting the stormy sky. He searched his brain, Victorian. Kind of. That was the look. A round turret on one side dominated the roofline. It was painted a maroon with black shutters. On the way up he'd noticed a more recent addition that was more of a rectangle and it protruded out the back forming an L with the rest of the building. The circular driveway framed a grassy area with a stone fountain with what looked like chubby angels in the middle. There was a turn off for a large parking area before entering the circle.

Flynn drove around the circle and parked the BMW to the side by a group of bushes. The spot was close enough to the door so he wouldn't get soaked and far enough out of the way so people could get by him. There was no way he was parking around back. The heavens had just opened and he would be drenched. He grabbed his stuff out of the SUV and bounded up the steps. He was soaked to the skin by the time he pushed open the front door. The door banged closed behind him, and he found himself on what he assumed was an expensive rug in the foyer.

"Mr. O'Connor," a tall elderly woman said as she entered the foyer from the back of the house. "Welcome to Everlasting Manor."

This must be Helen Carruthers. She ran the place or at least she was the overseer that answered to Archer. A place this size would have a few different department heads running it.

"Mrs. Carruthers. How are you?" He tried to keep his tone warm, but the woman put him in mind of an old nun, with her pinched lips, iron-gray hair, and frigid blue eyes. She gave the immediate impression she was disapproving of whatever was going on, including his visit.

Running a hand over her gray skirt she replied, "I am well." She gestured toward the stairs. "We've put you in the Seaview suite. If you'll follow me." She started up the long ornate wooden staircase. The carved spindles were beautiful and any other time, he would take a moment to admire the woodwork. He appreciated fine craftsmanship. Grabbing his bag he started up the stairs.

"I trust you have the appropriate clothing for this evening?"

"I'm sorry? This evening?" *Now what?* He wiped the water off his face with his hand.

"Yes. We are holding the first annual Halloween ball. Some will come in costumes of course but most will just use cocktail attire and a mask." She looked over her shoulder at him. "You do have something suitable, don't you?"

"Of course."

Fucking Sterling didn't bother to mention that part and the fucker knew. He had to know. He could have let Flynn wait one more day and miss it. Fly in Sunday morning and not have to deal but no. Here he was just in time for a ball. *Fuckin' hell.* Flynn hated attending these types of events. Not his usual scene, not being much of a jacket and tie guy.

"How is it that the Lock and Key Society is hosting an event? Hard to be secret if you invite the world in."

Reaching the top of the staircase, she turned and stared at him as he came to a stop beside her. "Here at Everlasting Manor, we interact with the local population much more than in most other Society locations. I would have thought Mr. Gray might have explained this to you." She sniffed. "To the outside world, we are known as the Rainy Day Club. A place where people can come and spend a few days golfing, or sightseeing, or just resting. Our Society members venture into town and attend local events. They are cautioned to watch what they say and only refer to this as "the club"."

"I see. And what happens when local people want to become members of the Rainy Day Club?" This was a dangerous move. The Society had purposely avoided being close to the public in the past.

"We refer them to our head offices in New York. The Rainy Day Club does indeed exist. Currently, our membership is full. I believe the wait list is several years long."

Flynn kept his lips tightly seamed to hold back the vulgarities he was gagging to release. Another damn thing he had to keep track of. Honestly, this is why he hated going to these little outposts. He liked sticking to the big busy locations like Miami where the Society had a hotel within a hotel. Or the members-only island in the Caribbean. New York was good, too. Several locations around the boroughs and no one asked any questions. Small town shit was going to trip him up. It always did.

Mrs. Carruthers turned and walked down the hallway. They were heading toward the newer section. The carpets here weren't quite as fancy and the paintings not quite as nice as the front part of the house. She stopped beside a door on the right. Gesturing to it, she said, "I'm sure you'll find everything you need. If not, please let me know." She held out a key to him. "Dinner will be a little earlier this evening. Six p.m. After that, hors d'oeuvres will be served during the party. The festivities start at seven-thirty."

"Thank you," he said.

She moved around him in the hallway and started to walk back. Pausing, she looked over her shoulder at him. "Do move your vehicle to the back as soon as possible." Then she moved on and disappeared around a corner.

Flynn ground his teeth and unlocked his door. No doubt working with her was going to be difficult. The room was larger and much more modern than he'd anticipated. There was a king-size bed and a nightstand against the one wall. The door next to the nightstand opened to a large bathroom with a huge walk-in shower. Room enough for at least two.

A flat-screen TV sat across from the bed on a dresser, and in front of the window was a wingback chair and a table. It was, like all Society locations, quite luxurious. He was sure the sheets had some huge thread count and the carpet was ultra-cushy. His feet sank into the thick fibers. It was the type of thing people paid through the nose for at high-end hotels. But he didn't understand the appeal.

He walked over to the window and admired the view. The driveway and then the Atlantic beyond on the right and the lawn and the trees dead ahead. It was a good space for him if he needed to keep an eye on the comings and goings of the guests.

The rain lashed the windows and the wind whistled as the storm picked up. Great night for a party. He sent a text to the head of security, Ravi Shah, and told him he'd be down in a few minutes. He needed to get the lay of the land so to speak before the party.

He glanced at the bedside clock; four-thirty. Just enough time to go down and get acclimated before dinner. Flynn glanced in the mirror and realized he looked rumpled. No wonder Mrs. Carruthers had looked down her nose at him. His shirt was wrinkled, and his dark jeans were damp. It would have to do for now. He'd change before the party.

Pocketing his room key, he walked back the way he'd come and descended to the foyer. He wanted to get the floor-plan of the ground floor in his head. He stood with his back to the doorway. To the left was a coat room and a little sitting area with a window over the drive. Further back past the stairs was an office.

There was a door at the back of the foyer that he assumed led to the new section. He started in that direction when Mrs. Carruthers appeared at his elbow.

"Is there something I can help you with?"

"No, thanks. Just learning my way around. What's behind that door?"

Her stare was frosty. "Two bathrooms, a room for watching television, a game room for cards, board games, and billiards, plus a bit of storage."

"I'll check them out later."

Leaving her and her chilly manner behind, he headed to the left of the staircase. The first room was a sitting room, filled on one side with several wing-back chairs positioned in front of windows. Each chair was flanked by a side table. The view was of the drive and the ocean beyond that. On the other side, plush sofas and coffee tables. A set of glass doors led to an outdoor deck. Those windows framed a large field rolling up to a tree line. The deck had some…he had to think of the word—Adirondack chairs. And the doors were

French doors. *Why the hell did they use so many place names when it came to decor?*

"Are you sure I can't help you?" Mrs. Carruthers hovered in the doorway.

"I am sure. I need to understand the layout of the house. The only way I can do that is if I walk around it."

She sighed. "I can give you a copy of the floor plan."

"That would be helpful." Mildly annoyed, Flynn strolled into the next room. It was the dining room. Each round table was surrounded by eight chairs. The house was much wider than it appeared from the outside because there were eight tables in the room and there was still a clear path through the middle with room to move around without bumping into chairs.

"I just said I would give you a floor plan. There is no need for you to skulk about the place..." her voice petered out as he turned and fixed a cold stare on the woman.

"I'm not sure what you're used to, but you need to check yourself." He walked right up to her, stopping just shy of her personal space. "What I do or where I do it is not your business. You will provide me with what I need because as long as I'm here, I'm in charge. If you have an issue with that, take it up with Archer Gray."

Her eyes widened. Fear lurked in their depths. *Good.* He wasn't big on leading by fear but nor was he going to be treated like he was less than. She needed to adapt her thinking and he was pretty sure he'd made the right impression to make that happen.

She trailed him at a respectful distance through the bar room into a kitchen with a little sitting room off of it. It would be bright and cheery on sunny days. It had sofas and tables and lots of plants. The kitchen was commercial grade.

He faced her and said, "Please send me the floor plan and a copy of the blueprints if you have them."

He walked past her and headed back to the foyer. He went around to the back of the staircase and found another set going down. The security room would be down here somewhere. He passed a billiard room on his right. Beyond that were doors that appeared to lead outside.

The first door on the left was the spa entrance. He knew from his site research that this place, unlike many of the larger locations, had no hospital. The spa was just that, a day spa, albeit a very nice one.

He walked by the spa without stopping. There were a few more doors. A wine and cigar room, a weight room, and a small library. But the last door in the corner had to be the one he was seeking. He tried the knob and pushed the door open only to come face to face with someone in a devil mask.

"Ahn!" the devil yelled and waved his arms.

Flynn's first instinct was to flatten the guy but instead he just gave the devil a cold stare.

"Oh shit," the devil said ripping off his mask to reveal a young, freckled face. "I'm sorry. I thought you were... someone else."

"Obviously." Flynn continued to stare.

The kid's face flushed. "Er, sorry." He blinked and had a hard time meeting Flynn's gaze.

Flynn sighed. "You gotta name?"

The young face flushed brighter red. "Um, yeah, I mean yes, sir. It's Donovan, sir. Donavan Wright. I work security here. That is, I am learning how to work security here. My father is the head of security." He glanced around and then stepped out of the way so Flynn could enter. It was a waiting room of sorts. The place where any guest could come to launch a complaint or look for a lost item or conduct any interaction with security.

Flynn spoke over his shoulder. "Is your father around?"

"He's down that way." The kid gestured to a hallway that ran off the back of the room.

"I'll find him, thanks." Flynn started to walk away.

"Er, sorry again," Donovan said.

Flynn turned. "How would you like to make it up to me?" He held out his SUV key. "Can you move my BMW around back? I left it parked in the front."

Donovan's eyes got big. "Ms. Carruthers won't like that." He took the key fob. "Happy to move it for you." He smiled and then hurried away. Flynn proceeded down the hallway in search of the head of security.

Ravi Shah was sitting at his desk in his office which was the last room on the right. He stood when Flynn knocked on his door.

"Mr. O'Connor, nice to meet you."

People knowing who he was without him introducing himself still freaked him out a bit. But he'd admit the automatic respect never got old. That was probably why Mrs. Carruthers bothered him so much.

Flynn walked in. "Mr. Shah." They shook and Flynn sat down in the visitor's seat across the desk from Shah.

"Sorry for the crap weather," Shah said.

Flynn shrugged. "Not unusual for this time of year, or so I'm told. Not a great night to throw a party, however."

Shah's lips curled into a sneer. "Yes."

"Not your idea, I take it." Flynn was glad to see that he and Shah were on the same wavelength when it came to the party.

"I think it's a horrible idea. Having non-members in here is a huge mistake."

"Who's idea was it?" He couldn't imagine Mrs. Carruthers thinking it was a great idea, not so much because of the members thing but because of the people in general. She would not want all those people messing up her space.

"Gina's."

"Who is Gina?"

Shah leaned back in his seat. "You've not met Gina yet? She's slipping. Usually, she's on the top step when anyone new shows up." He frowned. "Gina Ling is the… uh, membership manager."

"I thought that was Mrs. Carruthers' job."

"Mrs. Carruthers manages the operations but Gina specializes, I guess you'd say, in managing the members. She makes sure to supply anything they need that they may not feel completely comfortable asking Mrs. Carruthers for."

"Interesting," Flynn said. "I've never come across this type of situation anywhere else."

Shah shrugged slightly. "We're not the normal Society outpost. The members who come here are a little more…" Flynn stayed quiet while Shah tried to come up with a word that wasn't insulting to most members of the Society.

"They're more like regular tourists. Leaf peepers in the fall. Cross-country skiers in winter. People who just want some time out of the city. That sort of thing."

"So then why the need for Ms. Ling?"

Shah opened his mouth to speak when Donovan burst into the office. "Here are your keys, Mr. O'Connor."

Flynn turned to see the kid standing there soaking wet and making a puddle on the floor. He tried not to smile. "Thanks, Donovan. I appreciate it."

"No problem." He glanced at his father. "I'm going to head up and get some hot chocolate. Would you like anything, Dad? Mr. O'Connor?"

"I'm good," Flynn said.

"Me too," Shah agreed.

Donovan turned and left the office.

"Make sure you call your mother," Shah called after him.

"Tell her you'll be home late." Then he turned back to Flynn. "You must be wondering about Donovan."

"None of my business." And he meant it. He had enough of sticking his nose in people's private lives through his work at the Society. If he didn't have to know about it, he didn't want to know.

"I met and married Donovan's mother about eight years ago. He was ten then. His father died when he was five. He's called me Dad since the day my wife and I got back from our honeymoon. He's a great kid."

"Seems it." Flynn liked Ravi and Donovan. They came across as nice people, which made him wonder what the hell they were doing working for the Society. Not that everyone who worked for the Society wasn't nice. It was just not a place where good people spent a lot of time. Mostly people were like him. Willing to play fast and loose with laws and things of that ilk.

"Like I said," Shah repeated, "things are like that up here. I've worked in other Society locations. If Everlasting Manor was like that, I wouldn't let Donovan within twenty miles of the place. But here, well it's more like a luxury resort. Donovan doesn't know about Society business, and I keep him occupied with things that won't expose him to it." He frowned. "Or I did.

"In the last six months, we've had more of what I would consider regular Society members turning up. Gina showed up about five months ago. Archer Gray sent her after a few people complained that they didn't like Mrs. Carruthers' disapproving attitude."

Flynn understood that. She would make anyone feel bad no matter what they asked for. She was a very judgmental type or so she seemed. "So, in the last six months things have changed. Do you know why?"

Shah shook his head. "Not a clue. And to be honest, I

wish they would go back to the way they were. I think I'm going to make Donovan find another part-time job if things keep going like they are."

"And is that when the…" Flynn struggled to get the word 'hauntings' out. "Um…disturbances started?"

"No. Those are more recent. I'd say the last four months." He grinned. "I bet you never thought you'd be hunting ghosts, huh?"

Flynn shook his head. "Nope. Not once did that even enter my mind. Why don't you fill me in?"

CHAPTER FOUR

"Madam Mayor, who do you think is responsible for this?" a pushy reporter from Portland yelled over the crowd.

"I have no idea," Susan said. She stood under the picnic shelter in front of the trailhead, in a somber black sweater and pants that highlighted her steel-colored hair and dark eyes. "But we will use every resource possible to find out."

Chief Clark shifted beside her. He stood there in his uniform with a light police windbreaker over it. He appeared to be struggling for patience. Harper had known him a long time and knew his tolerance with the mayor was just about up. She was hogging the spotlight. So far, she'd behaved herself and not thrown any shade at him. But it was only a matter of time…a fact he was well aware of.

Susan held up her hands. "I'll turn it over to our police chief. I'm sure he has answers for your questions. At least he better." She looked at him and smiled, which was more like a baring of her teeth.

And there it was. Harper knew there was no way Chief Clark was getting away unscathed. And in a sense, fair enough. Susan had just been raked over the coals for the last ten minutes about how the crime rate had gone up during her tenure as mayor and questioned about why she'd trimmed down the police budget. Did she think there was a correlation between the two things?

As she stepped away from the microphones, Susan addressed Harper. "What do we know?" she demanded. Harper snapped open a large black umbrella and held it aloft over their heads as they started down the path. They ducked under the tape that a couple of the uniformed officers had put up to block off the path along the bluff.

"So far, not much. Jason is over there. He can fill you in on what they have."

"Is he that cute detective?" Susan asked as she moved quickly along the path.

Harper rolled her eyes which thankfully Susan couldn't see. The woman was a manizer. Was that a word? She'd dated most of the decent single men in Cedar Bluff who were over thirty-five and a few that were under. "Yes, he's the cute one." Before Susan could ask, she continued, "And yes, you look good."

Susan shot her a look but then smiled. "Can't blame a girl for wanting to look her best." She looked at her deputy mayor with narrowed eyes, and Harper braced herself. "You know, it wouldn't hurt to work on your appearance a bit. Then you might find a man."

"I don't want a man." They'd had the conversation more times than she could count. It came up whenever they had a glass of wine together after a long day at work. Susan just couldn't understand Harper's reluctance to start another relationship after the last one ended so spectacularly.

They were approaching the tent and Jason looked up. "Madam Mayor."

"Detective Merritt," Susan purred as she stepped under

the canvas covering. "Such a difficult situation." She touched his arm.

"Yes, it is." He shot the mayor a tight smile and then sent a panicked look over the top of her head toward Harper.

Harper turned away and stood still under the umbrella. She wasn't getting in the middle of that. Susan was in between men and as a woman in her mid-sixties with a self-described active libido, she was looking for companionship. On the prowl was more like it. *Rowrrrrr.* She was being catty. It was none of her business.

She walked down to the tent and glanced inside. Mandy was still there working on the body. She glanced up and Harper bit her lip.

Mandy frowned. "Did you know her?"

Harper nodded. "Yes, she was a close family friend."

"I'm sorry for your loss."

"Do you have any ideas on how she died?"

Mandy stopped what she was doing and stood up, stretching her back. "I can't determine an actual cause of death until I get her back to the morgue." She studied Harper for a second. "Off the record, she has a lot of broken bones. I can show you if you want."

Harper shook her head. She couldn't bring herself to get that close. It was hard enough to be here let alone get up close to Astrid's bones.

Mandy frowned. "It appears she was severely beaten. That may or may not be the thing that killed her."

Harper tried to force air into her lungs. She'd been hoping... She didn't know what she'd been hoping. A drug overdose, maybe? Something, anything not so traumatic and painful. She wanted to ask if Astrid had been sexually assaulted but she wasn't sure she wanted the answer. It would come out soon enough anyway.

Mandy seemed to sense her question. "I can't tell at this point and I'm not sure I will be able to even at the lab, but with a beating like this, I would be surprised if she wasn't raped too."

Harper swallowed and closed her eyes. The rain had temporarily lessened, and she let the steady drip on the umbrella center ground her. Maybe it was a blessing that Mandy couldn't confirm it. Astrid's father need not know that part.

She opened her eyes and cleared her throat. "Anything interesting or different about…"

Mandy shifted her weight. "See this right here?" She pointed to a part of Astrid's dress.

"The green bit?"

"Yes," Mandy agreed. "It's under her nails as well. Paint flecks. I thought it might have been car paint, like she'd been hit by a car, but that's not what the injuries look like. It's an odd shade of green."

"I see." Harper stared at the paint chip caught on the dress. Mandy was right it was an odd shade; one she knew very well. She remembered when her father had painted it on the walls in one of the rooms of Everlasting Manor all those years ago.

She backed away from the tent.

"You okay?" Jason stopped her retreat. "You look pale."

Harper wanted to tell him but something held her back. He'd think she was crazy. Her father had painted that room years ago. Jason would say it was thin at best and that she was just imagining things because she was upset. She needed to think about it more, so she gave him a tight smile. "It's just so upsetting."

He reached out and squeezed her arm. "Can you take the rest of the day off once you leave here?" Raindrops plopped on the top of his head and shoulders.

She shrugged. Originally, she planned to go to her sister's and see Audrey. But that paint made her change her mind.

"I'm leaving. Harper, walk me back." Susan said as she ducked back under the umbrella. "Jason, I look forward to hearing updates from you." She offered him another warm smile. Jason, for his part, gave her a cool nod.

Harper held the wooden handle aloft to protect them from the rain as they retraced their steps along the bluff. "Are you going to the party at Everlasting Manor tonight?"

"Yes, of course. I don't have a choice. So many of my supporters will be there. It's a good opportunity to check in with all of them and remind them why they supported me the first time around. I'll be running again in a couple years. It's never too soon to shepherd their support of me again."

"You don't think it's in poor taste?" she asked.

Susan huffed a bit. "Life goes on. I feel awful for Astrid and her family, and yours for that matter, but we can't stop living. There's work to be done and I'm hoping to corner a few donors tonight and get them to pony up to get certain projects underway."

"I see."

"It wouldn't hurt you to be seen there as well." Susan sent her a cold look. "If you want to be deputy mayor again, you need to be out there where people can see you. Even if you spend the whole evening saying how horrible Astrid's death is and how we're working closely with Chief Clark's office to find the killer. That's better than staying home where no one can see you or hear what we're doing."

She grimaced but let her shoulders drop. "I'll go."

"Good," Susan said. "And for God's sake find something decent to wear. None of that dowdy shit you usually wear."

They'd reached the trailhead. Susan strode into the picnic shelter and then faced the reporters again. She reiterated that it was a tragedy and that they would work very closely with the police to make sure the culprit was found. Then she was gone.

After throwing the umbrella into the back seat, Harper climbed behind the wheel of her SUV and headed home as well. She found the idea of going to the party repugnant. But, she knew on a deep level that she wouldn't be able to rest until she knew for sure if that green paint was still on the walls at the Manor. And if it was, well, it gave her a place to start looking. Because she knew with all the press around this, mistakes were going to be made in the investigation. How could they not?

The press would be looking for every snippet of information they could get and anyone who could provide a lead. Inevitably, there'd be a leak and then the finger pointing would start. With all that added stress, mistakes would happen. People were human. Except for the animal who did this. And Astrid deserved justice. She would do everything she could to ensure the girl got it.

"I'm coming to the party tonight," Harper declared over the phone to her friend, Dana Benoit.

"Oh, honey, are you sure you want to? It's been a hell of a day for you and your family."

She bit her lip. "It has and I'd call in sick to avoid it, but Susan insisted. And I can't blame her. A lot of her supporters will be present, and they need to see her out and doing things. She can stand there and tell them that she's going to make sure the chief does his job. If she stays home, then it looks bad."

Her friend snorted. "Susan wouldn't stay home if you paid her. She is not likely to miss a chance to hit on any single men."

"I know. I know. I keep telling her she needs to back off a bit. But you know Susan."

Dana sighed. "I do. She's a great mayor in lots of ways

but she'd be so much better if she could curb those cougar instincts."

Harper couldn't argue with that.

"Are you sure you want to go? Susan can live without you."

It was true but the green paint was going to haunt her. "Susan would be angry with me but the truth is I don't feel like sitting at home tonight." It was a half-truth. She wanted to be at her sister's.

"Okay then. What are you going to wear? I'm wearing my favorite blue cocktail dress and a blue mask. Do you have a mask? It's a Halloween party. You have to at least wear a mask."

"Shit. I didn't think of that." What the hell was she going to wear?

"I think I have a red mask from one of the Halloween parties last year. Just one of the kind that covers your eyes. I think it has a feather too. Do you have anything that will match that?"

"Hmmm. I don't think red is the right color for tonight. I have a dark purple dress. It's not ideal." The dress was quite sexy and she wasn't sure that was the look she wanted, but Susan didn't want her to look dowdy so it would have to do.

"The red mask might clash a bit but I don't think anyone will care. Do you want to ride with me and Derek?"

"No. Thanks, though. I'll drive myself. Easier to make an early getaway. With this storm predicted to get worse, I want to be home at a decent time."

"Okay. Let me know if you change your mind. See you tonight."

Harper disconnected the call as she pulled into her condo development. Two minutes later, she dashed through the rain and unlocked her front door. It had been messy on the bluff and she kicked off her shoes before entering her home. Dropping her keys and purse on the counter, she hung up her coat. A generous glass of wine would take the chill off. The idea of food wasn't appealing and instead she poured a robust red into a goblet and took it to the window to stare out at the Atlantic Ocean from behind her balcony doors.

As she sipped her wine, she reflected on how lucky she'd been three years ago, when this place had come up for sale. The two-bedroom condo right on the bluff overlooking the Atlantic was perfect for her. It was also expensive, but she's managed it and now she couldn't imagine being anywhere else. The view and the sound of the waves hitting the rocks were the two things that got her through the worst times in her life. It was hard to believe Astrid had been buried just a couple of miles down from her. And now she would go a few miles more and attend a party. It was all so surreal.

There was talk about building more condos along the bluff somewhere and adding tennis and pickleball courts, and a pool. Rumor around city hall was there was a bid to make the next set of condos a fifty-five-plus community. Someone else said no it was supposed to be some kind of private club that was super hard to get membership in. Nothing had come across her desk yet and Susan hadn't mentioned it.

There weren't many places left with enough space for those types of things. Susan had changed the zoning on a lot of the bluff property to stop overdevelopment and preserve local wildlife. It was how she got elected. Harper was glad she got her condo before all that happened. She'd never be able to afford those types of amenities.

Her mind went back to Astrid. It was so horrible. That Everlasting Manor was involved was not so surprising. The Rainy Day Club had hit Harper the wrong way from the beginning. The members came to town and mostly kept to themselves. The members didn't seem to interact with the locals other than to play tourist. Fair enough. But the fact that no one, not even Susan, could become a member? That was weird. The woman, Mrs. Carruthers, gave some song and dance about talking to the membership people in New York. Except the people in New York said there were no vacancies and there was a waiting list to join. It would be years before Susan's name would come up and then of course, there were rules about sponsorship and all kinds of stuff.

Bullshit. All of it. As far as Harper could tell. Her instincts said there was more going on up there at the Manor than anyone wanted to admit. The problem was the new woman, Ms. Ling, blew so much smoke up Susan's ass, Harper was surprised wisps weren't coming out her ears. Susan wouldn't hear any criticism of the Rainy Day Club and she certainly wouldn't ask them any hard questions.

And now Harper was pretty sure Astrid had been in the Manor before she died. The green paint was indelible in her memory because her father had painted the place and then brought the extra paint home and painted one wall in her bedroom the deep green. Harper had grown up with it. That's how she recognized the green. She'd painted over it when her folks sold the house she'd grown up in and bought themselves a one-story bungalow.

Her cell pinged and she swore as she checked the display. Susan was asking when she would arrive at the party. She grimaced. *Not late enough.* She needed to get her ass in gear. First though, she had to call her sister.

"Marnie," Harper said in a quiet voice. "How is everyone doing?"

"Harper, it's just awful. I mean we knew it was coming. None of us believed Astrid had run off but still, it's such a shock. Audrey is just crushed. I'm driving down to Boston to see her. I've asked the university and they've said she can take some time if she needs to, but she doesn't want to come home. At least not at the moment. She says everywhere she'll go she'll see Astrid or have a memory of the two of them together."

"Oh, Marnie. I wish there was something I could do. Astrid's father must be devastated."

"Paul's not doing so well. His sister Nancy is staying with him. First they lost Patti and now he's lost Astrid. I suppose it's a blessing that Patti went before all this happened. She suffered enough with cancer."

Harper stared out the window through the rain. "I'll call Nancy and maybe send her some food from Grace's Lunch Spot. I know Paul loves that place."

"That's a good idea," she agreed. "Bob and I are heading down to Boston tomorrow first thing. I'll let you know how it goes."

"Give Audrey a big hug for me and keep in touch."

"Will do. Love you," her sister rang off.

Harper swallowed a big gulp of wine and then put her glass in the kitchen sink. Time to haul ass. Ten minutes later, warm and pink from the shower, she stood in front of her closet and stared. Susan had said nothing dowdy which meant no pantsuits.

She pulled out a soft blue dress but it was too summery and wasn't appropriate for a Maine fall. She put it back and pulled out a brown one but one look and she knew Susan would call it dowdy and in fact, she would be correct.

She'd been right earlier; she would have to wear the dark purple one. She had a large selection of black clothing from her time with the Mayor's office in New York. Black was the staple that every New Yorker wore but sadly none of the little black dresses she had would work for tonight. The purple was sexy enough but the black ones were way over the top.

After a glance at her bedside clock, she swore. She shook off her robe and pulled on sheer nylons. Then she slid into her dress. It was short, mid-thigh and it hugged every curve.

She'd been thrilled when she bought it. The perfect going-out dress. It was less perfect now although it still fit like a glove and clung in all the right places.

She grimaced as she looked in the mirror. Not what she wanted to wear, but whatever. She'd pulled her dark hair back in a messy bun and let a few tendrils escape. Then she put on some dangly earrings and a bit of makeup and called it good enough.

Pulling on her over-the-knee boots, her one concession to the weather, she gritted her teeth and hoped that Susan was grateful for all this effort she was putting in, but knowing Susan, that was highly unlikely.

Fifteen minutes later she was pulling up to the doors of Everlasting Manor. There was a valet, thank God, and several young men standing around with umbrellas. The valet opened her door while one of the young men held a black umbrella over her head. "Sorry about the rain," he said with a good-natured smile.

"Perfect night for a Halloween party," she said as they climbed the stairs.

He waited until she was inside before stepping back again. She offered him her thanks, but he was already going back down the stairs to help the next guest.

"And you are?" a woman's voice said.

She turned and made eye contact with the young woman holding what appeared to be a guest list. So they were running a tight ship. No party crashers allowed. *Interesting.* The young woman had a smile pasted in place and waited expectantly. "Your name please?" she asked again.

Harper pegged her for no more than early twenties. Her blond hair curled over her shoulders, and she wore a strapless, black, body-hugging short dress with dark stockings, not unlike the outfit Harper was wearing but she'd paired hers with sky-high heels. She was about Harper's height, five feet six inches in the heels so she had to be just a little thing without them.

"Harper Edwards."

The young woman glanced down at the clipboard. "Um, I'm sorry but I don't see your name on the list." She glanced up again at Harper. "Do you have your invitation with you?"

"No, I didn't bring it," Harper said as she kept a tight smile in place.

"Well then, I'm sorry but you'll have to step aside. There are other guests waiting."

Harper clutched her small evening bag tightly. This was the last place she wanted to be and yet she had to fight to get in. It would be too humiliating to call Susan and have her come to the door. "I think you should check again. I'm Deputy Mayor Harper Edwards." She refused to glance behind her and see who was waiting. This was humiliating enough. She was always in Susan's shadow and normally she didn't mind, but this was just pissing her off.

"I'm sorry, I don't see—"

"Ms. Edwards," Gina Ling greeted as she approached through the foyer. "Wonderful to see you. Thank you so much for coming." She was dressed as a …something sparkly with wings, a fairy perhaps? And she practically elbowed the young woman with the guest list out of the way and brought Harper inside, hooking her arm through Harper's. "I'm so sorry about your niece's friend. It's just tragic." Gina never missed a beat. Not ever.

"Yes, it is."

Gina smiled at her. "It makes your presence so much more meaningful. Thank you for joining us." They stopped next to the young lady who was taking coats. She was dressed identically to the one with the guest list. "Payton will take your coat. Did you bring a mask?"

"No, but I believe my friend is here and has one for me," she said as she shrugged out of her coat and handed it over.

"Well why don't you use one of these until you find your friend." Gina handed her a black half-mask that covered her eyes.

"Thank you." She fastened the strings around her head.

"There now. Have a wonderful evening." Gina said and then sailed across the foyer toward the door again, her wings flapping behind her.

Harper smoothed out her dress and took a look around. A few people lingered in the area, but the majority of the crowd had moved into the room on the left. She glanced up the stairs. That's where she needed to go but it would have to wait. Too many people mingling by the door for her to climb the steps unnoticed. Once more people arrived, she could sneak up the stairs. Gina Ling needed to be otherwise occupied for sure. That woman had eyes like a hawk.

Harper walked across into the room and moved through the crowd, coming to a stop in front of the bar. "What can I get for you?" the bartender asked.

"Hey, Dave. Just a tonic water for me."

"Harper, is that you?"

She smiled. "Yes. How are things? How's Maggie?"

"Great. The school year is going well. We both have good classes this year."

"That's wonderful. Are you still teaching fifth grade?"

He put her drink in front of her. "Yes. Maggie's teaching kindergarten this year for a change."

"Nice. Well good luck with the crowd tonight," she said as she picked up her drink and then wandered away. She stood off to the side and watched the attendees. Susan was in the far corner and although she needed to say hello to her, she just didn't feel like it.

The room itself was done up nicely. Jack O' lanterns had

been used for centerpieces on all the tables, fake candles inside of course, along with black and orange tablecloths. Fake cobwebs shrouded the corners of the room and someone had added a couple of large spiders on the wall. Wafts of smoke rose from a big bowl of green punch at the end of the table. Assorted snacks were arranged on platters surrounding the bowl. Waitstaff dressed as witches and wizards mingled with the crowd, holding trays of offerings.

Several people greeted her, then she got dragged into a discussion about storm drains by one of the town councilors. She waved at Susan and got a nod in return. The mayor's arm was linked with a man Harper didn't recognize.

"There you are!" Dana wrapped her in a hug. "I brought your mask," she said waving it in the air, the red feather dancing. "You look divine." She took a step back. "That's a serious dress. How come you don't wear that more often?"

"Seems a bit upscale for Applebee's," Harper retorted.

Dana snorted. "True."

"I think I'll keep the black mask. I can blend in a bit more."

Her friend smiled. "Suit yourself but you're not successfully blending in with that outfit."

"Neither are you." Her friend was wearing a form-fitting red dress that displayed her ample cleavage. The black cape around her shoulders had a red satin lining. She had painted her face white and put fake blood drops on her chin. "You make a pretty sexy vampire."

"Thanks," Dana said with a laugh. "Derek didn't dress up of course. He says one vampire is enough. Between you, me, and the rest of the world, I think he looks damn good just as he is." Her friend looked over at her husband and Harper followed her gaze. Derek Covington stood with a circle of men at the far side of the room. Tall and handsome in a very conventional kind of way. Dana was over the moon about him and, more importantly, Derek was madly in love with her. They were the perfect couple.

Harper shifted her mask. The room was sweltering and the damn thing was itchy. Gina Ling had moved to the center of the room and tapped a knife on a crystal glass to get everyone's attention.

Harper decided it was now or never. "Do me a favor and take notes. I'm going to have a wander." She winked at her friend. "If anyone comes looking for me, I'm in the restroom. But text me and let me know."

Dana giggled. "A wander? Not sure that's a great idea in this creepy place, but I've got your back."

Harper strolled back to the foyer as if looking for some cooler air, she looked around. The coat check girl and the one with the list were chatting with the valet and the boy with the umbrella. Everyone else was in the salon listening to Gina's speech. No one was paying attention to Harper.

She took a deep breath and then quickly went up the stairs, her heart pounding. She expected someone to yell stop at any moment. Reaching the top, she turned and moved to the opposite wall so no one could see her from below. There was another staircase leading to an upper floor. Should she start at the top? The option was logical but somehow, she didn't think she'd have a solid reason to be on the third floor. She could always say she came up to the second floor to find a bathroom. She might get away with that ruse, but no one would buy that excuse for being on the third floor.

Looking left then right, she decided to start at the front of the house and then work her way down the hall. Standing at the foot of the stairs to the third floor, she tried the door to her left. It was locked. She went across the hall and tried the one directly opposite. The door opened but the room was dark. She quickly dug out her cell phone and turned on the flashlight. She didn't want to risk turning on the overhead light. The walls were a pale yellow. It looked like some kind of sitting room.

She backed out and shut the door again. Moving down the hallway, she tried the next door. Also locked. At this rate, she'd never find the green paint. *If it still existed.* She tried the next door and it opened. She hit her flashlight again but heard voices coming down the hallway. She closed the door behind her and leaned on it. Should she risk turning on the light? Then at least she'd look like she belonged. If someone opened the door and she was standing there in the dark, they'd know she was up to no good.

"I know what you're saying but we need to rethink how we play this," a voice said. "We're going to need local help to make this happen." There was a pause. He must be talking on the phone. *Oh my God, what if he's looking for a room to take the call in?*

"Possibly, but as I said, Davis, local help is going to be necessary. Circumstances aren't what we hoped in this location." The voice paused right outside the door.

Did she flick on the light? Try to lock the door? Shit, she sucked at this. *Note to self, don't take up a life of crime. It would be a short-lived career.* She held her breath. *Please go away.*

"I have to get back to the party before anyone notices I'm gone. Think about what I said. We'll talk soon." The voice died out.

Harper put her ear to the door and listened. Nothing. She was pretty sure the man had left but she wasn't about to open the door to check. Instead, she groped the wall until she found a light switch. Made more sense to be discovered with the light on.

She flicked the switch and a single floor lamp in the corner of the room lit up. She blinked in the sudden light. Then all her breath whooshed out of her lungs. This was it.

The room was the green she remembered. The green that was under Astrid's fingernails and on her dress. Astrid had been here.

Harper stared. Where the hell did she start looking for evidence? The room was a library. The walls were covered in dark wood bookshelves. An ornate wooden desk was by the wall on the left and some chairs with a small table between them were on the right. The windows were large and would flood the room with light during the day. Lightning flashed outside, scaring her. Where would Astrid scratch the green paint if this was the only green room? What if there were more? She couldn't think about that now. She looked all around the door. Nothing.

She crossed the room and went to the first window. If Astrid was clawing at the paint, then she was probably trying to get out. That thought made her stomach turn and she swayed on her feet. Closing her eyes for a second to regain her equilibrium, she clutched at the windowsill to keep her balance.

"What are you doing in here?"

CHAPTER FIVE

The woman clutching the windowsill jumped and put a hand up to her chest as she turned toward him. She was wearing one of those stupid black half-masks so he couldn't make out her face but he could definitely see the rest of her, and damn if she wasn't a walking wet dream. Her dress was deep purple, and the fabric kissed every curve. One of those, what was it called…bandage dresses, stopping mid-thigh. The tops of her breasts were exposed in the deep vee of the neckline. As he approached, her hazel eyes appeared startled behind the mask.

"What are you doing in here?" he asked again. He came to a stop beside her. Her scent wafted up to him and a sudden wave of lust caught him off guard. He stared down at her. Energy charged off her and he felt an immediate pull in his groin. Excitement danced across his skin.

"I—I was just looking out the window when the lightning hit. It scared the life out of me."

Her voice was low and sexy but he was having trouble concentrating on what she was saying. "Lightning?" Just then the sky lit up and the crash that followed was so loud, the house shook.

"Oh." She jumped and swayed.

He slid an arm around her to steady her.

She rested a hand on his chest. "It's getting bad out there."

Touching her had been a mistake. It took everything he had not to curl his arm around her waist and draw her against him. What the fuck was wrong with him?

He dropped his arm and stepped back. "It does seem to be getting worse."

Of all the inane shit to say. *Jesus.* This woman had fully thrown him off his game. The electricity between them rivaled the storm. He'd never felt the pull to a woman so strongly before. It was as if…his Irish mother would say it was as if they knew each other in a past life. He gave a mental snort. Too much talk of haunted houses and this close to Halloween. He was letting it get to him. He didn't know this woman. They'd never met before. He didn't forget a face or especially a figure like that. But she seemed so damn familiar somehow. His mother was laughing at him from wherever she was. He could feel it. She'd always said out of all her seven children he was the only one with her gift. *Gift for trouble was more like it.*

"I think it's probably time for me to go." She offered him a small smile and moved to step away when he shifted his weight to block her exit.

"Maybe not just yet. I think you should tell me what you were doing in here first." He had her backed against the window. He wasn't touching her, but he was close enough for the energy to arc off her skin to his. And close enough that the sound of her quickened breathing reached him.

"Um, like I said, the lightning startled me." Her eyes widened behind the mask.

"You're not telling me what you are doing in here. You're not a member, are you?" There's no way he'd miss it if her picture had crossed his email. He got headshots of all the new Lock and Key Society members when they joined, and he'd never seen those eyes before.

"I was...looking for the bathroom."

Flynn smiled. "Nice try, but no." He leaned in. "Try again."

A flush rose up her neck. The telltale giveaway. *Never lie unless you're good at it.* That's what his father taught him. This woman wasn't good at lying. Not at all.

"I—I was just looking around."

He cocked an eyebrow. "For what? What was it about the library that caught your attention?"

She licked her lips. "It was..." her voice trailed off.

He leaned one arm against the window. "What exactly?" The urge to kiss her was intense. Those big eyes and her scent played havoc with him. He reached out and ran a finger over her jaw. She tilted her chin slightly allowing him access to her neck. She was feeling it, too.

"One more time," he said as he rubbed a thumb gently over her full lips. "What are you doing in here?"

She surprised the hell out of him when she pressed forward and kissed him. Slanting her lips across his and demanding access to his mouth. Access he was only too happy to oblige. He wrapped his arms around her and kissed her back, trapping her between him and the window. She leaned into him and deepened the kiss. Pure fucking bliss as far as he was concerned.

A loud thump forced them apart. The sound came from the wall behind the desk. Flynn turned and stared. It wasn't the type of thump as if something hit the wall in the other room. It was as if it came from the wall itself. All the hair on the back of his neck stood up. He scanned the wall and the bookcases. They were not alone. He could feel another presence. He knew someone was watching them like he knew his own name. Lightning flashed once again with another loud crash and then everything went black.

The woman let out a small squeak. Then the thump sounded again. Flynn pulled his cell phone from his pocket and flicked on the flashlight. Though the light was powerful, it wasn't enough to banish the shadows that seemed more menacing than benign.

"Are you okay?" he asked. At her nod, he walked over toward the desk, scanning the wall of books behind it. Nothing. There had to be something though. Something that made the sound. Something that made all his senses go on high alert, including his sixth sense. Oh. he had one and it had kept him alive more times than he could count. He just didn't believe in ghosts or past lives. At least maybe not until now.

"I need to check something," he said and then strode out of the room, trying the next door over. He opened it and shined the flashlight inside. A broom closet. It didn't go very deep, not deep enough to be where the thumping came from.

He closed the door and went back to the library. "I'm sure they'll have the lights on…" his voice died out. The woman was gone. He shined his flashlight all around the now empty room. What the hell? He looked up and down the corridor but it was empty. Had he imagined her? Was she the ghost? *Jesus.* He needed to get some sleep or get laid or get… something. Ghost or not, he wanted to bed the lady in the library very badly.

The lightning flashed one more time, followed a heartbeat later by the crash of the thunder. The storm was intensifying. The lights flickered, died, and then turned back on. Flynn glanced around the library. The woman hadn't left a trace. What was he expecting? A fucking trail of bread-crumbs? *Get your head in the game.*

Pushing thoughts of the woman from his mind, he exam-ined the bookshelves behind the desk. They seemed solid. Nothing seemed amiss. But he knew he'd heard the thumps and so had the woman. Not for a minute did he believe in ghosts. He'd honed his senses over the years with all the things he'd done, and he knew for a fact that when that thump happened someone was watching him.

"What are you doing?" Mrs. Carruthers asked. She had one hand on the doorknob and one on the door jamb. She was wearing a black witch costume with a tall witch's hat that had glitter on the band. "I asked everyone to stay out of these rooms this evening."

Flynn swore under his breath. This woman needed to back the fuck off. He didn't need to explain himself to her. He took a breath. No point in alienating the locals any more than necessary. "There was a woman in here, looking out the window. I came in to see what she was doing."

Mrs. Carruthers looked around the room and then raised an eyebrow at him. "No one seems to be in here now. If you wouldn't mind?" She stepped back and made room for him to walk out of the library.

As he came even with her, he stopped. "That's twice now you've questioned me. I wouldn't go for a third time. You might not like what happens."

As Flynn exited, he knew immediately why Gina Ling was there. Members of the Society were not used to being spoken to like that. Mrs. Carruthers must have ruffled feathers left and right. Not that he was a member, but usually people who understood what his job was didn't speak to him like that either. If he was on site, there was a problem. The people in charge usually wanted his help solving the problem and did not want the blame for causing the problem. Ordinarily, he was given a wide berth. An employee questioning his presence was new for him and he didn't like it one fucking bit.

He came out into the hallway and glanced down the stairwell. People were leaving in a rush as Mrs. Carruthers preached about the storm getting worse. A flash of purple caught his eye. The woman paused and looked up at him. Their gazes locked. And then she was gone. At least now he knew for sure she existed. And his gut said she'd been up to something in that room. He would have to track her down and find out what, exactly, was going on. He smiled. That idea appealed to him in all kinds of ways. This might be an exciting chase, making a trip to Maine less of a horror. He snorted. Even with a potential ghost.

As he stared down at the crowd, a young woman in a tight black dress holding a clipboard caught his eye. She smiled up at him. *Shit.* He hadn't been smiling at her. He nodded back. She looked young, early twenties maybe. Way too young for him. At thirty-six, he had no interest in twenty-year-olds. They were like French pastry, beautiful to look at but sticky as hell. He wasn't interested in any kind of serious relationship, and they always seemed to want more. Nope. He liked women his own age. They knew what they wanted and they took it, generally speaking, and when they were done, they were gone. At least, the ones he dated were that way and he liked it.

Flynn's phone went off and he glanced down at the screen.

How's Maine? Meet any ghosts yet?

Cash. Figures he would rub it in. He was on his way to Italy. Lucky asshole.

No ghosts but it's early yet. I've got you on speed dial in case I get scared. He hit send and put his phone back in his pocket.

"Hi there," a voice said and he looked up. The blond had ditched the clipboard and come up to talk to him.

"Hello," he responded. Up close she looked even younger than he'd thought. No more than twenty. Was she a local here to help with the party?

"I'm Calli." She offered her hand.

"Flynn." He took hers but dropped it almost immediately. He didn't want her to get the wrong idea.

"I hear you're with Society security."

That answered one question. "Who told you that?" he asked, his voice hard.

Her eyelids fluttered. "Sorry. Gina said."

"You're not from here?"

Calli laughed and tossed her long blond hair over her shoulder. "God no. I'm up from New York. Gina brought me and Payton up from the city for this event. There was also supposed to be a golf outing, but the weather is shit so that's been canceled."

"I see."

She offered him a smile and captured his gaze. "Now we have nothing to do but hang out all…weekend…long." As she said it, she let her fingers touch his blazer sleeve and then his wrist.

Yeah. No. He straightened, moving his arm away. "I'm sure Gina will find you something to keep you busy."

"I'm sure." She moved closer to him. "But I can think of other things that would be more fun, especially with you."

He gave her a dead stare. "And just what do you think would be fun, Calli?"

She looked at him uncertainly. He wasn't falling for her charms.

Her brow furrowed. "Oh, I don't know. I'm sure we can think of something." She brushed her fingertips on his chest.

"Are you getting paid, Calli?" He was sure now that his instinct was correct.

"What?" her brows drew together. "Of course. Like I said I was hired by Gina."

He leaned in. "To do what exactly?"

She glanced around as if looking for a way out. "To help her keep the guests happy."

Fuck. She was an escort. "Do you work for Gina often?"

"What is this? Twenty questions?" She took a step back and started to turn away but he grabbed her arm and held it.

"Answer my question." His tone said he wasn't going to put up with any shit.

She glanced over the railing and then licked her lips.

"Calli?"

"Fine," she snarled. "I work for her all the time. Permanent like. Me and Payton and a few others. Gina tells us where to go and when."

What the fuck was going on? "Is she always with you or does she just send you out?"

Sighing, she tossed her hair again. This time it was in annoyance. "She tells all of us where to go via text or a phone call and we go."

"I see." So now the Society was running girls? There was no way Gina was doing this on her own. Archer Gray had to know. It made Flynn's stomach roll. Of all the things the Society was involved in, and a lot of it was bad shit, this was…beyond fucked up. What the hell was Gray doing *supplying* girls to members? If the members asked, there were madams to call but running their own stable? The concept sickened him. But here they were, women on a menu. Members could probably call up and order what they wanted, no questions asked.

He let go of her arm. "Let's get this straight right now. You're here to work? Then go work. Do not talk to anyone but the members. Leave everyone else alone." He made sure his voice was icy. He wasn't dicking around. If she started hitting on Shah or, God forbid, Donovan, there would be hell to pay. Shah said the boy knew all about the Society but Flynn had his doubts. If he did, there was no way he'd have his kid anywhere near it.

She took a step back, a red flush crawling up her neck. "You don't have to be a dick about it," she snarled as she turned on her heel and went back down the stairs.

Yes, he did. He was a dick about it because it would be his responsibility to sort out whatever mess these girls were going to end up in and that would piss him off royally. Pulling his phone out of his pocket, he punched in a number.

"We're running girls now?" he growled into the phone.

"And a good evening to you too, Flynn." Archer Gray's voice was smooth and unruffled as always.

"What the fuck are you doing? Do you know what kind of evil these girls are going to face with certain members?" It was one thing to run the Society but did he really know what he was doing?

There was a long silence. His voice was deceptively soft when he answered. "I assume you've met Gina and that's what you are referring to."

Archer did not like to be challenged. *Too goddamn bad.* "I haven't met her yet but I've met one of her girls. Archer, this is not good. These girls...they're kids."

"They are not, in fact, children but I understand your hesitation and I am inclined to agree with you." There was a sigh. "However, sometimes I do not get to make certain decisions."

Flynn blinked. *What the fuck?* Archer made all the decisions, didn't he? "The board?"

"Yes," Archer ground out. "Months ago. Remington

Tanger was the only one who voted against it and then he died."

Flynn's blood ran cold. He'd liked the old man. A lot. He didn't know the granddaughter at all but had heard good things from Rush. He met her down in the Caribbean. "Are you saying someone killed the old man?"

"I'm saying the board voted in favor of offering the new service after his death."

Flynn ground his teeth. Someone had murdered the old man. "Who suggested the service?"

There was another silence. Finally, Archer said, "Austin Davis."

"Fucking asshole," Flynn ground out.

He should've known. Davis and Eli Fisher and their cronies were all garbage. Pure evil. He'd take great pleasure in killing them one by one if Archer would let him.

"If they killed Remington Tanger that would be breaking the rules. Aren't they supposed to be punished for that?"

"Yes," Archer agreed. "But all in good time. There are… things that are in play." He paused. "Regardless, there's nothing we can do about Gina's operation." He paused again then added, "At the moment."

At the moment. So, maybe there was hope to stop this train wreck.

"How goes the ghost hunting?" There was a smile in Archer's tone.

Archer was ending the discussion. Nothing more would be said on the matter. Flynn just had to let it go. "Funny," he growled. "Ghosts. Really?" he asked.

"So I've been told. I'm sure you'll get to the bottom of it."

"Yeah, sure," Flynn agreed reluctantly.

Archer spoke to someone else, but the words were

muffled and then he was back. "Watch out for things that go bump in the night," he advised and then he was gone.

"Smart ass," Flynn grumbled as he put his cell back in his pants pocket.

He leaned over the railing and stared down at the crowd below. The two young women in black stood chatting. This was a nightmare in the making. Nothing, and he meant fucking nothing, good would come of it.

CHAPTER SIX

"Hell of a night," Shah said as he joined Flynn at the railing.

"Do you have cameras in the library?"

Shah frowned. "Yes. Why?"

"I'm going to want to take a look in the morning." He raised an eyebrow. "There was a woman in the library. I want to know who she was, and what she was doing in there."

"Okay. I'll bring up the video feed whenever you want."

"What is next to the library?" he continued.

Shah frowned. "There's a sitting room on one side and a broom closet on the other. Why?"

Flynn shook his head. "Just wondering." It was a lie and Shah knew it, but he was also smart enough to know that Flynn wasn't going to answer any more questions.

"How's everything else?"

"Aside from the power going out and all the guests wanting to leave at once?" Shah snorted. "Good."

"No lasting effects from the power surge?" Flynn asked.

"Not that I know of. Everything appears to be functioning normally at this point but the storm isn't over and according to the forecasters, it's only going to get worse from here."

"Gentlemen," a voice said. Eli Fisher had come around the corner with two other men in tow. "How are you all this evening?"

"Fine, Mr. Fisher," Shah responded. "Mr. Bryson, Mr. Lockerby. I hope you enjoyed the party?"

Steven Bryson snorted and shook his head. "The facade is just ridiculous. I'm surprised Archer is allowing this sort of thing. Only a matter of time before a member screws up and reveals something he shouldn't. Rainy Day Club. Just stupid."

"I admit, I think it's slightly bizarre," said Richard Lockerby, "but Archer Gray is not a stupid man by any stretch of the imagination. If he is allowing this, there must be a reason for it."

For once Flynn agreed with Lockerby which was slightly surprising. Lockerby was known for being a smart, ambitious businessman, who didn't rest on his family's name, although he could have. The Lockerby name was synonymous with old money New York. He also didn't suffer fools gladly which was another thing he and Flynn agreed on, but Flynn grew up a street kid, involved with gangs before he was even a teenager. Lockerby grew up on the Upper East Side and in the Hamptons. He'd had private jets and yachts since he was a kid. Flynn had brass knuckles and guns.

"Flynn," Fisher said, "I hope you can reason with Archer about this."

"Not my job to reason with Archer."

He wasn't getting involved especially with anything Fisher was selling. He and Steven Bryson were grade-A assholes as far as he was concerned. Although, Bryson was more of a puffed-up peacock than anything else. Full of bluster and great at nagging. Completely useless. That's how Flynn thought of him.

Bryson sneered. "No one can reason with Archer." He shook his head. "The man needs to be replaced. He runs the Society like it's his."

Fisher shot him a look and Bryson stopped talking.

Lockerby smoothed the moment over by saying, "It's been an eventful evening. I will say I appreciated the effort, and the food was divine as always. Now if you gentlemen will excuse us, I think we're going down to play some billiards."

Shah piped up. "Enjoy yourselves."

"I always do," Fisher responded as the men headed down the stairs.

Flynn growled lowly as the men disappeared around the corner toward the back of the foyer and the door to the billiard room.

Shah mumbled, "Those are the kinds of members I like to steer clear of."

Flynn made a noncommittal sound as he stared at the slowly dwindling crowd. Everyone wanted to leave at once… Was that done purposely? Did the lights legitimately go out because of the storm, or had someone deliberately cut the power?

He turned to Shah. "Aren't there backup generators for this site?"

"Yes, but they didn't kick in. I have no idea why. I've called maintenance to take a look."

Flynn's gut knotted. His instincts were bang on again. Something was off. "Are they checking now?"

Shah shook his head. "Nah. I couldn't in good conscience bring the guy out on a night like this. Darrel's wife is due any moment with their twins. I just couldn't ask him to come now. He said he'd be here in the morning as long as Linda didn't go into labor."

Flynn sighed heavily. He'd forgotten he was in a small town. In NYC or Miami, someone would come out immediately, regardless of the weather especially since they'd be paid double time or more. "Right. Where's the electrical panel?"

"Why?" Shah asked. "Are you going to take a shot at the generator? That's outside behind the bushes beside the parking lot near the back right corner of the house."

"No, I just want to see something." He wasn't going into it with Shah. At least not yet. He needed to take a look at the setup first.

Shah shrugged. "Follow me." He turned and started down the stairs. Flynn followed, making note of all the cameras they passed on their way to the basement. At the bottom of the stairs, they headed back toward the security offices but instead of using the door on the right, they went through the one on the left.

Shah stopped as soon as they walked through the door and flicked on the weak overhead lights. "I hate this place," he muttered.

Flynn said nothing, but at first glance he was inclined to agree. The damp air settled on his skin with a cloying chill as he followed Shah through the labyrinth of exposed pipes and forgotten corners.

The thunder crashed and Shah put his hand up and touched the concrete walls as they walked. "This place gives me the creeps," he said in a quiet voice.

Flynn's senses were on high alert. There was something about this place that set him on edge as well. "We're just here to check out the electrical equipment," he said ostensibly to calm Shah down but he wasn't sure if it was Shah or himself he was trying to reassure. *Stupid.* He was letting the stories he'd been told get in his head. He had to be logical about this.

As they moved deeper into the basement, the musty scent of old wood and dust filled the air. Their footsteps echoed eerily, the weak light from the naked bulbs hanging from the ceiling painted grotesque shadows on the walls. Flynn's hand instinctively drifted toward where his gun would be, if he was carrying one.

They stopped by the very back corner and Flynn's gaze swept over the exposed wires and circuit boxes that lined the walls, his trained eye seeking any sign of tampering. It all looked old and unsafe as fuck. "How the hell…?" He didn't even know what he was looking at.

"I know," Shah said, his voice tense. "It's one of the reasons I hate being in here. The wiring is ancient. I feel like the whole place could burn down around our ears."

That was not a comforting thought. "Wait, you live here?"

Shah shook his head. "Not permanently but I do stay here on occasion. I have a room in the new section that Mrs. Carruthers keeps for me. Just down the hall from yours."

Flynn chuckled grimly. "You must be the only person she likes then."

He grinned. "No. She tells me when she wants me to stay there and I don't have a choice, so I negotiated with her. It has to be my room where I can keep my stuff and grab a shower or a nap if I need."

Flynn laughed. "Smart man."

The conversation had relaxed him. He was being stupid to let the circumstances get into his head. He knew better… was better than that. He raised his cell and let the flashlight play over the panel. The master power switch was flipped to the *On* position, its once-white label now faded and smudged with age.

He looked closer. The switch glistened in the glare of the flashlight. Reaching out, he touched the switch and frowned.

"What?" Shah asked.

"It's sticky." Flynn glanced down at his fingers. The tips had a pale substance on them, along with some glitter.

Shah's lips thinned. "What's that?"

"No idea." He smelled the smudge, but with everything in the basement smelling damp, he couldn't tell what the faint scent was. "Regardless, I think the lights going out was on purpose. Someone hit the switch."

Shah's eyes widened. "But who could've—" Before he could finish his sentence, a distant, chilling sound echoed through the basement. It was the faint, almost ghostly sound of laughter.

"What the hell?" Flynn's pulse raced and he hustled back along the wall. The laughter got louder. He exchanged a wary glance with Shah, his instincts urging him to be cautious.

"Stay alert," Flynn instructed in a low voice.

As they ventured deeper into the basement, the darkness seemed to close in around them. The light from the naked blubs wavered with each crash of thunder. Flynn's pulse jumped as he rounded a corner, his flashlight beam falling upon an old mirror that had been propped against the wall. In the warped reflection, he saw a flicker of movement, a figure standing just beyond the edge of the light.

His muscles bunched. "Who's there?" he called out, his voice echoing through the damp silence as he whirled around.

The figure stepped into the light and Flynn blinked. There were horns coming from its head and its eyes were black. *What the fuck?*

"For Christ's sake, Donovan," Shah's voice was harsh.

"Sorry, Dad. Didn't mean to scare you." Donovan pulled the mask off and had the good manners to look sheepish.

"Mrs. Carruthers sent me down to find you. She'd like you to talk to some the people from the party. They're claiming someone stole their jewelry. She sent them to wait for you in the salon. She would like you to come up right away."

Shah swore under his breath. "I have to go deal with this."

Flynn waved him off. "No problem. I'm going to poke around down here a bit and then I'll be up. Send Donovan down here to get me if you need any help."

Shah nodded and waved as he walked back toward the door, Donovan in tow.

Flynn waited until they were gone, and the basement had gone silent once again. Then he cocked his head and listened. No more laughter but there was a faint tinkling. What the hell could that be? He strained his ears in the silence trying to pick out what could be making the soft sound he was hearing. A sudden bark of laughter made him jump and he whirled around again. He glanced at his reflection in the old mirror. His dark hair was over the collar of his white shirt and navy blazer. His brown eyes looked black in low lighting but mostly what he noticed was how unsettled he looked.

"Shit," he said again and then started back toward the electrical panel.

"Oh God," a voice said.

He stopped dead. Then he cocked his head once more. Was that...yes it was the sound of someone having sex. What the actual fuck was going on? He looked up and then took a few steps backward. Above one of the exposed pipes was a vent, set high on the wall. The noise was coming from there. Somewhere in the building, a couple was actually fucking and the sound was carried through the vents.

Flynn grimaced. *At least someone was having fun.* He let out a long breath and went back to the electrical panel and the switch on the wall. He shined his flashlight beam over it again, but the mysterious substance was gone. He'd probably gotten it all off when he'd touched it, but he looked around nonetheless.

Finally, he decided to head back. There was nothing else he could glean at the moment. He needed to check the cameras and see who was in the vicinity when the power went out. He also needed to get a set of blueprints for the house. A better feel for the structure would be key if he was going to find the 'ghost.'

A large flash illuminated the window high in the corner and the thunder crashed.

All the lights went out.

"Fuck," Flynn grumbled. No one had gotten by him and he'd just left the panel so he knew the power had been knocked out by the storm this time.

He raised his phone flashlight and tried to pick his way back toward the door, but he must have gotten turned around because as he rounded a corner, he found himself in a narrow corridor, the walls lined with crates and debris. He heard some muffled sounds but he couldn't distinguish what they were, and they were growing fainter. Since he was already there, he decided to keep following the dank hallway. Flynn pressed on, his flashlight cutting through the darkness. Suddenly, he found himself standing in a dead-end. He swung his flashlight around. It was just a small empty space. Strange.

He shrugged and turned heading back the way he'd come. He got as far as the turn where he first discovered the hallway and then everything went black.

Flynn came to in pitch blackness. Lying on his side on the cold hard floor, it took a moment for him to recall he was in the basement. His head hurt as adrenaline filled his veins. He got to his knees slowly cursing as his stomach rolled. He didn't think he had more than a slight concussion but it was too soon to tell. The worst part was he must have dropped his cell and now there was no light.

He felt around on the floor with his hands searching for the missing phone when he heard another bark of laughter coming from the vent. Apparently, the couple had finished screwing, because now they were quite chatty. He couldn't quite make out what the person was saying but he was sure it was a woman.

Of course, that knowledge didn't help his current situation.

The search was pointless. He couldn't see a damn thing and his fingers kept jabbing into boxes and bags. The phone could be right next to him, and he wouldn't know.

"Fuck," he swore again and sat back on his heels. Getting out of this section of the basement without a light would be damn near impossible. He'd bang into everything and no doubt hurt himself even more. He needed a game plan.

Just then he heard a small creature scurrying nearby. Fucking awesome. Rats. Just what he needed. Jesus, could this day get any worse? He took a deep breath and let it out, trying to remain calm and let go of the anger burning in his chest. Being pissed off wasn't going to help him here. It would just cloud his thinking.

At times like this he asked himself if he should pull the rip cord. He had an escape plan for leaving the Society. Archer Gray might be all-knowing on one level, but he had no clue when it came to Flynn's people. His Irish clan could make him disappear, he just needed to say the word. He'd been thinking more and more about it lately. He pushed out a heavy breath. As much as this sucked, today wasn't the day to go.

He tested the lump on the left side of his head. It was growing but it didn't appear to be bleeding. That was a plus. Flynn slowly stood. The room seemed to stay in the right place, not that he could see it but at least he didn't feel dizzy. Another plus. Now to find his cell phone.

"Hey, Siri? Find my phone."

"Which model?" The electronic voice cut through the darkness and started listing them. He turned his head toward where the sound was coming from and spied the illuminated display of his phone. It had fallen into the box on his right. No way in hell he'd ever have found that without light. Thank God for smartphones. He picked up his phone and used the flashlight to get back to the door. He opened it and walked out into the hallway.

Raised voices came from upstairs. Ideally, he wanted to look at the video of the hallway and see who the hell had come into the unfinished side of the basement and whacked him on the head, but since the power was still out and the generator wasn't coming on, he had no way to do that.

He started up the stairs two at a time, each step sending a jarring shard of pain through his head. Slowing his pace, he gingerly walked the rest of the way up and turned to the right as he reached the top. The voices were coming from the room where the party had been held. He made his way in to find Shah along with Mrs. Carruthers and a woman wearing fairy wings whom he assumed was Gina. Another older woman was with them, along with a gentleman who he assumed was her husband. Someone had set hurricane lamps on a couple tables, giving a room a dim, eerie glow.

Why were these people still here? He glanced at Shah who cocked an eyebrow at him and frowned but then turned back to the couple.

"I'm telling you, when the lights went off, someone grabbed my necklace and pulled it off my neck. It hurt. I'm not imagining things and it couldn't have just fallen off. It was pulled viciously. If there were lights, I'm sure I could show you the bruises." The woman finished with a huff.

Obviously not the truth. Flynn bit back a sigh. If that had happened, she would've screamed bloody murder. She didn't say anything until after people started to leave.

Mrs. Carruthers said, "Mrs. Addison, I can assure you—"

"You can stuff your assurances. I know what happened. Charles," she said, "you were there, tell them."

"Marjory is correct. Someone pulled the diamond necklace off her neck."

"And you saw this?" Shah asked. "When the lights were off?"

"Er, well…" The older gentleman glanced at his wife. "If Marjory said that's what happened then that's what happened. We need to call the police."

Police. Yeah. No. That would be a serious problem. Police were never allowed in a Society location if it could be avoided. Hell, half the locations were hidden so the cops didn't even know they existed.

Shit. He was going to have to step in and try to smooth things over. *Not his forte.*

"As I started to say before," Mrs. Carruthers broke in. "I can assure you that—"

"Mrs. Addison," Flynn said, overriding Mrs. Carruthers' voice, "I'm Flynn O'Connor, one of the lead security officers for the Rainy Day Club worldwide. I'm sorry this happened to you. It's been a traumatic evening, but maybe you'd consider dealing with all of this in the morning. It'll give us a chance to review our security protocols and search the Manor for your missing necklace." She started to speak but he cut her off. "If we don't find it, then if you'll provide us with the insurance documents for it, we'll be happy to cover the cost of the necklace." He was making it up on the fly, but he needed these people to go home.

He watched her expression closely. Her eyes narrowed and her mouth pursed. Cash wasn't working for her.

"Or," he continued, "we could have your necklace remade at…" What the hell was the name of that jewelry store… "Harry Winston in New York." Her eyes got narrower still. "Of course, if you have a preferred jeweler, I'm sure we could get it remade with them." Ryker was going to have his ass for this if it didn't work out.

Mrs. Addison blinked. "Harry Winston," she murmured.

"My wife's necklace had sentimental value," her husband stated. "Merely replacing it will not be the same as finding the original."

"Of course. Understandable," Flynn agreed. What the hell would make this woman happy? "Maybe we could add matching earrings? We will, of course, search the Manor for your necklace. Everything possible will be done to find it."

"Matching earrings?" She grabbed her husband's arm. "From Harry Winston?"

Flynn nodded.

"Well, I'm sure…that is, I am of course devastated that I lost my necklace, and nothing can make up for the loss of such a beloved item, but I can tell you're sincere in your apologies and well, these things can't be helped sometimes. What is this world coming to? Having the necklace remade at Harry Winston along with matching earrings would, of course, be acceptable."

Flynn did his best not to smile. He just bet it would be acceptable. "Thank you for being so understanding. Someone will be in touch to make sure we get everything set up for the replacement." He turned and offered her his arm, which she took promptly, and walked her toward the door. "Please drive safely and once again, our sincerest apologies for this evening's happenings."

"Of course." With that, Mr. and Mrs. Addison were escorted out the door by a young kid with an umbrella and taken down to their waiting car.

Flynn turned and looked at the small crowd that had walked over to the door with him. "Someone want to tell me what the fuck is going on?"

Shah rubbed his face. "At least they're happy now. Good thinking on throwing in the earrings."

"Has this type of thing happened before?" Flynn asked.

"Yes, but only small things, and I'm Gina Ling, by the way," said the attractive woman wearing the fairy wings. "We didn't get a chance to meet earlier." She extended her arm.

He shook her hand and waited for more details.

"Mrs. Carruthers would know more than I would. Mrs. C.?"

Mrs. Carruthers said, "Gina is correct, we've had a few small things disappear. A brooch, a favorite pen, a book. Small trinkets mainly. This is the first time something of extreme value was taken."

Shah eyed him. "What are you thinking?"

"I'm thinking the first power outage wasn't an accident. In the morning, Mrs. Carruthers, organize a search for the necklace. I don't think we'll find it but who knows."

There was a loud bang and Flynn spun to his left. Then swore and put his hand to his head.

"It was just a shutter hitting the side of the house. Are you okay?" Shah asked.

"Yeah. Fine." He fucking hated small towns and all their nonsense. Give him an apartment building any day. "Okay, let's call it a night. Keep your eyes open and let me know if anything else goes missing." Flynn turned and went back to the stairs.

Whatever the hell was going on here, whoever was involved, they'd just upped the ante by hitting him in the back of the head. He could guarantee they weren't ready for the hell he was going to rain down on them. They weren't even gonna see it comin'.

CHAPTER SEVEN

Harper curled up on her sofa, her legs tucked under her. Today had been as long as it had been brutal. She was just glad to be home as the wind howled and the rain pelted against the windows. The weather seemed to reflect her own inner turmoil. She pulled a blanket around her shoulders as the fire crackled in the fireplace, casting a warm, flickering glow across the room.

She breathed in the soothing aroma of the tea she held in her hands, its steam rising to warm her face. She'd changed into her favorite flannelette pajamas and a pair of big wool socks. Comfort clothing. Shadows danced along the walls, casting an aura of warmth and solitude. Storms had a way of making the world feel small, encapsulated in the cocoon of her seaside haven. This was what she needed tonight; a balm to her frayed nerves.

The encounter in the library had just about done her in. She'd only just managed to get her hands to stop shaking. She'd thought for sure the man was going to discover what she was up to. Thank God for the ghost. She smiled. She never thought that would be something to be thankful for, but the unexpected noises had proven to be the best distraction. Otherwise, she could have been in real trouble.

She still couldn't believe she'd gone with her instinct and kissed him. She'd needed to distract him from asking her questions and, well, he was so close and smelled so good that she just went for it. The kiss left her unsteady. The man knew what he was doing. Her knees had gone weak and he had her wanting more in seconds. Intense electricity had arced hotly between them, but she hadn't expected that they would fit together so seamlessly. Like they were made to be together. She snorted. *Hallmark movie much?*

The mystery man was too damn sexy. She had no idea who he was and probably didn't want to know since he had to be a member of the Rainy Day Club. She didn't want to be near any of that.

But those dark eyes of his. Had her senses been heightened because of the situation? She'd never had chemistry like that before with anyone.

Just as she took a cautious sip of her tea, a knock echoed through the room, pulling her from her reverie. Harper's fingers tightened around the cup. She wasn't expecting company after midnight, especially not during a storm like this.

Setting her tea on the coffee table, she rose from the sofa and made her way to the door. She glanced through the peephole. Why in the world was Jason Merritt waiting on the other side? She'd changed her mind about telling him about the paint chips and left him a message earlier that she wanted to speak with him tomorrow but that didn't explain why he was here now.

Her heart lurched. Had something else happened? Was something wrong? She unlocked the door and wrenched it open.

"Jason, is everything okay? What are you doing here?" she demanded.

Jason's tall frame was soaked from the rain, droplets clinging to his blond hair and overcoat. He gave a weary smile as he stepped inside. "Sorry, Harper. I didn't mean to scare you. Everything is fine. I just got your message as I was passing. I saw your lights were still on so I thought... I hoped it would be okay to stop. Tomorrow is going to be a long one and I wasn't sure I'd have time to see you."

Harper put a hand on her chest. "Oh, thank goodness. Sorry for being so abrupt. I'm just a bit on edge. Would you like some tea? Or I can make coffee if you'd like. Or something stronger?" She was rambling. She did that when she was nervous. Why was she nervous around Jason? Because now she had to tell him what she'd found and she knew he wasn't going to like it, that's why.

Jason stepped further into the room, raindrops falling from his coat onto the wooden floor. "Tea would be great," he said, his voice carrying a note of gratitude. He removed his coat and hung it on a nearby hook before turning to face Harper. "It's nasty out there." He walked over and looked out her glass doors to her deck. "Be careful with your chairs. They could break something if the wind picks up." He came back across the room and Harper handed him the tea she'd just poured. He smiled his thanks. "Your message mentioned that you wanted to talk to me about Astrid."

She motioned for him to take a seat on the sofa and then settled into an armchair across from him, her gaze locked onto his. "What were you doing out in this storm?" she asked stalling for time.

"It's an all-hands-on-deck situation. I was over at the Bradley's. They couldn't get in touch with their son Danny and went into a panic since... Well, you know, since we found Astrid today."

"Is Danny okay?"

"Yeah," Jason said and then took a sip of this tea and swallowed. "He'd gone over to his girlfriend's place and fell asleep. He'd plugged his phone in but then the power went out and his phone died."

She sat back in her chair. "I'm glad he's okay."

"Yes," he agreed. "Now you wanted to discuss something about Astrid's case?"

She took a deep breath. "Today at the bluff, Mandy pointed out a green flake of something on Astrid's skirt and under her nails."

"Yes, they came from some kind of green paint."

"I...I recognized it."

Jason's gaze narrowed. "What do you mean you recognized it?"

She licked her lips. This was the tricky part. She knew it sounded farfetched, but she also knew that she was right. "When I was growing up, my father did a lot of work at Everlasting Manor for the previous owners. During my teen rebellion years, I wanted to paint my room black but he and Mom said no way. The compromise was that I could paint one wall a dark color. He brought home a dark green paint that had a touch of sparkle to it and I used that."

"I'm sorry." Jason frowned. "I'm not following you. Do you think Astrid went to your parents' old place?"

"No." She cursed under her breath. "I'm not being very clear. I used the green paint that he brought home, but he had it because he used it at Everlasting Manor. He painted one of the rooms there in that color."

Jason's eyes narrowed slightly. "So, you think Astrid was at Everlasting Manor before she died?"

"Yes, I do."

"Well...I guess it's a possibility but as you just pointed out, that green paint could be from anywhere. I mean maybe

Astrid did go to your parents' place. She was best friends with their granddaughter, so maybe she ran into the paint there."

"No. No. I painted the room over years ago before my parents sold it. She had to come in contact with the paint at the Manor."

Jason set his tea down on the table. "I think you're grasping at straws a bit here. You painted over your room, maybe the new owners of the Manor painted over their rooms as well. She—"

"They didn't," she blurted.

He stopped and stared at her. "And you know this how?"

"I checked this evening while I was at the party."

His brow furrowed. "You went to the party? I'm…surprised."

"It wasn't my choice. Susan demanded that I attend. I spent most of the night reassuring people that there wasn't a homicidal maniac on the loose."

"I see. What room did you see the paint in?" he asked.

"It was upstairs in what I think was a library." He needed to believe her. This could be a real lead that would take them to Astrid's killer.

Jason sat back on the sofa. "I thought they didn't let non-members of the Rainy Day Club off the ground floor," he stated, his eyes accusing.

"Yeah, well…it was a party. I wandered around some."

He let out a breath. "I'd advise you to leave this to the department. I know you're hurting, but seriously Harper, stay out of it and let us do our jobs."

"But the paint, Jason. She had it under her fingernails." Harper got to her feet. "You know as well as I do there's something weird about the Rainy Day people. The whole thing stinks. It needs to be investigated."

Jason got to his feet. "Okay," he said raising his hands as if to appease her. "Okay. I will see what I can find out and if anything else leads to the Manor, I will check it out. Your word on paint color isn't going to cut it."

He was placating her, and she couldn't understand why he wasn't jumping all over this lead.

She crossed her arms over her chest. "Fine."

He nodded and then tried unsuccessfully to stifle a yawn. "It's been a long day. I'm going to head home." He walked over to the doorway, and grabbed his coat off the hook.

Harper followed him but had the sneaking suspicion that Jason was feeling disappointed somehow. Did he think she would invite him to spend the night? If so, he was sadly mistaken. She wasn't one to jump into bed with anyone. A quick flash of the stranger at the party entered her brain. She'd wanted to jump into bed with him, no question.

"Keep dry tonight. Try to get some rest." Jason offered her a tired smile.

"I will. You, too."

He leaned over and squeezed her arm. "Please trust me, Harper. I will do my absolute best to find out what happened to Astrid." He gave her another quick smile and then he was gone.

She watched him get into his car and then closed her door and locked it again. He'd said he'd 'find out what happened to Astrid, not find Astrid's killer. Did that matter? Was she splitting hairs? Maybe, but his phrasing bothered her.

A lot.

Harper woke with a start, her heart hammering against her ribcage. She stayed frozen, listening. What had woken her up? The wind howled. Could that have been it? Maybe a shutter banged or something…except she didn't have any shutters.

She turned her head and glanced at the clock. And was disoriented by the lack of display. *Great. No power.* She didn't think she'd been in bed for a couple of hours. The storm was still raging. Willing her body to relax again, she settled deeper into her pillows. She closed her eyes and took a deep breath. Her eyes popped back open as she caught a smell that didn't belong in her room. The scent of lavender filled the air. What the hell? She strained her ears but could hear nothing.

Sitting up, she swung her legs over the side of the bed and got up. Lavender filled her nose. She hated lavender with a passion. Nothing she owned had that scent so how could it be in her house? Grabbing her cell phone off the charger, she started to dial for help. She got as far as the nine-one and then stopped. What the hell would she tell the dispatcher? *Hi, it's the deputy mayor. I smell lavender in my house. Can someone come check, please?* Yeah. No. That wasn't happening.

She bit her lip, hit the second one but didn't hit the call button. Instead, she kept her finger close to it and then slowly walked across her room toward the hallway, sniffing quietly as she went. The scent was stronger in the corridor. She shivered. Only wearing her boxer shorts and tank was a mistake. With the power off, her condo had cooled down.

Shadows flickered on the wall where the hallway opened to the great room below. A cold sweat broke out across her body. Her hands were slick on her cell phone case. There was nothing that could cause those shadows. Nothing at all. She leaned on the wall and peeked around the corner, looking into the room below.

A small gasp escaped her throat as she clutched the corner. She tore her gaze away and searched every inch of the room below but saw no one. She stayed still and tried to sense if someone other than her was in the condo. She waited for at least a full minute, but she was sure she was alone. At least she was now.

Leaving the safety of the wall, she tiptoed over to the stairs and made her way down, studying the scene before her. She even brought up her phone and snapped a few pictures as she crossed the room and came to stand in front of her coffee table.

In the middle of the table, in a glass jar, was a lit candle. Lavender. The flame danced as the wind blew causing air currents to move in her condo. Leaning against the candle was a piece of paper, folded over once with her name on it.

Her hand shook as she reached out and picked up the paper. Opening it, she sucked in a breath as she saw the words. The message was handwritten in a scrawling cursive.

You need to stop poking around in things that don't concern you. It's not good for you. You could end up like her.

Her gaze darted around the room and then back down to the paper. Who the hell could've left that? Were they still there? Her shaking hands made the paper rattle. Swallowing hard, she reminded herself that she was alone. Whoever did this was gone. But how did they get in?

She dropped the paper on the table and hurried to the front door. Her knees were weak and she stumbled but she caught herself and continued on. Reaching her front door, she checked the locks. All locked and the security chain was in place. No one had come in that way.

Asshole. Someone had purposely come in to scare her. The overwhelming fear she'd felt moments ago was rapidly turning to anger. Her blood pounded through her veins. She fisted her hands, her right one curling tightly around her cell as she headed toward the balcony doors. Pushing aside the blinds, she checked the lock. Open. Her balcony door was open.

"Son of a..." Harper wanted to scream or throw something. She'd locked this door before she went to bed. Someone had broken in while she slept. Who the fuck would do that? Who even knew she was poking around in Astrid's murder? At least that was the *her* she assumed the note referred to.

The man in the library was the only one who'd seen her up there. It had to be him. Her heart thumped as her breath came in gasps. Asshole didn't cover it. If he thought he was going to get away with this, he had another think coming. Who the hell did he think he was trying to intimidate her?

Jason wanted proof? Well, this was proof. She grabbed her phone and deleted the nine-one-one and then dug up Jason's number. She started to hit the call button and then stopped. He hadn't wanted her to interfere with his investigation. Her word wasn't good enough about the paint. She stared at the candle.

The note was too generic. That's what Jason would say. It could be referencing anything not necessarily Astrid's murder. Also, there was no way to be sure the note had been left by the guy in the library. How did he find out that she hated lavender? All valid points. Oh, she could argue with each one but it wouldn't help her any nor would it improve her case with Jason or the police department.

That was the thing about being a public figure; whatever she did, everyone would notice. She stared at the candle in trepidation. Telling anyone in law enforcement wasn't going to help. She needed stronger evidence. She brought her cell up and took a few more pictures. She held the note open and took pictures of that as well.

Then she retrieved a flashlight from a drawer in her kitchen and turned on the gas burner under her kettle. She was up now and there was no pretending otherwise. Marching back into the great room with the flashlight, she blew out the candle. The smoky scent helped mask the lavender, a welcome relief. Whoever pulled this shit wasn't going to get away with it, she vowed silently. She'd find out the truth no matter what the cost. Her stomach rolled. Somehow, she knew that the information she was seeking wouldn't come cheap.

CHAPTER EIGHT

Flynn stared at the ceiling. The power was still out and his room had gotten chilly. It was hard to believe this morning he'd been nice and toasty warm in Miami. Fast forward a couple hours and now he was freezing his arse off in Maine. He closed his eyes and attempted some breathing exercises to relax, but it was no use. The dull ache in his head and the self-recrimination in his heart for getting hit in the first place were enough to keep him awake for days.

He threw back the covers and got out of bed. Pulling on a pair of jeans and a sweater, he quietly padded out of his room and down the hall. He was hungry. Dinner had been hours ago, and he'd only managed to snag a bit of food as he'd been late to the dining room and Mrs. Carruthers hadn't wanted to feed him. She was stomping on his last nerve.

He understood why the members didn't want to deal with her. Rounding the corner by the library, his thoughts went back to the sexy mystery woman. That kiss had been fucking hot, there was no denying that, but what was she doing in the library, and did it have anything to do with the theft of that woman's necklace? Best option was to find her and ask her. A smile tugged at the corners of his lips. Maine might be interesting after all.

He roamed around the ground floor until he found the kitchen. His stomach rumbled as he opened the fridge. He shined his flashlight inside and was choosing between roast beef and a roast chicken dish when the hair on the back of his neck went up again.

He whirled around but the kitchen was empty, but he sensed he was not alone. He shined his flashlight all over the kitchen but saw nothing out of place. Everlasting Manor was joining Carruthers on his last fucking nerve. *Goddamn ghosts, my ass.* Someone was playing around.

He returned his attention to digging in the fridge. He pulled out the chicken and put it on the counter. Cold chicken he could do. Pulling off a chunk, he pulled out a stool and sat down on it while he started munching. He kept his gaze roving around the kitchen but the eerie feeling of being watched didn't return. Damn good thing. The ache in his head throbbed and he didn't trust himself not to shoot someone at this point if they annoyed him. The fact that he'd have to go to his room to get his gun just meant more time to plan on how to make it as painful as possible.

After finishing most of the chicken, he put the leftovers back in the fridge with sudden haste. It had occurred to him that someone might get up and find him there and the last thing he wanted to deal with was getting yelled at by Mrs. Carruthers. He'd end up snarling at her or worse. He grabbed a bottle of water from the pantry and headed for the stairs.

As he crossed through the salon, he heard a voice. He stopped, cocked his head, and turned off his flashlight.

"Yes, Austin, it is unfortunate. But I think we're making progress. If it's handled just right, it should work."

Flynn recognized Eli Fisher's voice. He'd know that cockroach anywhere. And what the hell was he doing in Maine of all places? His presence, although Flynn knew he'd be there, was unexpected. Eli liked bright lights and big cities and all that they offered a vulture like him. Maine was far too sedate, too colloquial for the likes of Eli Fisher, so what the hell was he up to? Did it have something to do with Bryson's comment about Archer running the place like it was his? Something serious was brewing. The nerves in Flynn's shoulders tightened.

"Things have been put in motion. As you know there are ways around everything. Great strides were made on finding a solution last night." A smile in Eli's voice made Flynn wish he'd not just eaten cold chicken. Fisher snorted. "Just leave it with me for now. Anyway, I must run. I have a few more calls to make overseas. I'll be back in D.C. at the end of next week. When will you be back?" There was a silence. "Right. I'll call you with any updates." He clicked off the call.

Flynn's instincts told him nothing good would come from that phone call. It never was good when it involved monsters like Eli Fisher and Austin Davis. The two of them were evil incarnate in Flynn's mind. Just like a two-headed snake operating from the same dark heart. Good thing he was a monster slayer. It was his job and he enjoyed it immensely.

Fisher stood up. He'd been sitting in one of the wingback chairs. His face was briefly lit by the light of his cell phone screen. He was wearing a sweater and what looked like some kind of sweatpants. Not his normal attire at all. The light from the screen faded and Flynn heard him curse as he walked into the table that had been beside the chair.

Flynn could offer assistance but he'd rather let the man stumble around in the dark so he remained frozen in place. Fisher cursed some more and his cell phone screen lit up again. Fisher flipped it over and used it to light the floor in front of him. Idiot didn't know how to turn on the flashlight feature.

Flynn stood, arms folded across his chest and waited. Eli got within a few feet of him before he finally spoke. "Good morning, Fisher."

The man let out a small scream and then cursed. His phone screen turned off again and they were plunged into darkness once more.

"Having difficulties?" Flynn couldn't keep from chuckling.

"Who is that?" Fisher demanded. He hit the screen on his phone once more and started to hold it up when Flynn turned on his flashlight and shone it directly in Fisher's face.

"What brings you to Maine?"

Fisher threw up his arms to block his face. "Get that fucking light out of my eyes," he demanded. Flynn reluctantly lowered it. "O'Connor, is that you? What are you doing lurking here in the middle of the night?"

"I asked you first," Flynn replied.

Fisher glared at him. "I'm here relaxing. Maine is wonderful for that type of thing."

"Uh-huh. Sure."

"I have more calls to make," Fisher huffed "I guess I need to find a more private location."

"Your room is private. Why not make the calls there?" He was curious why Fisher was downstairs in the first place.

"I would but there's no signal. It worked perfectly fine last night," he pointed out. "I have no idea why it's not working now."

"The house uses repeaters to boost the signal. With the power out, the repeaters are down."

"Shameful. I will be complaining to Archer about this. A Society facility should be top-notch at all times. This is most decidedly not."

"Archer can do a lot of things but he cannot control the weather, nor can he fix the power grid. But go ahead and complain. I'm sure he'll note it down."

Fisher glared, let out a snort, then scurried toward the stairs. There was a thump and then Fisher swore again. Flynn grinned in the darkness. Served him right. He let out a sigh and headed back to his room. Maybe now he could get some sleep.

Flynn made his way up the stairs. At least he knew how to work the flashlight on his phone. Other than the library and the kitchen just now, he hadn't heard, or felt, anything that could remotely be considered ghostlike. Shah had said people heard thumps and voices. No one had seen anything weird though or at least no one Shah believed. Flynn theorized the voices were traveling through the vents like in the basement. The thumps he'd heard in the library could be anything.

Shah did share a story about some elderly member who was visiting and claimed to have seen his dead mother. Flynn gave a mental shrug. The last thing he wanted to see was his dead mother, or father for that matter. He rarely saw his siblings and that was the way he liked it. Too much family and togetherness got to him.

As Flynn climbed back in bed he decided on what to tell Archer. He would use logic to explain everything and add that people's imaginations were getting carried away. It was close to Halloween. He could practically hear Archer and Sterling in his head. *Did you check every angle? Are you sure there's nothing to this? What are we going to tell members who ask? We need rock-solid answers…*Fair enough. He'd have to stay a little longer and investigate the thumps.

He might have been able to figure it out earlier if he hadn't been so distracted by the woman. She was an easy scapegoat. He hadn't felt that level of… connection, electricity, whatever the hell it was in…forever. She had overloaded his senses to the point where he'd lost his focus. Stupid of him.

On the other hand, the kiss had been worth it. A few more days in Maine might not be a bad thing if he could track her down and get her in his bed, or anywhere else for that matter. Yes, further investigation was required…

The sound of a crash in the hallway outside of his room woke him. Who the fuck was out there banging around at this hour? He glanced at the clock. It was dark so he picked up his phone and glanced at the screen. Eight a.m. Jesus someone needed to get a life. He rolled out of bed and pulled on his jeans, then padded to the doorway thinking he'd tell off whoever was working but then he stopped. Carruthers probably put whoever was out there up to making a racket this early. He didn't need gut instinct to know she was trying to drive him and certain other members out of town. She hated him and he wasn't so stupid as to think he was the only one. No, she wanted everyone she didn't like, that she didn't think belonged, to leave town.

He glanced through the peephole at the young woman cleaning. He hadn't seen her before but that didn't mean much. He opened the door and leaned against the jamb.

"Excuse me," he said. She didn't hear him. "Excuse me," he tried again. The woman turned around and a blush immediately filled her cheeks. She took Air pods out of her ears.

"Sorry. Did I wake you? I was told to clean this hallway now." Her young face was filled with embarrassment and a touch of fear. She looked down and didn't meet his eyes again. "I'll be finished shortly."

"Who told you to clean this area now? Is this the normal time you clean?"

She bit her lip, her dark eyes getting larger. "Um, no. It's usually later in the day but Mrs. Carruthers insisted. I told her people would still be sleeping but she said we had other things to do since clean up after the party was delayed due to the power outage. She said people would just have to deal with it."

Bingo. He knew it. Now he knew her game. Two could play and she wasn't going to like it one bit. "Why don't you stop now? Call it good enough. You don't have to finish it. I am sure it will be fine until the next time."

"You really think so?" she asked shyly.

"I do." Flynn smiled at her and then closed his door again. He glanced at the bed. No point in trying to go back to sleep now. He'd have to tough out a cold shower and then go in search of food. The chicken was long gone from his stomach. And he needed about a gallon of coffee.

Shah was waiting at the bottom as he went down the stairs. "Any news on the generator?"

"Monday at the earliest. With the storm, they have a lot of people in desperate need."

They turned and started toward the dining room. "What's for breakfast?"

"Oatmeal. They can only cook on the gas stove so no individual orders this morning."

Flynn groaned. "Yuck. Is the power out all over town?"

Shah shook his head. "No, the main part of town is fine."

"And is there a coffee shop in that area?"

"Yes. The Coffee Cake bakery is there. It's sort of a trendy coffee shop that serves great baked goods and sandwiches."

Flynn's stomach rumbled. "Great. A real breakfast. Where is it?"

Shah stood by the entrance to the dining room. "It's on Main Street, about mid-way down the block."

"Excellent." Flynn turned on his heel and started back toward the stairs.

"Bring something for me when you come back. I hate oatmeal," Shah called after him.

Flynn waved his agreement.

He drove slowly down the street checking the storefronts. It was a typical New England downtown with all kinds of regular stores like sporting goods and hardware mixed with the cutesy touristy things and a lot of clothing stores. Flynn spotted the bakery Shah had mentioned and snagged a parking spot right out front. Maybe the gods were smiling on him today. He sure as hell wasn't going to take any chances with Carruthers' oatmeal and coffee. The woman might poison him or at the very least spit in it.

The air was cool and the sky was still gray. Rumor had it there was another storm rolling toward them. This one was a nor'easter. People seemed more excited about it though, kind of like a it was a hurricane. A storm is a storm but whatever. Hopefully, if his luck held he'd be long out of here before it hit.

He pulled open the door to the shop and the tantalizing aroma of fresh baked goods hit him in the solar plexus. His stomach rumbled again. He looked around the shop. A few booths lined the windows and he counted a half dozen tables around the room. The counter on the left held an assortment of baked goods in a case with a cash register at the end. The counter on the back wall had another glass case with more pastries but also sandwiches and salads. The line snaked from the cashier all the way across to the door but it seemed to be moving quickly.

Flynn was studying the case when his sixth sense tingled. He looked around the room. The tables were full, as were the booths. He studied the people but didn't recognize anyone until he got to the last booth in the back corner. He could see just an arm and a bit of hair, but he knew immediately it was the woman from last night. He didn't know how he knew and if someone asked him under oath, he'd have to make some shit up but he knew it was her as sure as he was standing there. He smiled. Luck was definitely swinging his way.

After getting a half dozen pastries and a massive bucket of coffee, he ventured over and swung into the booth, dropping onto the bench across from the woman. He set his bag down on the table. She looked up from the file she was reading, startled. Yes, he'd know those hazel eyes anywhere.

"Hello again," he said quietly.

"I-I'm sorry. Have we met?" She was wearing a deep green sweater and her hair curled about her shoulders.

"Nice try," he said taking a sip from his paper coffee cup. "Damn, that's good."

"First time tasting Kim's coffee? People have moved here for it."

His gaze met hers. "This town keeps surprising me in all kinds of ways."

She smiled and closed the file she'd been reading. "I hope that's a good thing, Mr..."

"Flynn O'Connor. And you are?"

"Harper Edwards." She started to stand. "I'm done here. Take my table, I hope you enjoy your coffee and pastries. Kim's an excellent baker as well."

"You should stay and chat with me," he said in a soft voice.

"I'm sorry, Mr. O'Connor, I'm very busy," she said as she smoothed out her long brown and green plaid skirt. "Maybe some other time."

Flynn put a hand out and caught her wrist. "Do you usually call the men you kiss by their last names?"

Her eyes widened. "I-I don't know what you're talking about."

He cocked his head. "Should I kiss you again just to confirm it? I don't mind an audience but I'm guessing you do."

Harper glanced around quickly. Several people were watching them. She smiled at them and then sat back down. "You know I could just walk out of here. If you did anything I could call the police."

"You could," he acknowledged, "but then you would have to explain to them why you were poking around in the library during the party, an area strictly off-limits. Why don't you explain it to me like I'm four."

She stared at him and he knew she was trying to figure a way out.

"Rather than waste time creating a lie, just tell the truth. It's simpler and less taxing."

"Always threatening. That seems to be your style. The candle was a bit weak though. Hard to be afraid of a piece of wax."

He frowned. "I have no idea what the hell you're talking about. I haven't threatened you. If I had, you'd know it."

She narrowed her eyes at him but whatever she saw must have convinced her she was wrong because she dropped the topic.

"Did someone threaten you?" Now he wanted to know. The thought of someone terrorizing this woman unsettled him.

"It's none of your business. Just like what I was doing in the library."

There was something in her eye, a glint that made him think maybe she was in trouble. Maybe she needed help.

"That's where you're wrong. You weren't supposed to be in the library. You have a reputation to uphold, and I could tell everyone how you were drunk and you made a pass at me."

"I wasn't drunk."

He grinned. "No, you weren't. Can't use that as an excuse. But only we know that. They'll all believe it because people love gossip. So, what were you doing in the library?"

She jutted her chin forward. "Alright. I was there looking for proof that Astrid Windsor had been in that room."

He frowned. "Who is Astrid Windsor? Some historical figure?" Was the woman some kind of history nut?

"She was an eighteen-year-old girl, my niece's best friend in fact, and she was found dead yesterday, buried up by the bluffs. She's been missing for months."

Flynn stilled. He studied Harper's face. She wasn't making it up. Her eyes were bright with unshed tears. It made him want to pull her into his lap and soothe away all her pain. "I'm very sorry to hear that."

"Thank you," she said as she leaned back in the booth. "I have a lot on my plate. I need to go."

Flynn wasn't letting her off that easily. "Why do you think she was up at the Manor?"

Harper grimaced. "I shouldn't have said anything. It's part of an ongoing police investigation."

"Are you a cop?" Shit. That would be bad. But she sure as hell didn't look like a cop with those big hazel eyes and full pink lips.

"No, I'm Deputy Mayor of Cedar Bluff."

"Harper," a shrill voice called.

Flynn didn't bother to turn to see who it was because he didn't know anyone in that town, but Harper's face blanched and fatigue haunted her eyes.

"Susan, I thought you were staying home today." Harper started to rise but the woman came and stood at the end of the booth. She was tall with silver hair cut bluntly so it hung like a curtain around her head. Her blue eyes were cold and assessing. Frown lines appeared permanently etched around her mouth. An angry vibe rolled off her in waves. She was dressed in a long sweater and leggings with long boots. She was styled to the *nth* degree as if she had— what did they call it?—a glam squad working overtime before she even left the house. Her whole image screamed *look at me.*

"No. Too much to do. The Halloween Extravaganza is this Wednesday night and Jed Thompson is threatening to pull our permit if he doesn't get to go over what he thinks are the necessary steps to protect the statuary and gardens in the square with me. I told him I would meet him here." She turned to focus on Flynn. "I don't believe we've met." She offered her hand.

Harper seemed to grind her teeth. "My boss, the mayor of Cedar Bluff, Susan Duggan."

"Flynn O'Connor." Flynn took her hand and shook it briefly. It was like shaking hands with a skeleton.

Susan gave him an assessing look. "Didn't I see you at the party at Everlasting Manor last evening?"

"Yes, I am with the Club's security." He hoped his terse tone signaled to the woman he didn't want to chat. He wanted more information from Harper, like why she thought the dead girl had been at the Manor.

"I thought that was Ravi Shah's job," Susan persisted.

"He is in charge locally. I am with the global team. I'm just here for a site visit."

"I see," Susan purred. Her voice had taken on a deeper tone and now she was looking at him like a piece of choice meat in a butcher shop window. "Welcome to Cedar Bluff. Please come see me if you have any questions. Perhaps we could have lunch and you can tell me all about the ins and outs of the Rainy Day Club. I've been trying to become a member for a while now."

Not happening in a million years. "You would have to talk to the head office about that."

She let out a bark of laughter. "So closed mouth about things, all you club people."

A chill went across his skin. He recognized that laughter. He'd last heard it through the air vent when he'd been in the cellar. This was the woman having pretty vocal sex with someone. It had to be a member.

Note to self: figure out which room the vent in the basement was connected to. That was going on his list of things to do immediately because for all her attention seeking, he recognized a shrewdness in her eyes. She was someone worth keeping a close eye on.

"Well, I'm off. Harper, first thing tomorrow morning I want you in the office. We have much to go over." With that, she sailed out after nodding hellos to half the people in the bakery.

Flynn cocked his head. "I can see why she makes you tired."

Harper's hazel eyes widened. "What makes you say that? She—"

He waved her off. "It's written all over your face if you know where to look."

She snorted. "And you know me that well, do you? One kiss and you know all my secrets?"

Flynn leaned forward so his lips were inches from hers. "Not yet, but I will."

Harper leaned back in the booth and stared at him. "I-I must go," she shot to her feet and grabbed the file folder. "Take care," was all she said before she left the bakery like it was on fire.

Flynn watched her through the window. He needed to

talk to Shah and find out about this Astrid person. The last thing they needed was cops sniffing around the Manor. This whole openness to the community was a big fucking mistake. A bomb just waiting to go off that Flynn didn't want to be anywhere near it when it did because there would be lots of casualties.

CHAPTER NINE

Harper plopped down behind her desk and fanned herself. She'd practically run from the bakery to the sanctity of her small office in the township building. Flynn O'Connor was something to behold. She'd thought he was sexy last night in his navy blazer and white shirt, but he was a fantasy come to life today with his black sweater and worn jeans. The stubble on his jaw only made it worse and those coal-black eyes; she was sure they could see into her soul.

She continued to fan herself. What the hell was the thermostat set to in here? She rubbed shaking hands over her face and chided herself for being ridiculous. O'Connor was just a guy who, admittedly, she had amazing chemistry with, but he was also from the Manor. And anyone from that place was suspect, as far as she was concerned. She needed to be careful around him.

Leaning back in her chair she looked out the window to the square below. There were days when she missed New York. The excitement of it, the energy. She loved that she could, at any hour, go out and buy milk, go to a club, or eat food from anywhere in the world. But the City also wore her down. And in the end, she was happy to move even if Cedar Bluff wasn't her choice. Although, she'd missed small town life. Things like having dinner with her folks on Sundays and going to the square for the holiday functions. There was something so fresh, so pure in that.

At least that was how she'd thought of it before Astrid's death. Now she wasn't so sure. Someone had killed the girl and tossed her away like she was trash. It was easy, but unfair to blame it on outsiders. It could just as easily be someone from Cedar Bluff. She would be a fool to discount a local just because she knew them.

Flipping open the file one more time she picked up the sheet she'd been reading. It was the autopsy report on Astrid. Jason had sent her a copy. He'd wanted to come over and talk with her as she read it, answer any questions but mostly soften the blow. She liked him for that, but it wasn't what she needed.

The fact was, working in New York City for ten years had hardened her in certain ways. She'd seen all kinds of things, dead bodies among them. As an assistant to one of the city's Deputy Mayors, all kinds of things had crossed her desk. It was what got her the job here, it was also what made her leave the city. She'd seen too much. Knew too much about too many things.

She read over the report one more time. Astrid had been beaten but that was not the official cause of death. Someone had broken her neck. In short, she had been tortured. Maybe not in the traditional sense like waterboarding or pulling out her fingernails, but she was tortured and then someone killed her.

Because of the state of Astrid's body, the findings were inconclusive in whether she'd been raped or not. But Mandy had privately told Jason, as she had Harper, that she thought it likely. How she knew was a mystery to Harper and there was nothing about it in the report but Mandy had been quite sure. She must have a feel for these types of things after doing so many autopsies. Kind of like when Harper knew when Susan was going to do something that would purposely piss certain people off and she headed her off at the pass. She just had a gut feeling about it.

Her phone rang. "Hey, Dana. How are you feeling today?"

"My head still hurts but not too bad. Derek took the kids out for breakfast, so I got to sleep a bit."

"Nice."

Dana yawned. "You took off in a hurry last night. Did everything just get to you?"

If by everything Dana meant a tall, dark, sexy-as-hell stranger whom she'd kissed with abandon... yup. "Well, when the power went out, it felt like the party was over. It was just time to go, you know?"

"Did you find what you were looking for?" Dana asked.

She tapped a pencil on her desk. "Maybe? I need more time to go back and check it out."

Dana yawned again. "That's not going to be easy. What are you up to today?"

"I'm at work."

Her friend *tsked*. "You work way too hard."

"That is not a lie. But, I was sitting here thinking about New York and Kenny and how I dodged a bullet with that one."

Dana snorted. "I'll say. What an asshole. Throwing you under the bus for his mistake. If he'd kept his mouth shut and not blabbed about the deal your boss made to get the backing of the union boss to that reporter, you would still be in the Mayor's office."

"Maybe, but honestly, probably not. My boss knew what Kenny had done, which is why once the whole thing blew over, Kenny got shipped out to Staten Island to work for the borough President. I was told I could stay, but fundamentally, I knew the day was coming when I would be seen as a liability. No one got to just fade away. They either got fired and discredited, got new jobs with their old bosses when they left or they disappeared off the face of the earth, hiding in some little town somewhere never to be heard from again. I chose option three before anyone could force my hand."

"Personally, I'm glad you did. I missed you while you were in the city."

"Thanks. I missed you too."

"So, back to the Manor. How are you going to do more exploring?"

Glancing out the window, Flynn came into view. He was carrying his bakery items but also some other bags. Shopping? Didn't seem like something he'd do. Not that she knew him at all...but maybe she should. A smile slid across her face. "I've got some ideas."

"Ooh. Do you need any help?" Dana sounded excited. "Being a full-time mom and part-time school secretary is not the most exciting job in the world.

Harper laughed. "I'm not sure. I'll let you know." Flynn got into his SUV and pulled out of the parking space. "You know," she said, "there is something you can help me with." The smile got wider.

Two hours later they were at Harper's condo.

"Are you sure you want to do this?" Dana asked.

She shook her head ruefully. "No, but it gets me back into the Manor and it gets Susan out of trouble with the town council. She's been trying to get everyone on her side before the Halloween Extravaganza on Wednesday, but they are all giving her grief, especially Jed Thompson."

"But we do all the other holidays in the square, why is this Halloween thing so different?"

"It's not, but the rest of the events, Santa's North Pole Fair, and the Turkey Trot, are all grandfathered in. The council can't change them, but Halloween is new at the town square. They used to do it at the school but it's too big and the school parking lot can't handle the event and all the cars. You remember what happened last year."

Dana rolled her eyes. "Jesus, I'd thought I'd seen it all until Jim Thorp lost his shit at Ken King for putting a dent in his new car."

"Yeah. So, what location has lots of parking and plenty of space and is spooky?" she grinned.

Dana shook her head. "You are pure evil. Switching locations of the whole event to suit your personal needs is a bold strategy."

"I like to think of it as being creative. Solving two problems at once."

Dana hugged the pillow in her lap. "Uh-huh. How are you going to get the Rainy Day Club to agree?"

Harper sat on the other end of the sofa sipping her tea. "I have some ideas. First and foremost, if they host then we can get their generator fixed. It moves them up on the list."

"But their power will be up by then."

"True but they still need their generator fixed. Honestly, I think Susan might have some connections she can use."

Dana snorted. "That wouldn't surprise me one bit. And you know it would make her happy to piss off the town council. Everyone knows she hates most of them." She glanced at her watch. "Shit, I've got to run. The kids have a play date this afternoon and I have to drive them." She got up off the sofa. "Let me know how I can help."

"Will do." Harper gave her friend a quick hug and walked her to the door. She made sure she locked the door after her. Unease set in as soon as Harper was alone. How had they gotten her patio door open? And who were 'they'?

She'd thought it was Flynn but the look of confusion on his face when she brought it up was enough to tell her he had nothing to do with it.

She stared at her door for a second. Short of installing more locks to make it more secure, there was not much she could do. Installing an alarm system would take days. She could, however, set some traps so if the person broke in again, she would at least know they were there.

She went about laying her trap. It wasn't pretty but it was serviceable. That done, she called Susan. "How did the talk with Jed go?

"The man is an ass."

Harper's stomach dropped. "I hope you didn't tell him that." It would take her weeks to get him over it. Jed could hold a grudge.

There was a sigh. "I may have mentioned it. Regardless, we can use the square just not the part by the monument in the middle or the edge of the duck pond area and only part of the parking lot."

"For Pete's sake, that's almost the whole square. How are we going to throw this Halloween Extravaganza now? I knew it was a bad idea to entertain any conversation with him at this point. It was all settled before this. Everyone agreed." She was laying it on a little thick but not by much. Would the world end if they couldn't hold their Halloween Extravaganza" Probably not. But it would suck.

"I tried but he just wouldn't compromise," Susan huffed.

Harper knew that was probably true. He did it on purpose because this was the first time he had any power. People really were the worst.

"I have an idea but it's going to take some doing. You might have to use whatever connections you have." She tried to make it sound like Susan had to save the day because she knew that appealed to the other woman's ego.

"I mean you will have to work your magic for this to happen."

"Stop trying to sell me on being the hero and tell me what it is," she demanded.

Susan was one shrewd cookie. "Where's the one place around town that has plenty of parking, lots of outside space and a reputation for being haunted?"

There was a pause. "That's a brilliant idea! Everlasting Manor is perfect to host this event."

"It is, but we need them to agree to it and they may not be so keen. It will be a lot of people, including a ton of kids running around their grounds."

"Leave it to me. I'm pretty sure Gina will get on board. There might be one or two other people that I can whisper in their ear about this as well."

"I have another suggestion. Get Bert to shift some guys and restore the power over there but make sure they know you made it happen. Then they'll owe you. Also, get Darryl's boss to move fixing their generator up on his list as well. He's going to be out since his wife gave birth last night but I'm sure they must have someone else who could do it."

"I like the way you think," Susan said, a smile in her voice.

Harper bit her lip. "I have one request. I want to come with you when you go talk to Gina and whoever. I think you should do it face-to-face. You're far more persuasive that way."

"I'm not even going to ask you why because you'll just make some bullshit up, but okay, you can come with me. Meet me there this afternoon at five p.m. We'll hit them up during cocktail hour."

Harper let out a breath she didn't even realize she was holding. "Are you going to call them and tell them we're coming?"

Susan laughed. "No way. The element of surprise is always helpful in these cases. It gives them less time to prepare and come up with a good reason to say no."

"How will you get past the guard at the gate?"

"Leave it to me. I'll get our names on the list. See you at five," she said and hung up.

Harper put her phone back down on her counter. That gave her time to prepare. She needed to find a way back into the Manor's library, but she suspected it wouldn't be too hard as long as Flynn O'Connor was there. She'd get him to let her back in.

Picking up her phone again, she made another call. "Hey, Mom."

"Hi, honey. How are you? I spoke with your sister, and she told me about yesterday. I am so sorry you had to see that, sweetie."

"I'm fine. How is Audrey? Did Marnie say? I know she said they were going down to Boston. Did they go?"

"They're in Boston and everyone is doing the best they can under the circumstances."

It was always nice to hear her mom's voice. Nicer to know she could go see them when she wanted. Family was more important to her these days. Possibly because of all she saw in New York or possibly because she realized they wouldn't be around forever. Brushing those thoughts aside, she asked her mom about the storm. "Any damage?"

"Nothing major. Lost a few shingles. Your father wanted to go up on the roof and check but I told him I would kill him myself if he got the ladder out." Mom laughed hollowly. "Pete Henderson will come on Monday and take a look. What about you? Any damage around the property?"

The truth was she hadn't bothered to look. The building maintenance team took care of all of that. "Nothing that I noticed."

"Well, that's a relief. I'm making seafood chowder for dinner. Why don't you join us?"

Just the mention of her mother's seafood chowder made her mouth water. "I have a five o'clock meeting but if I can get out at a reasonable time, I'll stop by. Don't wait for me though."

Her mother *tsked*. "You work too hard."

She almost laughed. Dana had said the same thing. It must be a small town thing. "Quite possibly. Is Dad around?"

"No, he's gone out to the hardware stores. He wanted to get some recycle bags and a new rake. The rest of the stubborn leaves will fall like snow with all this rain and wind. He wanted to get a start on getting them up."

Disappointment rocked her. She wanted to talk to her dad about the Manor. "Okay. I've got to go but hopefully I will see you later."

"Love you, honey."

"Love you too, Mom," she said and hung up.

She'd have to wait until tonight to quiz her father about the Manor but she knew he'd know the inside scoop. Everyone always said it was old women who gossiped but she'd always found that they couldn't hold a candle to old men. If there was anything to know about Everlasting Manor, he would know it.

In the meantime, she grabbed the file on Astrid and headed back over to the sofa. She wanted to re-read every word and make a list of questions for Jason and Mandy. There had to be something there that pointed to Astrid's killer, something besides green paint.

CHAPTER TEN

F lynn leaned forward in his chair. "Do you know the exact date Astrid went missing?"

Shah frowned. "It was over the Fourth of July weekend. She went out supposedly with friends and never returned home again."

A weight settled on Flynn's shoulders. He'd been involved in a lot of shit in his youth and even more in the military as a sniper, but none of that held a candle to the shit he saw working for the Society. And yet, the idea of a young girl going missing like that made him ill. He was angry and sad all at once and he didn't even know her. Life was never what he'd thought it would turn out to be and now hers was over.

"Do we have video of that weekend?'

Shah glanced across the desk at him. "What kind of video?"

"Of the rooms in the Manor."

"We do." Shah studied him. "Do you think someone here might have had something to do with Astrid's death?"

"It's been suggested." He wasn't going to give more details than that.

Shah blew out a breath. "That would be horrible but also make things very difficult."

"Yeah. Cops sniffing around would not be helpful. So do you have video?"

"Yes." Shah stood. "Come on I'll show you now that the power is back up." He moved from around his desk and Flynn followed him into another room. One wall was filled with computer screens with a desk below it that held a few keyboards and mice. Equipment racks loaded with computer servers lined the opposite wall. "This is the in-house security video room." He sat down at a chair in the center of the desk and started typing.

Flynn took the chair next to him as the screens came to life.

"Okay, first let's start with last night, just before the power went out the second time. See if anyone entered the unfinished section of the basement."

Shah frowned. "Okay. Why? Did something happen?"

"Not really. Just thought I heard something and wanted to be sure no one had come into that area." He sure as hell wasn't going to confess someone got the drop on him.

Shah pulled up the video but the only people who went into the unfinished area were him and Flynn. Then Donovan. So, the ghost struck again. Curiouser and curiouser.

Flynn was not amused. "Show me the date when Astrid disappeared."

Shah pulled up another video. "This is the night Astrid went missing. I'll start at the main door around five p.m." He hit a button and the video started, not that it was easy to tell only the time counter moved. Shah hit fast forward and the screen picked up speed. He stopped it when someone appeared on screen. It was Mrs. Carruthers going out. Then the time counter said fifty-three minutes later, she came back.

Groups of people went out and came back for the rest of the night. They stopped at eight a.m. the following morning.

Shah let out a long breath. "She wasn't here." His shoulders sagged. "I've got to say, that's a relief."

Flynn didn't comment. He wasn't convinced. "Can you show me footage of all the outside doors?"

"I can…but do you think it's necessary?"

"I do."

Shah frowned but brought up the footage of the back door in the salon and when that was empty, he did the same for the dining room. Still nothing. Flynn wanted to call it after each one but knew it paid to be thorough. It was his job to protect the Society and if someone had done something that threatened the organization, then he had to make sure that threat was neutralized.

"This is the last one. It's a side door off the storage area." Shah started the video. They zoomed through until ten-oh-five and then the door opened. Someone came in but they were wearing a hat that was pulled low and the collar of the jacket was pulled up to block the face. The cameras didn't record in color so it was hard to discern if they were male or female. It was hard to discern anything about them.

A second later, a young girl walked in. She was wearing a dress and her hair was down around her shoulders. Shah swore.

"Astrid?" Flynn asked.

"Yes." Shah typed furiously on the keyboard. The video fast-forwarded. There was nothing else. No one left again.

Flynn stared at the screen. "How is that possible?"

Shah shook his head. "It isn't. I don't have a fucking clue. We've been through all the video of the entrances of the house. She didn't leave. At least not that night."

"Yeah, that's what I thought. What are the options? She

left a few days or weeks later? She was carried out in something a day or two or a week or two later? Is it possible to secret someone in this house for a long period of time?"

Shah's mouth hung open. "Are you serious? Do you think someone killed her here and left her body on ice until they could get it out?"

"Right now, I'm just throwing out ideas. What we do know is someone knew about the cameras so they knew they could possibly be seen. How often do you check the cameras?"

Shah shrugged. "Never, unless I have a reason. You know the types of things that go on here. I don't look at the video unless it's necessary. At the gate, Karl keeps people out for the most part. If something bigger crosses our outside cameras, we check it but it's always deer. No one comes into the house uninvited." He pointed at the screen. "She was obviously invited but I have no idea by whom, if she left alive, or was smuggled out dead."

"Check with Karl and see if anyone signed her in." It was doubtful. Not if they smuggled her in the side door, but it was worth a shot. If this came out, the cops would be asking. Flynn would have to destroy any evidence of Astrid ever being on the property. "You're going to have to watch the video for the next few days after she arrived. See if you can pinpoint when she left and how. But first, show me the video for that area of the house."

Shah hesitated. "I can't. There is no video in that area. It's mostly storage with a second billiard room, a TV room, and a game room. The truth is, when the new section was built, whoever it was did a crappy job and we've had all kinds of problems with the area. Can't get it hardwired for the cameras. We've tried for the last year to get it set up. No dice. After a while Mrs. Carruthers told me to stop trying. The camera by the door works and the rest didn't matter. I take my cues from her. She didn't want to have to keep making excuses to the guests as to why those rooms were off limits as we tried to get the installation right."

This was a fucking nightmare. He wanted to yell at Shah but there was no point. He was going to have to sit down with the man and explain his job to him a little better... But even more Mrs. Carruthers was going to have to go. She was a menace to the Society, and likely her meddling was the reason they were in real trouble now.

"Okay show me the one in the foyer. If they left that area without leaving the house, they must have gone through the foyer."

Shah brought up the feed quick time and they reviewed it. No evidence that Astrid had crossed the area. "I don't get it," he said.

"Neither do I." Flynn was mystified and that pissed him off. There was something they were missing. Harper thought Astrid had been in the library. Maybe she had. It was time to check it out. "Keep trying. I'm going to go upstairs and poke around."

Shah nodded. "I'll see if there's anything on the system that indicates a window was opened for any length of time or if the camera was turned off or..."

Flynn didn't bother to listen to the rest. He left the room and headed toward the hallway. A window was an option, he supposed. But that would require more than one person. He couldn't imagine one person opening the window, pushing Astrid's body out, then climbing out themselves and shutting it again. Then what? Pick Astrid up and lug her to a car?

Maybe she hadn't been killed until later. She could have gone through the window of her own volition. But why would she do that? What possible explanation could be given to make her crawl out a window?

He came to the top of the stairs in the main foyer and paused.

"Susan, Harper, what brings you here?" Gina's voice floated over to him.

"We came to speak to you," Susan said and linked her arm through Gina's. Flynn came around the corner and watched them go into the salon. Harper was a few steps behind and she waited for them to get further ahead and then she turned toward the stairs.

"Going somewhere?" Flynn asked as he leaned against the banister.

Harper jumped. "I didn't see you there."

"Obviously," he said with a smile. She was wearing a dark pair of jeans and a deep burgundy sweater that accented her coloring and cleavage quite nicely. Her black rain jacket was much too big for her and made her look like she was swimming in it. Her hair was back up in a messy-looking bun. She looked like a sexy waif and damn if his dick didn't stand at attention. "Would you like to go check out the library?"

She narrowed her eyes at him. "You would let me?"

"All you have to do is ask."

"Fine. May I see the library?"

Flynn smiled. "Sure." He came around the banister and grabbed her hand pulling her up the staircase with him. He liked the feel of her hand in his and although he should probably let it go, he didn't. Instead, he crossed the hall to the library and opened the door, ushering her inside ahead of him mostly so he could try and get a glimpse of her ass in her jeans. The fabric kissed every curve and his lips twitched. She turned.

He reluctantly brought his gaze back up to hers. "Go ahead and check."

She paused, but he just walked over to the desk and

leaned his butt on it, crossing his legs out in front of him. Huffing out a breath, she went over to the windows and moved the curtains back from the frame. Her oversized jacket caught on the edge of the windowsill and she swore. He tried to watch what she was doing but mostly he just watched her ass and then her back and any other part of her in his line of vision.

The hair on the back of his neck stood up. He turned and stared at the wall. Someone was watching them. It wasn't a ghost. It was a real live human. Flynn knew it in his bones but how were they doing it? Was there a camera?

Harper sighed. "I was so sure Astrid was in here. Positive in fact. It just made sense." She came over to stand beside him.

Part of him desperately wanted to tell her that she was right just to wipe the dejection from her face but that was not in the best interest of the Society, so not in his best interest. Besides, if he told her, she'd run right to the cops no matter what she promised and then there'd be a shit ton of problems that he'd have to deal with.

"Satisfied?"

She remained silent for a beat. "No. There could be other green rooms in the house. She could've been in there. I want to keep looking. I have to keep looking. Astrid was like family. Her murder can't go unsolved."

Flynn let out an exaggerated sigh and sat back down on the desk. The feeling hadn't gone away but he didn't want to call attention to it and give Harper any ideas. "And if I tell you there are no other green rooms in the house, would you believe me?" Her scent engulfed him as the heat from her body penetrated his arm. He was having difficulty focusing on anything other than this alluring woman. He should be keeping her at a distance but what he wanted to do was take her now, here on the desk, in the library. They could make it a game. Where would he take her next? On the desk in the library, on the dining room table downstairs, or his personal favorite, on the pool table …like a game of Clue only with sex toys instead of weapons. He sucked in a deep breath trying to get his shit together. She was too fucking distracting for words.

"I suppose I have to believe you," she said finally.

"But you don't."

She turned to face him. "No, I don't."

That stung. He didn't like that she didn't trust him. Not one bit. "At least we know where we stand. You don't trust me and I—" The door to the library opened.

"And this is—" Mrs. Carruthers broke off. She glanced at Harper and then back at Flynn. "I'm sorry, Flynn. I didn't realize you had a guest. You know you're supposed to give me prior warning."

"She's not my guest," he said, eyeing the men who had now filed into the library.

"Jason, what are you doing here?" Harper said as she swung around, her jacket hooking the stapler on the desk and knocking it to the floor. Flynn reached down and picked it up, putting it back in place.

The blond man spoke. "We're here looking into Astrid's death." He turned to Flynn. "I'm Detective Jason Merritt," he walked over and offered his hand.

"Flynn O'Connor."

"You're a member here at the club, Mr. O'Connor?" Merritt asked as he looked at Harper.

Flynn knew immediately that Merritt was pissed to see Harper there. The fact that he was at the club meant that either they had evidence of Astrid being there or she'd already told Merritt about the paint. Flynn was annoyed. He felt betrayed which was a little irrational, but he didn't give a fuck.

He straightened. "No, I'm not a guest. I am part of the security team."

"George! You're back. How are you doing?" Harper asked the man behind Merritt. The chief obviously thought better of only having Jason and Lazlo on this case.

"Hey, Harper. Doing well. Got bored sitting at home watching shit TV. Had to get back in the saddle." The large man came across the room. "I'm Detective George Crawley. I thought Ravi Shah was the security guy around here." He was over six feet but heavy. All his muscle turned to fat and now he was just bulky. Probably a linebacker in high school but by the way he was moving, he was in pain.

"He is. I'm part of the global security team, just here on a site visit."

"I see."

"Sorry," another voice said. "I got lost." The kid that came through the door was tall. Taller than Flynn's six foot-one inch height, and he was built. All muscle but the way he moved made it seem like he was uncoordinated. Like an over-excited dog. He stumbled as he came across the room. "I'm Billy er, Detective Lazlo." He offered his hand.

Flynn shook the kid's hand. Lazlo squeezed and Flynn met his gaze. This kid was no overzealous puppy. There was a coldness in his eyes that Flynn recognized because he saw it in the mirror every day. Then in an instant it vanished. Lazlo was a man to watch out for. He was far more dangerous than the other two combined.

"Why are you here?" Flynn asked.

"We're looking into the death of Astrid Windsor. We received an anonymous tip that she might have been here." Merritt tried hard to keep his gaze from Harper but failed.

Harper had the grace to blush as she straightened. Flynn

had the urge to put his fist in Merritt's face if for no other reason than the possessive look he just gave Harper.

"Did you speak to Shah about this?" he asked.

Mrs. Carruthers's back went ramrod straight. "They spoke to me about the matter, and *I* said they could search the library."

Flynn pulled out his phone and sent a text to Shah. "This is why we have security. To deal with things like this, among other reasons." He turned to Merritt. "You may search this room but only this room. You aren't going on some wild fishing expedition across the whole house."

Mrs. Carruthers opened her mouth to speak when Shah arrived.

He greeted the newcomers. "Gentlemen, it's nice to see you. Sorry it's under these circumstances."

"Shah," Merritt said and the other two nodded to him.

"George, how are you feeling? I heard you had surgery." Shah moved further into the room and came to stand on the other side of Flynn.

"It hurts but I'm fine," the large man said.

"Glad to hear it. As I'm sure Flynn said, you are welcome to search this room but I'm afraid I will have to limit it there."

Mrs. Carruthers put her hands on her hips. "I see no reason why—"

"Thanks for your help, Mrs. Carruthers," Flynn said. "Shah and I can take it from here."

Her face flushed and her eyes narrowed. Flynn coldly stared her down. If she opened her mouth, he'd make sure she was gone by the morning. He couldn't have cops wandering around this place no matter how innocent she thought everything was. It wouldn't be one and done. Letting them in was a mistake. They could claim they saw all kinds of things that they could later get a warrant for. As it was,

Flynn wasn't comfortable with having them in the building at all. There was no way in hell he was going to turn them loose to search the whole thing.

Carruthers turned on her heel and stormed out.

Flynn turned back to Merritt. "Do your search. We will wait outside." He turned to Shah. "You stay by the door." Then he put his hand on the small of Harper's back and ushered her out of the room. Merritt watched them go with a look of hatred in his eyes. *So noted.* The feeling was mutual.

Harper turned to him in the hallway. "I should stay—"

"No, you shouldn't. You came here with Susan for another reason. I suggest you find her and do whatever it is she came here to do because if you go back in that room everyone will know that you're the anonymous source and I'm guessing you don't want that."

She stared at him weighing his words. "I guess you're right, but I would like to continue our…chat later."

"Fair enough. Have dinner with me." Flynn knew it was a mistake the moment the words left his lips but fuck it. He truly wanted to have dinner with her.

Harper hesitated. She stared at him and then glanced over at the library door. "Okay. Dinner. Where?"

"You tell me. This is your town. I have no idea where to eat. As long as it's not here."

She nodded. "Come to my place. We can order in."

"Don't want to be seen with me?" It stung a bit, he had to admit.

"No. I don't want to have to answer all kinds of questions about you."

He wasn't sure he liked that answer any better but knew it was the best he was going to get. And, of course, there were benefits to being at her place where no one was watching…

"Is there a restroom up here?"

Flynn gave her directions and watched her walk down

the hallway. Dinner was definitely a bad idea, and he hadn't looked forward to something this much since coming home from Iraq.

He had plans for Harper Edwards and very little of them involved food.

CHAPTER ELEVEN

Harper felt the weight of Flynn's stare all the way down the hallway to the restroom. Once inside she closed the door and leaned against it. Disappointment filled her. She'd been so sure. So freaking positive Astrid had been here.

After washing her hands, she took one of the towels and dampened it, then ran it over her face. She was hot and tired and annoyed. Mostly she was off-center. Flynn O'Connor did that to her and now she'd agreed to have dinner with him. What the hell had she been thinking?

Who was she kidding? She'd been thinking he was sexy as hell and that she trusted him. She'd been amazed how safe she felt around him and having him in her condo would make her feel if not better, at least more comfortable about what had happened last night. And, if she were being honest, she would admit she was thinking about having him in her bed.

She stared at her reflection in the mirror. But who needed to be that honest?

She straightened up and turned to throw out the paper towel, hooking her jacket on the tap. "Shit," The damn jacket was too big and was always getting caught on things. She knew she should give it away, but it had been her dad's and wearing it always felt like he was hugging her. She needed that today.

Harper left the restroom and headed back down the hallway. Sundown was long gone, and the scant light that had filtered in earlier was gone, making it hard to see her way. The library was dark. They must have finished their fruitless search. She did feel badly about that. Jason had trusted her; trusted her information, and her instincts, and she'd let him down. He wouldn't be so trusting next time.

She arrived at the top of the stairs and grabbed the banister. The dark carpet made it hard to see anything more than a foot in front of her face. Flynn must have gone down as well. She'd just put one foot on the top stair when a hard shove came from behind. She yelped and tried to hold on to the banister, but her grip slipped. Her jacket, however, caught around the top of the ornate newel post. The fabric ripped, but in the end, held. She managed to grab on again with both hands and look behind her. Footsteps pounded away but the person was too far away, and the dimness made it impossible to locate whoever had pushed her. She sat down heavily on the stairs. It was a long way to the bottom.

Someone had just tried to kill her.

Flynn appeared at the bottom of the stairs and turned on the light switch. He took one look at her and sped up two steps at a time. "What is it? What happened? Are you alright?" He pulled her to her feet.

Tremors had seized control of her body and she had a hard time forcing the words out. "S-someone just tried to push me down the stairs."

Flynn looked down the hallway.

"They're gone. I heard them running away."

The pulse in Flynn's jaw jumped. His eyes were black as they looked her up and down. "But you're sure you're okay?"

"Yes," she said her voice still a little breathy but now she wasn't sure if it was from the fall or from being this close to Flynn. This man represented safety, and she didn't want to be anywhere else.

"Harper, are you okay?" Jason called up from the bottom of the stairs. He was shooting Flynn a death glare and she realized he still had his arms around her.

"I'm fine," she said reaching for the banister once more and moving away from Flynn. "I just ripped my jacket on the banister. I knew I shouldn't wear this one. I'm always getting it snagged on stuff." She started down the stairs holding the balustrade for dear life and hoping her knees would hold her.

"I'm about to head out," Jason said. "Do you need a lift?"

"No, thank you. I drove here." Thunder rumbled as she spoke. She glanced out of the windows in the foyer. "Again?"

Susan appeared at her side. "Yes. Apparently, another storm is blowing through." She glanced Harper's way with a frown. "Are you okay?"

"Yes. Just slipped on the stairs and ripped my jacket. How did it go?" she asked. Now that the library was a bust, she wanted the chance to look around some more.

"Fine. We're working out details but I think it will come together." Then she lowered her voice. "What is the entire detective division of the Cedar Bluff police force doing here?"

"I'll explain later."

"Jason," Susan said, "how are things progressing?" she asked as she looked over his shoulder. "George Crawley. I'm surprised to see you here. Didn't I hear you were out on leave?"

"I'm fine. Thanks for asking." The big man grimaced as if

he was anything but fine, but no one was going to say anything about it. Being back on the job was his choice.

The sudden pelting rain on the windows startled them all. The ferocity of it hitting the glass made them all pause. "God, there's going to be more flooding," Susan commented.

"We should be going," Jason said. "They're going to need all the help they can get in town." He gave Harper a cool look. "We'll talk later," he announced and then proceeded out the door.

Crawley and Lazlo nodded to everyone and then followed.

Susan arched an eyebrow. "Who pissed in his Cornflakes?"

Gina came up beside her. "I've just checked with Mrs. Carruthers, and she is on board so all we have to do now is convince Ravi and I think we're good."

"Convince Ravi of what?" Flynn asked.

"The mayor wants to hold the Halloween Extravaganza here on Thursday night. It's like a pre-cursor to trick or treating on Friday night. I think it's a lovely idea." Gina gave him a sunny smile.

"No."

Gina frowned. "What do you mean no? It's a great idea. We get to foster good relations with Cedar Bluff and provide a safe environment for the kids to celebrate."

Flynn clenched his jaw. "No."

Susan immediately sidled up to Flynn. "Come now, Mr. O'Connor, I am sure we can find some way to persuade you." She offered him a huge smile.

Harper gritted her teeth. Susan never knew when to quit. She had to know Flynn wouldn't fall for her tricks. But that didn't stop her from making the attempt.

Susan took Flynn's arm and Harper was quite sure the

woman deliberately brushed a breast on his bicep. Was she fucking serious?

Harper cleared her throat. "I think we should go, Susan. The weather is deteriorating."

"Nonsense. I think it makes more sense to stay here until it lets up." She tried tugging Flynn back toward the salon. "Mr. O'Connor, do you mind if I call you Flynn? I was wondering if you could tell me more about the Rainy Day Club."

Flynn dug his heels in, resisting her efforts to get cozy. He didn't even respond to her question. "Holding the event here is a bad idea. You'll have to find somewhere else."

"Susan!" A man stepped out from the salon. "I didn't realize you were here."

"Eli!" She immediately dropped Flynn's arm. "And Richard. What are you gentlemen doing here? I thought you were leaving town."

"We got held up," Eli said. "Why don't you join us for dinner? The club is doing a nice hearty stew this evening with fresh crusty bread."

"Sounds delicious. I would love to." She followed the men into the dining area, her hips swaying like a starlet from the Fifties.

Harper turned to Flynn. "Do you need some time? You could follow me to my place."

He glanced up and swore softly as the front door opened. Jason, along with Crawley and Lazlo, trucked back into the foyer. "The canal overran the Thompson Bridge. I'm afraid we're stuck here for a while."

Harper didn't know whether to cry or celebrate. She wanted to check out the rest of the rooms in the house and search for green paint and this could be her opportunity. On the other hand, she wanted to be alone with Flynn. She let out a long breath. Shit. She'd been jealous of Susan a few moments ago. How stupid was that? Maybe it was better if they stayed with other people. God only knew what would happen if they went to her place.

Crawley and Lazlo shrugged out of their coats and went into the salon. Jason came to a halt beside her and Flynn.

Flynn glanced at her. "Excuse me for a minute." He walked by them and went down the back stairs.

But she knew exactly what would happen if he came to her place and now she was seriously disappointed that it wasn't going to happen. She wanted Flynn as much as she wanted to breathe. That kiss had rocked her world and she wanted more of that. Much more.

"Harper?" Jason scowled at her.

"Sorry, what?" She'd been staring after Flynn and Jason's face looked as ominous as the sky outside.

"I said what are you doing here? Didn't you trust me to look into what you told me? And thanks for the tip, by the way."

She wanted to hit him. There was no other way to describe it. She wanted to smoke Jason Merritt right in the nose and hopefully break it. "Sorry if I was wrong. Just trying to find out who killed Astrid. It was the same paint, by the way. The library is just one room with it. There could be more in here." She fixed him with a glare. "And for your information, I'm here because we need a better place to hold the Halloween Extravaganza. Jed's giving the mayor a hard time. This place has lots of space and parking. It's close to town and spooky as fu...uh, in its own right. Perfect for the event. We're here trying to convince everyone. Flynn is the only holdout."

Jason glanced in the direction Flynn disappeared to and then back at her, uncertainty sprawled across his features. "So, you're here to what, help Susan?"

She wanted to tell him the truth but didn't trust his very

judgmental attitude. Exactly what she didn't need right now. She knew her infatuation with Flynn was stupid. She didn't know him from Adam, and he emanated danger, but she also knew a compelling chemistry existed between them. More powerful than anything she'd ever experienced.

"I'm here to keep Susan on task and stop her from pissing people off. We wouldn't be in this mess if she'd played nice with Jed." She let out a loud sigh.

Jason smirked. "That sounds like Susan." He inclined his head. "Where is she?" Just then a peal of laughter came from the dining room. He glanced in that direction and then back at Harper. "It's like that, is it? She's schmoozing and leaving you to do the real work?"

Harper made a non-committal sound. She didn't want to throw Susan under the bus. Instead, she asked about the bridge. "How high was the water?"

He shrugged out of his jacket. "It's a good foot over the bridge. If it keeps raining like this, we'll be stuck here for a while."

"It's been such a wet fall. I'm not surprised there's flooding. Climate change is real." She peered at the back stairwell but still no Flynn.

"Well, since you're here, you might as well eat," Mrs. Carruthers said from the middle of the salon.

"Not the friendliest invitation I've ever had," Jason commented. "But I'm starving so I'll take it." He stepped back and gestured. "After you."

Harper didn't have a choice but to head into the dining room unless she wanted to tell Jason that she had dinner plans with Flynn. That wasn't an option. She wasn't in the mood for another sarcastic comment from him. It would be criminal to lose her temper and hit him. Besides, the flooded bridge sort of put a pin in their plans.

She strode into the dining room behind Lazlo with Jason

at her heels. Mrs. Carruthers stopped beside a table for four. "You may sit here."

They all took their seats. A young woman came to take their drink orders. She was dressed in a white blouse and black pants with her dark hair tied back in a ponytail.

"I didn't know you were working here, Blair," Harper said to the server after everyone had ordered.

"Yeah, just part-time. Gives me some spending money." She frowned. "I was so sorry to hear about Astrid. Please tell Audrey that I'm thinking of her, 'kay?"

Harper's heart panged. "Of course. That's very kind of you."

The situation was just horrible. She wanted to throw open the door of every room in the manor and see if there was any more green paint. There must be. She needed to talk to her dad. Maybe he would remember.

"Did you know Astrid well?" Jason asked.

"Oh, no." The young girl's face flushed. "She was a year ahead of me. I'm still in high school."

Jason nodded.

"I used to see her sometimes at The Clam Shack, though."

Harper frowned. "Did you guys go to The Clam Shack often?" Despite the name, it was one of the most expensive restaurants in Cedar Bluff. It was fine dining. Not a place teens would normally hang out.

"Oh no. We both worked there when they needed an extra hand, like with an event or something. She was a server, and I was mostly cleanup crew. I know she made good tips. I want to be a server there next summer." Blair said, her cheeks flushing pink and then she disappeared into the kitchen.

Jason leaned on the table. "Did Astrid know a lot of the kids in the year behind her?"

"Yes and no. I mean they were on teams together and had

some classes together, but she wasn't super close with any of them so far as I knew. Why do you ask?"

"Her father said she was going out that night. I just wondered if you knew anyone who might know who the mystery date was."

Harper fidgeted with her fork. "I'm pretty sure it was an older man."

"Why do you say that?" Crawley eyed her as he bit into a buttered roll.

"Because if it was just some guy, she would've told Audrey all about it. I think she didn't say anything because she knew Audrey wouldn't approve. Audrey is a great kid but she's pretty opinionated. Astrid liked that about her, but I think this was one time when she didn't want Audrey's opinion, which tells me there was something about the guy she was seeing that made her slightly uncomfortable."

Lazlo leaned forward, "That's an interesting theory. Do you know who it could've been? How many adult men was she around?"

Harper turned and stared at him. It was a good point. Where would she come in contact with an older man? School was the obvious answer, but Harper didn't like to think that was the case. Maybe it was naïve, but she knew a lot of those people, they'd taught her as a student, or she worked with them on special projects. The thought that one of them might have killed Astrid made her queasy. The Clam Shack? That place would have a parade of men going in and out.

"I guess The Clam Shack for one, school would be another place. Not really sure after that. Possibly the hospital. Her aunt works there and she used to go visit her at work sometimes."

Blair arrived with their drinks and another woman who Harper didn't know brought their food almost immediately afterwards. She moved the food around her plate in silence while the men discussed football. Soon enough the meal was over.

Jason answered his cell. He nodded at Lazlo and Crawley. "The river has gone down and the road is clear. We're good to go." Jason ended his call and got up from the table. "You ready to go?" he asked Harper.

She wanted to say no, that she was going to wait for Flynn but suddenly she was pissed off. He'd said he'd be right back and he hadn't bothered showing up. If he wanted to see her, he would've come looking for her. She wasn't allowed to look for him. *Screw it.*

"Yes." She stood. "I'm ready."

She looked around and realized that Susan had left the room. Chances were good, knowing Susan, she'd gotten the message before Jason and already headed back to town.

They started toward the door when Gina came around the corner. "Thank you for putting up with us."

"Of course," the other woman replied. She smiled sweetly at the men but there was a look in her eye that made Harper slightly wary. Gina was no fool. She knew where her bread was buttered. She reached out and touched Jason on the arm. "Please get home safe."

"Thanks," he said with a smile. "It was nice of you to feed us and take such good care of us."

Harper did a mental eye roll. Kiss up much?

"Please stay in tonight, at least until the water levels drop a bit. I wouldn't want you out on the roads on a dark night like this one." Jason flashed a concerned grin at Gina.

Yeah, he was smitten. She couldn't blame him. Gina was the entire package; long black hair and dark eyes, a smooth complexion that made her look about mid-twenties although Harper figured her for at least ten years older. But Jason's over-the-top comments and flirtatious smile made her want to slap him upside the head for being such a friggin' hound dog.

Hold the phone... was she jealous? First Susan with Flynn and now Jason with Gina? She thought about it but quickly realized it wasn't the case, at least not with Jason. He was nice and attractive, but he just didn't do it for her and this performance wasn't helping matters.

They all trooped out and Harper said good night to Jason, Lazlo, and Crawley. Then she headed to her SUV.

"Wait, Harper," Jason called and came over to her vehicle.

She got in and put the window down. It had stopped raining, but it was still windy. "What's up?"

"How about I follow you and make sure you get home safe? Then you can make me a cup of tea."

Was he kidding? After that display? Yeah. No. "That's kind of you to offer, but honestly, I'm pretty damn tired. I think I'll just head home and turn in early. But thanks for your concern. Have a good night and drive safely," she said and then put up her window.

He stepped back and she pulled out of the parking lot.

CHAPTER TWELVE

F lynn muttered an oath as he watched Harper drive away on the video monitor. He'd wanted to go out there and take her to his room where they could have dinner together… and see where that might lead. But he had work to do. He'd have to drop by her place tomorrow.

He ran his hands over his face. "Got anything?"

Shah shook his head. "It's just too damn dark. I have no idea who did it or how they did it but someone put something over the lens. I can't see anything and I can't make it any brighter."

"Fuck. Someone tried to push Harper down the stairs."

"But why?" Shah stared at him. "It doesn't make any sense."

Flynn threw the pencil he'd been holding down onto the table. "Because she's been looking into Astrid Windsor's death. She told Jason that the green paint they found on Astrid is a match to the green paint in the library."

Shah gave a low whistle. "Well, that changes things."

"Yeah. Would be nice if we could figure out how the hell

Astrid ended up in the library without ever walking through the door into the foyer."

Shah raised his eyebrows. "You think she was in the library?"

"It's a possibility." He wasn't going to elaborate and say he was sure he was being watched in there which led him to believe anything was possible in that room. He just had to figure it out.

"Did you get anything on the jewelry theft?" The theft had been playing around in the back of his mind.

"On that front I have made some progress." Shah brought up video from the party on the screen. "See here," he pointed at the top screen. "Mrs. Addison is still wearing it. That's ten forty-five." He fast-forwarded for a bit and then stopped. "And see here at eleven thirteen? It's gone. She hasn't even realized it yet."

"So it wasn't stolen after the lights went out. And she didn't raise any alarm so there's no way it was pulled off her neck like she said."

Shah smiled. "Agreed. She was just trying to make it sound more dramatic but more importantly, the necklace was stolen when the lights went out the first time."

Flynn stared at him. "You think that whoever stole the necklace had something to do with the lights going out."

Shah nodded.

Flynn swiveled his chair back and forth. "Makes sense. I know they searched after the lights came on today. I'm assuming no one found the necklace."

"No."

"Any progress on finding out who turned out the lights?"

Shah's shoulders slumped. "No, not with that one either."

Flynn glanced at the clock. It was already eight-thirty. "Let's go get some dinner. We can regroup in the morning."

Shah stood up. "Sounds good to me. I'm staying here again tonight."

He looked at Shah. "Why?"

"What do you mean?"

"Why did you stay after the party and why are you staying tonight? Why not go home?"

Shah sighed and his shoulders slumped a little bit. He rubbed his hands down his face. "Donovan's mom and I are having some…issues."

Under normal circumstances, Flynn would stop right there. He didn't need to know anyone's personal life unless it impacted his personal job performance. But his gut told him there was more to this story. "And?"

Shah leaned forward and placed his elbows on the desk and then sunk his head into his hands. "She wants me to get Donovan more involved with work. He's interested in the security field and she thinks this is a great opportunity."

The light bulb went on. Flynn grimaced. "She has no clue about the Society."

"No. That's the rule. She's not allowed to know. I don't want her to know." He rubbed his face again. "I started with the Society years ago in India. I came over here and the Society paid my way through university. It gave me a life and I was…am grateful and then I met Linda. Suddenly, the confines of the Society were hard to maneuver. Archer looked after me. He moved me out here and left me alone so I could create an outside life, but now my worlds are colliding and I don't know what to do. Linda knows I'm not telling her everything and she's pissed."

Flynn did not envy the man. Working for the Society was different than working anywhere else. It did provide a great life but there was a steep price for that life. "Sorry. That sucks."

"Yeah. Anyway, I used the party as an excuse to stay.

Things at home are a bit tense and I just needed the break. I'll stay again tonight as well in case you need me."

Flynn ate a bowl of stew in record time and then left the dining room. He was restless. There was work to do but concentrating on any particular task would be difficult. Especially with Harper on his mind. How did the woman drive him crazy without even being there? Instincts that had served him well throughout his life told him that she might be in trouble. He tried to talk himself off that cliff, but his mother's thickly accented voice in his mind told him that he was an animal like all the other animals and he should listen to his instincts. They wouldn't steer him wrong. *Fuck it.*

He got in the BMW and headed into town. He'd asked Shah where she lived and he told him where the condo was but he didn't know the number of her unit. It wasn't a problem. Her SUV was parked right outside the door.

He knocked and then waited. Nothing. He checked her vehicle again to confirm it was hers. Pulling out his phone, he called her and knocked again. She didn't answer her phone or come to the door. His heart rate ticked up a notch below panicked, and his gut tightened. She could be in the shower. That could be it. Or she could be dead on the floor. Icy fingers gripped his heart.

He pounded on the door. "Harper!"

Still nothing.

There were no windows by the door but there was one that was over a small garden. He stepped onto the mulch and tried to peer in the window. A lacy curtain covering the glass made it hard to see through, but he could see an island in the kitchen and another room beyond. This had to be the window over the kitchen sink. He tried to open it.

The sound of a shotgun racking made him freeze. "I suggest you don't move, son. I already called the police."

Flynn raised his hands in the air and turned around slowly. The man holding the gun was an elderly gentleman with a shock of white hair. He was wearing a plaid jacket with a puffy vest over it. "I'm not trying to break in," Flynn said but then thought the better of it. "Actually, I am trying to break in. I'm worried about Harper. She's not answering her phone or the door. Her car is parked right there so I know she's home or at least should be." He didn't want to say Astrid's name so he said, "And with everything that's been going on lately, I'm just… I'm worried."

"What's your name? I don't know you." The old man pointed the muzzle at Flynn's knees, which was progress, but still an issue.

"No, you don't. I'm Flynn O'Connor. I work for the Rainy Day Club in security. Harper was out there earlier today and she left before we could speak about the Halloween Extravaganza. She wants to hold it at the club." He had no idea why he was adding all that detail but anything to help him appear less dangerous.

"I heard Jed was giving Susan a hard time about using the town square." The man lowered the shotgun. "I'm Bob Ross. Harper came home a while ago. You sure she's not answering?" He went over and knocked on the door, but it remained closed.

Flynn tried to rein in his impatience. Harper could be in there lying on the floor.

Bob said, "Let's go around to the other side. See what we can see from there."

"Agreed. Should we maybe call off the cops?" The last thing he wanted was to have to deal with Merritt and his band of mighty men.

Bob snorted. "I never called 'em. I've known most of

them since they were in short pants. Hard to take 'em seriously, know what I mean?"

"I do."

He followed Bob toward the water side of the condo complex and looked up at Harper's windows. Flynn knew he could jump up and grab a hold of her deck and then hoist himself up but he wasn't sure how Bob would feel about that and since he was still holding the gun, it seemed prudent to ask. "Do you think I should go up onto the deck?"

"Well, her bathroom light is on so maybe she's just in the shower. We just need a way to get her attention. How's your arm, son?"

"Excuse me?"

"Your throwing arm. Grab some pebbles and throw them at the window. See if she answers."

Was this guy for real? "I think it would be better if I just went up on the deck and checked—"

"Trust me, son, women love this shit. It's how I got my wife to marry me."

What the fuck? How did Flynn always get into these situations? Cash wouldn't be out here throwing pebbles. Cash would've grabbed the shotgun and quite possibly hit Bob Ross with it. *Just breathe.* He went over to the edge of the walkway and grabbed some stones. He threw one and hit the window. He threw a few more and all of them hit their target.

"Say, you're really good. You gonna be in town long? We sure could use a man with an arm like that on our baseball team. Kennebunkport beats us every year."

Flynn was going to beat the man around the ears with the gun in a second if he didn't stop talking. This was getting desperate. He needed to know Harper was alright. Nothing else mattered and the old man was starting to piss him off.

Throwing one last handful of pebbles, he drummed his fingers on his thigh and waited.

"I'm going to go up on the deck." He started forward when he heard a sound.

"Who's out there?" Harper stuck her head out the window.

"It's Bob Ross and your young man, Mr. O'Connor."

"Flynn?" she called. "What the hel-heck are you doing?"

"Trying to get your attention." He let out a breath and the knots in his stomach eased slightly.

She stared at him for a beat and then started to laugh. "Okay. I'll meet you at my front door. Just give me a minute."

Flynn started back around the building.

"See?" the old man said. "She'll be putty in your hands now."

Flynn certainly hoped so but probably not in the way the old man was thinking. He glanced over at him and there was definitely a twinkle in his eyes, so it was possible Flynn was mistaken about that.

They came to the front of the condo building and Flynn started toward Harper's door but Bob put the shotgun across his path. He looked up and met the old man's gaze.

"Harper's been through a lot lately with Astrid and a few other things. You be careful and treat her right. A lot of us would be upset if you hurt her in some way."

Flynn admired the man. He was sticking up for Harper and that was okay by Flynn. He was glad someone was keeping their eye on her, someone who didn't want to bed her.

"I hear where you're coming from. I'll do my best." He offered Bob his hand and they shook.

"Take care, son," Bob said and disappeared into the darkness.

Flynn made his way over to Harper's door where she was waiting. "Seriously? You threw rocks at my window? You know that's going to be all over town tomorrow."

She moved out of the way and let him into her apartment, closing the door after him.

He turned and gave her the once over. She was wearing a pair of black boxer shorts and a pale pink sweatshirt. Her hair was pulled up in a bun. She made that casual look so damn sexy that he wanted to take her right there on the carpet. But relief overrode his libido. She was okay. Safe.

And he intended to keep her that way.

"You left without saying goodbye," he said.

She cocked her head and propped her hands on her hips. "*You* left *me* and said you'd be back. You never showed. What was I supposed to do?"

"Fair enough," he agreed. "So, I've eaten and so have you but I could use a beer if you have one."

"What makes you think you're staying? It's late. I was having a bath listening to an audiobook when you started throwing rocks at my window."

"I called and pounded on your door but you didn't answer. The rocks were Bob's idea." He stared at her. "I'm open to a bath if you want to get back in."

Her cheeks went pink. "I'm finished." She turned on her heel and went to the fridge.

He pulled off his jacket as he looked around her apartment. He hung his coat on the back of the stool at the granite-topped island and then started into the living area but stopped. "Why do you have a string of pots hanging across your balcony door?"

"Oh um, well, I…" her voice died out and her cheeks got pinker. "Someone broke into my place last night."

Flynn's heart stuttered. "I'm sorry… what?" He started toward her. "Someone broke in here last night," he growled, "and this is the first time you're mentioning it?" She had backed up until she was leaning against the fridge door, staring up at him.

She licked her lips. "It's not anyone's business, is it?" She raised her chin as if to challenge him. "And I did mention it this morning when I made reference to the candle."

"Tell me what happened," he demanded.

"Fine." She sighed. "I woke up because I smelled lavender. I hate lavender. I don't own anything that would smell that way. I got up to investigate and there was a lavender candle lit on my coffee table with a note addressed to me telling me to stay out of Astrid's murder."

Flynn stared at her. Someone knew she was poking around. "Did you call the police? Tell Jason?"

She hesitated. "No."

He cocked an eyebrow. "Why not? Someone just broke into your place and threatened you. Why not ask for help?"

"Jason had been at my place earlier—"

Flynn's gut tightened. "Why the fuck was Jason here? It had to be late because you were at the party until after eleven. What was he here for?"

"He came because I called him to tell him about the paint."

"And he couldn't take that information over the phone?"

She swallowed. "I left him a message and he showed up."

"I'm sure he did," Flynn grunted. "Go on. So why didn't you call for help?"

"I guess I just thought it would be silly to call him back and show him a candle. I mean it's not exactly the most threatening thing… and with the storm and everything, he already had a lot on his plate."

Flynn rubbed his face with his hands. She was lying to him. He hated being lied to.

"Harper," he said, his voice low, "if we're going to work

together, you need to tell me the truth. Why didn't you call for help?" he demanded as he put a hand on the fridge on either side of her head.

"Are we going to work together?"

He didn't want to, but it appeared cooperation might be necessary. "Yes," he grunted.

She stared at him. "Fine. Because I was super pissed off. How dare they break into my house and threaten me? I'm not some shrinking violet. Sending me a note with a candle scent that I find annoying isn't exactly scary. It's just fucked up. I figured I would just keep doing what I'm doing and the hell with them."

"The hell with them…" Was she serious? Did she not get it? "Harper your niece's friend is dead. This isn't something you can protect yourself from on your own. You need help."

"And I suppose you're going to give it to me? You're going to keep me safe?"

He gritted his teeth. "Better than a bunch of pots can. I want you to move into the Manor where I can keep an eye on you."

"I can take care of myself. I don't need twenty-four-hour surveillance. Don't be silly."

He knew she couldn't be this obtuse. Just stubborn. There was no way he was going to leave her on her own. No way in hell. "There's a killer out there. Now isn't the time to play action hero. You need help."

"Are you for fucking real? I lived in New York City for years on my own." She started poking him in the chest with her finger. "Took the subway at all hours. Ate muggers and businessmen with wandering hands for breakfast. Don't tell me what I can and can't do. You've got no right," she snarled.

"I've got every right," he said and then kissed her hard on the mouth.

He pinned her to the fridge with his body. There was no

escape for her. He was too damn angry and scared to let her go now. If something happened to her, he'd kill whoever was responsible.

She shoved against his chest and then slowly gave up and as he deepened the kiss, she wrapped her arms around his neck and kissed him back with a ferocity that rocked his world. He buried one hand in her hair and ran the other down her hip and over her ass, pulling her against his erection. God, he fucking ached for her. There was no way he was going to leave her alone so someone could hurt her. No way in hell.

She pushed her hips against his and broke off the kiss. "Fuck me, Flynn."

The sound of his name on her lips broke him. He ripped his mouth away and fastened his lips over her neck, sucking hard. She made another one of those sounds and he knew he needed to be inside of her—like right this second. He pulled the two of them away from the fridge, picked her up, and settled her on the counter.

She tugged at his sweater, pulling it over his head so she could run her hands up his chest.

She wanted him. She wanted him as badly as he wanted her. The electricity between them had made this inevitable, but the all-consuming nature of his lust was wholly new to him. She was his in every way shape and form and he was going to make sure she knew it.

He pulled her sweatshirt over her head, and sweet mother of mercy, she was braless. He tossed the garment to the floor. Then molded his hands over her breasts and captured her mouth once more. His kiss was punishing, and she was there for it. All of it.

"Take off your jeans," she muttered.

He removed his gun and set it on the counter next to her

and then unbuttoned his jeans. She stared at the gun and then back at him. "Were you expecting trouble?"

"With you, that's a given." He dropped his jeans on the kitchen floor and then captured her mouth again. She ran her hands down his back and then cupped his ass as he brought her to the edge of the counter so he could rub against the apex of her legs as she wrapped them around his waist. She fisted his hair and deepened the kiss.

He dropped down to his knees and wasted no time. He pulled off her boxer shorts and licked her clit while she moaned.

"Say my name, baby," he grunted before sucking her again.

"Flynn," she moaned. "Oh God, Flynn."

He slipped a finger inside her, then added a second digit. He moved them at an increasing rate while he licked and sucked her.

Harper bit her lip. "More," she whimpered as she lifted her hips in rhythm with his fingers. He added another finger and increased his speed. Within seconds, she bucked her hips hard once and the strangled sound she let out was like water to a thirsty man. Pure nirvana.

She called his name as she came. Music to his ears. Blood rocketed through his veins. She was his and now she knew it as well as he did.

She opened her eyes as he stood up. Harper reached for him. She pulled his cock free of his underwear and wrapped her legs around his waist. He entered her slowly, but she reached back and cupped his ass, pulling him in deeper. "Fuck me hard, Flynn."

He let out a soft curse and then pulled out and thrust into her again. Within seconds, he was slamming into her, and God, she was tight and wet. He bit her neck and sunk one hand into her hair as he thrust deep inside her. It was pure animal lust, and it was fucking amazing.

"Flynn," she moaned as she came a second time.

He buried himself to the hilt and pulled her head back as he shot off inside her.

Three hours later, Flynn was lying on top of the covers, his body intertwined with Harper's. "You should go," she said.

"Excuse me?" He went up on one elbow. "Did you just kick me out?"

She looked up at him. "I have a reputation to protect. As it is, Bob Ross will be telling the whole town you threw pebbles at my window. I don't need him telling the world you spent the night."

He stared at her. "Are you serious? This is the shit you care about?"

"This is a small town, Flynn. People talk. I'm in local government. It's just better if they don't talk about me."

Flynn was shocked. No one had ever kicked him out of bed before. Not once. He'd gotten up and left more times than he could count but women usually wanted him to stay. Correction--they *always* wanted him to stay.

Except this one. And somehow, this woman was the only one that mattered.

"Okay then." He swung his legs over the side of the bed and got up. He went down to the kitchen in search of the clothes they'd so aggressively ripped off.

Harper followed him wearing only a robe. "Thank you for understanding."

"I don't understand but I'll go." He walked over and pulled a chair out from under her table and then wedged it under the knob to her balcony door. He came back over to her. "Keep your phone next to you and call me if you hear anything."

She nodded.

He hated leaving her, but he wouldn't stay where he wasn't wanted. Not ever. He put on his jacket and then bent his mouth to hers and kissed her. He moved his hand under her robe and stroked between her legs. She leaned into him. He broke off the kiss and went out the door without another word.

As he got into his SUV, he glanced back at her condo. Harper Edwards was a nightmare. His nightmare. The electricity between them was enough to light Manhattan. He had no idea why she thought she could fight it. There was no getting away from something like this no matter how much either of them might want to. Maybe it was his Irish ancestors or maybe it was on a more cellular level but either way, Flynn knew he and Harper had a connection that was beyond the normal. He'd give her a bit of space but the sooner she came to realize this was the truth of it, the better. Harper wasn't going anywhere without him.

He pulled out his cell and made a call. "Karl, how would you like to do me a favor?"

Flynn arrived at the manor with his stomach rumbling. What was it about Maine that made him hungry all the time? He headed for the kitchen and was walking across the salon when Carruthers passed him. "I trust that you won't eat all of the chicken this time?" she said with a sneer.

"You just never know," he replied and kept walking. That woman was sitting on his last nerve and it was getting thinner and more stressed with each interaction with her.

Flynn made himself a roast beef sandwich and poured a

glass of milk. Finishing up his snack, he was heading out of the kitchen when he bumped into Eli Fisher again.

"O'Connor."

"Fisher."

The sound of rain hitting the windows made them both turn and look. "Does it ever stop raining in this place?" Flynn commented.

"I'm told this is not the norm and soon it will turn to snow."

"Lovely," Flynn growled.

Fisher had a peculiar smile on his face. "Oh, it's not so bad. I am coming to appreciate Maine more and more." Then he turned and went into the kitchen.

Flynn stared after him. Not sure what that was all about, but one thing was certain, something sure as hell was going on with Fisher.

He shrugged and started out of the dining room when a blood-curdling scream pierced the darkness followed by some thumping. Flynn took off toward the sound. He rounded the corner and slid to a halt in the foyer. The lights were off. He hit the switch as Fisher came up behind him.

There at the bottom of the stairs was Calli, dressed in another mini dress. This one was forest green but now her legs were at an unnatural angle and so was her neck. Her eyes stared unseeing toward the ceiling. A bolt of lightning lit up the area and then thunder crashed, shaking the house.

"Don't just stand there, help her," Fisher demanded.

The stew in his gut was suddenly heavy as a boulder. "She's past any help I can give her." He squatted down beside her and felt for a pulse in her neck. That's when he noticed that her dress was on backward. His heart slammed against his ribcage.

He studied her face. It had taken him a minute, but he knew her face looked wrong somehow. It wasn't just that her eyes were lifeless, no there was something more. Her nose. It was flatter than it had been. He peered closer. Some fucker had broken her nose. She must have cleaned herself up and then added more makeup to cover it. There was some slight bruising around her eyes that the makeup didn't quite cover.

"What is it?" a voice demanded. "What happened?"

Flynn looked upwards. Mrs. Carruthers was standing at the top of the stairs. Doors were starting to open and the murmur of voices was getting louder. Members were coming out to check what was wrong.

"A young lady has fallen down the stairs," Fisher supplied.

Flynn glanced up at him. Their gazes locked and Fisher set his jaw as if daring Flynn to say more. Seemed like Fisher knew there was more to this than a fall. Flynn remained silent. There would be no hiding this from the other members but for now, he was willing to allow the lie to stand. He'd deal with all the questions once he had more time to discuss things with Ryker and Archer. This was a murder, no doubt, but did they report the crime, or did he call a cleanup crew to come take care of it? He knew what he would advise.

"Who is it?" Mrs. Carruthers demanded.

"Yes, what's going on?" Another voice joined hers. Peter Webber, one of the Society's more prominent members, appeared at the top of the stairs demanding answers. Flynn grimaced. Webber was an officious ass-wipe, but he was not surprised the man was here. He loved to hunt and fish. This would be the perfect place for him.

Flynn stood. "A young woman has fallen down the stairs. She is dead. Please go back to your rooms and let me handle this."

There was grumbling and a few of the members peered over the banister trying to see the dead girl. Flynn wanted to turn off the lights again so people couldn't see but that wasn't logical.

There was another scream. This time it came from the other young blond woman. Flynn thought her name was Payton. Her eyes were wide and staring as she covered her mouth with her hand. "I can't believe it. Is she...?"

Gina appeared by her side, taking her by the shoulders and turning her away from the banister. They disappeared from sight. Everyone remained motionless, staring at the dead girl.

Mrs. Carruthers came to the rescue. "Go back to your rooms everyone, please. Let us handle this." She shooed them away and then started down the stairs. "I need to—"

"Stop," Flynn growled. "I need you to go back up and go to your room. I'll let you know when you can come out."

She froze. Her mouth opened and closed several times. She pulled herself up to her full height. "I am in charge here—"

"Not anymore. I am in charge." Flynn's stern tone cut across hers. "And I am telling you to go back to bed." He turned to Fisher. "There's a set of stairs by the kitchen; use those to go back up to your room."

Fisher opened his mouth to argue but must have thought the better of it because he turned and walked back through the salon.

Flynn turned back to Mrs. Carruthers. "Now, please."

She glared at him but finally, pursing her lips she turned and went back up the stairs and disappeared. Flynn only hoped she hadn't destroyed any evidence that was up there. He needed to find out who did this. Not just because a young woman was dead but because she was killed on the premises and that was against the rules. Someone would have to pay and pay dearly.

He pulled out his cell phone and hit a preset to call

Archer. Calling the man was not something he did often if he could help it and two times within a forty-eight-hour period was unheard of, but the situation warranted direct contact.

"Flynn, I don't have time for any more complaints," Archer said sounding tired. He must have been in bed.

"There's been a death here in the house in Maine. She was one of Gina's girls. How do you want me to handle it?"

Archer swore. "How many people know?"

"All the members I would guess. Someone threw her down the main flight of stairs," Flynn said matter-of-factly.

There was a pause. "Are you sure it was murder? Could she not have just fallen? Maybe she tripped in the dark."

"Her dress is on backward."

"How do you know?" Archer asked, in a neutral tone, which meant the man was pissed.

"Because the zipper was in the front and it should be in the back. And her nose is broken. She has slight bruising around her eyes and makeup is covering it. This was no accident. I think she was dead before she went down the stairs and someone just wanted to make it seem like she fell. They added a scream for appearance's sake."

"Fuck," Archer snarled. "Has anyone called the police?"

"Not yet," Flynn stared at the dead girl. "I was thinking maybe we could avoid that since Calli, the dead girl, came up from New York."

Archer's response was quick. "Do you think that's possible? It would be the most prudent course of action."

Flynn cocked his head. *Shit.* "I think…that ship has sailed."

"How do you mean?" Archer demanded.

"I hear sirens." Flynn's gut tightened. Cops were never a good thing in his world. Everything was about to get a lot more complicated. This. *This* was why mixing the Society with anything in the outside world was always a mistake.

Now there would be cops in the building asking questions and poking around. How the hell was he going to keep a lid on this?"

Archer let out a string of curses and then fell silent. Finally, he said, "Do you think you can keep everything under wraps?"

Flynn wanted to immediately say yes but he stopped himself. He had to be realistic. "It's going to be hard. Someone is obviously working against us. They called the cops. And as this is a case of murder, it's not like the cops won't be asking a shit ton of questions. I'll do my best but Archer, I can't promise something won't get out."

"Do you want me to send Ryker up?"

"No. Too many of us here will raise suspicion. I'll do what I can and if I see it spiraling then I'll call. In the meantime, I'll work out a plan B."

"Keep me in the loop. Don't fuck this up."

Flynn wasn't sure how to respond to that, but Archer had hung up, saving him the effort.

CHAPTER THIRTEEN

The sound of the sirens grew louder, and red and blue flashing lights strobed off the windows. Flynn quickly sent a text to Shah and then tucked his phone away.

A second later, there was a banging on the door. "Police,"

Flynn mumbled a curse. His headache was back and the last thing he wanted to deal with was cops. God, his evening with Harper had been so spectacular, and had deteriorated from there.

He opened the door. A uniformed police officer stood there. He was Flynn's height but with a much heavier build. The guy's hat was pulled low, making it hard to see his face. "Evening sir. Someone reported a possible death?" The voice was deep, and Flynn thought the cop was possibly his own age.

The sound of more sirens reached his ears and he glanced over the cop's shoulder. An ambulance was arriving along with a second patrol car.

Flynn decided no words were necessary at that moment and just moved back out of the way.

The cop came in and stopped, staring at the dead body.

"Shit," he murmured.

Flynn immediately lowered the cop's age. No officer with any kind of experience was going to say that in front of people. He bit back a sigh. On the bright side, if the kid was new to all this, it would make Flynn's job much easier.

The cop keyed his radio. 'Dispatch. It is confirmed, we have a dead, ah that is we have a…Just send the detective, please, Ruth."

A response crackled over the open line, "Roger that."

The two ambulance attendants arrived at the door and moved into the foyer. It took everything Flynn had not to roll his eyes. He leaned on the wall by the coat closet and crossed his arms over his chest. Part of him wanted to kick the attendants out because they were wrecking any possible evidence and he needed to find out who did this. But, the way he saw it, these rookies trashing his crime scene helped him keep the local cops from getting anywhere in *their* investigation. He needed them to shut it down very quickly. One way was if they couldn't find anything. The other way, well he didn't want to think about that just yet.

Mrs. Carruthers emerged from the salon and entered the foyer. "What are you doing?" she demanded.

The cop turned and looked at her. "Ma'am, I'm gonna need you to step back into the other room."

Pointedly ignoring the cop, she said, "Oh, for goodness sake. You're too late to help her," she gestured toward the body as she spoke to the two attendants, "and you're destroying any evidence there might be here in the foyer. Go back outside."

Dammit. Exactly what he hadn't wanted to happen. Flynn scowled at Carruthers.

The two attendants looked at her and then back to the uniformed cop, who said, "Confirm she's dead and then go back out."

The taller of the attendants leaned down and touched the dead woman's neck. "No pulse. She's dead." He stood and shrugged. Then he and his partner picked up their gear and went back out into the rain.

Shah appeared next to Mrs. Carruthers. His gaze met Flynn's. *Interesting.* Where the hell had he been? Did he spend the night in his room? If so what took him so long to get down here? They were going to have to have a chat but not now.

The cop took note of Shah. "Sir, ma'am," he said addressing both Mrs. Carruthers and Shah. "Please go back to the other room."

A second uniformed cop entered the foyer. "Detective Merritt is on the way," he announced and then took in the dead body. Flynn figured this guy to be older, maybe late forties. He was on the short side at maybe five feet six inches but his muscular build more than made up for it.

The first cop turned to Mrs. Carruthers. "Ma'am, do you know how many people are currently on the premises?"

Her sigh was full-on exasperated. "Officer…?"

"Watson," the first cop said.

"Officer Watson, I am Mrs. Carruthers. I run the Rainy Day Club here at Everlasting Manor." She looked at the second officer. "And you are?"

"Sergeant Vincent."

"Sergeant," she nodded. "I can certainly tell you how many people are here." Then she pointed to Ravi. "This is Mr. Shah, our head of security. I'm sure he can help you with any questions you might have."

Shah cleared his throat. It was hard to look official wearing a pair of sweatpants and a ragged T-shirt. It didn't help that his hair was standing on end. He used one hand to try and smooth down his hair as he offered a tight smile to the officers. "I will be happy to answer any questions I can."

Vincent shook his head. "Mr. Shah, why don't you take Mrs. Carruthers back into the other room? Once Detective Merritt gets here, we'll get you…sorted out."

More uniformed officers arrived. If Flynn had to guess, it was probably all the cops currently on duty. He stayed in the corner, nonchalantly leaning against the wall, trying to look invisible. It was dark in the corner so he was in the shadows. No one seemed to notice him.

The uniforms worked getting organized, putting calls into the police chief and the medical examiner. An officer was stationed at the top of the stairs to ensure the guests stayed in their rooms and Mrs. Carruthers showed them how to go up and down using the back stairs.

Shah hovered but stayed out of the way. Flynn wanted him downstairs reviewing the video of the foyer before the cops got there and started asking about it. That's what he'd been texting him about, but it was obvious that Shah hadn't gotten the text. There were quite a few things they were going to have to discuss. Flynn didn't tolerate dereliction of duty and his conversation with Shah would be a bit of a come-to-Jesus lecture.

Flynn stayed immobile in the shadows. He'd learned to spend hours this way back when he had been a sniper in the military. It was a skill he'd honed. Blending into the background. It was like he could just disappear into the woodwork. The trick wasn't just remaining motionless, it was about keeping his energy as quiet as possible.

At last, Jason Merritt walked in. He was wearing jeans and a sweater this time with a windbreaker over it. His hair was damp from the rain.

"Detective Merritt," the sergeant said. "Sorry for calling you out so late, or rather so early."

Merritt waved away the man's concern. "What have we got?"

"Body of a young girl. Identified by the housekeeper as Calli Gant."

Housekeeper. Mrs. Carruthers was not going to like that. Flynn bit back a smile.

"What do we know about her?"

The sergeant shrugged. "Not much. I understand she is from New York City. We're trying to get some contact information for her next of kin now. Gina Ling, an employee of the Rainy Day Club, has more details. We are waiting on her to find them."

Merritt nodded as he stared at the body. "Do we know what killed her? Were there any witnesses?"

The sergeant shrugged. "None we know of so far."

Merritt squatted down next to the body. "When is the ME getting here?"

"The medical examiner said she'd be a little while yet. Flooding has blocked some of the roads."

"Okay then. I will start by interviewing the housekeeper. Let me know the minute Mandy arrives." He stood and was about to head into the salon when there was a commotion at the top of the stairs.

"I am the mayor. I need to be down there," said a woman in a shrill voice.

Flynn cocked his head. *Well, well, well.* Susan was showing her face. He'd noticed she was still here when Harper left but he'd not bothered to track her down. It wasn't up to them to kick invited guests out and she was obviously someone's guest because she was coming from the bedroom area, unless she'd been in the library. By the look of her hair, he'd go with a hard no on that one.

"Ma'am, you can't go down this staircase," said a voice. Flynn assumed it was Watson at the top of the stairs.

"Jason?" the woman called. "I need to see you."

Flynn was pretty sure Merritt swore under his breath.

The detective called, "Madam Mayor, just wait a moment." He turned to one of the uniformed officers. "Is there a back stairwell?" The officer confirmed it. "Ms. Duggan, I'm going to need you to go down the back stairwell. I'll meet you in the room next door."

There was a harrumphing sound but then footsteps receded.

"What the hell is she still doing here?" he asked Vincent.

"No idea. I didn't know she was in the building. Maybe she's a member or something."

Merritt shook his head. "She's not a member."

A commotion got louder as she entered the salon. "Jason," she said a little breathlessly, "what is going on?"

"Madam Mayor, what are you doing here?"

"I was here earlier with you. I just stayed to discuss some business."

"I see," Merritt said. It had just gone one a.m. and the woman looked like she'd spent the last few hours in bed, but Merritt didn't bat an eye. Flynn had to give him credit on that score.

"Now I want to know what's going on, Jason. This is just horrible for Cedar Bluff. This death on the heels of Astrid's murder...well, we just have to move quickly on this. This needs to be sorted so you can go back to working on Astrid's case. It's clear this poor thing fell down the stairs in the dark. There's no need for an investigation."

"We have to follow protocol, so I won't know what happened until the medical examiner gets here."

"Surely this is obvious. You can't possibly mean to launch an investigation into this. This is the Rainy Day Club, not some back alley operation. The girl tripped and fell down the stairs, probably broke her neck."

"Until the medical examiner tells me otherwise, I will treat this as a suspicious death."

There was movement by the door. A woman wearing rain gear and carrying a bag walked in. She pulled down her hood. Flynn immediately felt a tug below his belt as he recognized Harper. What was she doing here? And why hadn't Karl told him she'd gone out? He'd arranged for the man to watch her place to make sure no one else broke in. He pulled his phone out of his pocket and saw he had a missed call and a few text messages. He quickly sent off a text saying Karl could go home and thanked the man. He'd pay the ex-cop well for keeping an eye on Harper. It was the only reason he hadn't stayed in the parking lot outside of her condo.

"Susan," she said and then crossed the foyer, glancing down at the body, and then scurrying past.

"Oh, Harper. It's about time." The mayor put her hand out and snatched the bag from the other woman. "I need to…" she glanced around the room and then fell silent.

"I came as quickly as I could. Denise said she couldn't find exactly what you specified but she hoped this works."

The mayor snorted. "Sometimes that woman is useless." She turned to Merritt. "I need to go powder my nose, but I'll be back. Hopefully, by then you will have come to your senses. Harper, get him to see reason," she barked and then turned on her heel and strode back toward the kitchen.

Merritt reached out and squeezed her arm. "I'm sorry you got dragged out in this."

Flynn's temper sparked. He narrowed his eyes and cocked his head. There was that possessiveness again. Were they lovers? Is that why she'd kicked Flynn out? That would be unfortunate, at least for Merritt.

Harper gave him a small smile. "Not your fault, Jason. You must be exhausted."

"You, too. I hope you got some sleep."

"Some," she said which Flynn knew was a lie. Harper

nodded toward the body. "Who is the girl?" Harper asked.

"Not a local. Someone up from New York. We think she fell down the stairs in the dark. Mandy is on her way, but I've got to go through the motions just in case."

She bit her lip and Flynn's jeans tightened again. Harper wrapped a hand around her neck. "It's not related to…"

Merritt shook his head. "No, we have no reason to think it's got any relation to Astrid's murder." He touched Harper's arm again. "Why don't you go home? We've got this. There's nothing for you to do here."

"I can't leave until Susan goes." She sighed and tucked a stray hair back behind her ear.

Merritt shook his head. "I don't know why you ever wanted to become deputy mayor. She's a real piece of work."

Harper's back went ramrod straight. "Probably the same reason you work for the police chief. Because I like my job and I'm good at it."

Merritt held up his hands in surrender. "Sorry, didn't mean to offend. It's been a long day and an even longer night." He let out a breath. "I need to interview people and find out what the girl was doing here."

"She was in charge of the guest list for the party," Harper supplied.

"You saw her at the party?" Merritt's voice had gone hard.

Flynn didn't like the tone he was using. It was accusatory.

"Yes, I had to go to support Susan. I told you I was here."

"Right. The library."

Again with the accusing tone. Flynn struggled to keep his energy low-key, nearly impossible given how much animosity for the detective was surging through his system.

Harper glared at Merritt. "I am just telling you what I know."

"Jason," the mayor barked as she strode back into the foyer, "I need to go but it is very important that you treat this with discretion. The Rainy Day Club is a valued institution in Cedar Bluffs."

"As I said, I have to do my job."

The mayor frowned. "I don't like the sound of that."

"Madam Mayor, I can't help that. We all have jobs to do."

"Harper, stay here and make sure Jason is respectful to the members, will you? And where's the other detective? What was his name?"

"Lazlo?" Harper supplied.

"Yes, him. And Crawley. Why are you here alone?" she looked accusingly at Jason. "Harper, you must stay and help Jason."

Merritt's shoulders squared up. Like he was spoiling for a fight. "Harper is exhausted. She needs to go home. I'm going to do my job and that's all I can promise. Lazlo will be here shortly."

"I am sure Harper can speak for herself," the mayor said. Turning she fixed her gaze on Harper. "Well?"

Harper opened her mouth and then closed it again.

Flynn had seen and heard enough. "I'm sure, we can accommodate the deputy mayor if she would like to stay. We have many spare rooms and of course we can make her very comfortable while she is here," Flynn said as he crossed the foyer and came to a stop across from Harper.

Her eyes widened as he came into view.

Someone had tried to push her down the stairs earlier, likely to kill her. And now someone succeeded with Calli. He wanted her far away from here, but he also knew she was about to say yes because she wanted a chance to search the whole house for more green paint. It was better to place her under his protection than to let her wander on her own. Plus, the chance to have Harper under the same roof with him was too great to ignore.

CHAPTER FOURTEEN

Harper stayed silent. She'd wanted a chance to be at Everlasting Manor so she could look around but now that the poor girl was dead, it didn't seem like such a good idea. It did, however, prove her point; Astrid's death had to be connected to this place. There weren't two murderers running around Cedar Bluff. The odds were just too great against it.

Susan just nodded at Flynn. "Good, glad that's settled." She turned to Harper. "I'll call you in a bit and we can make some decisions on what we're going to say about this. I want to think about it a bit, and loop in Denise." Susan started toward the door.

There was no stopping Susan. A woman was killed and she was all *bring me work clothes and my make-up*. Of course, if she'd left earlier, like Harper had, they wouldn't have to worry about what it looked like to have the Mayor in the house when a young woman died.

"I didn't agree to this," Jason interjected. He glared at Flynn. He redirected his attention to Susan. "And you're not going anywhere, Madam Mayor."

Susan whirled around and gave him a death stare. "Excuse me?"

Most men wilted under that look, but Jason held his ground. "You were present in the house when someone died. Until we know more, no one is leaving."

Just then Alvin Clark, Chief of Police, walked into the foyer. The snaps of his police-issued windbreaker strained over his significant belly. "Jason. On me," he ordered.

The detective joined him, and they moved over to where Calli's body still lay. Their discussion was carried out in low tones that Harper couldn't make out.

Susan came back to stand beside Harper. "Jason better watch himself. It's ridiculous to make me stay. I'm the mayor for Christ's sake."

"He's doing his job." She didn't know why, but she felt obligated to come to Jason's defense.

"Let's hope Alvin has more sense."

Harper looked for Flynn but didn't see him. Tension snapped over her shoulders The only way she was willing to stay was if he was with her. He made her feel secure. Like nothing could touch her. That attitude might be stupid, but someone had tried to push her down the stairs in this place. As long as Flynn was next to her, she knew she'd be okay. Well, at least safe from harm. Safe from Flynn was a different matter entirely. Her body still ached so good from their earlier escapades, not that she was complaining.

Harper sighed as she wrapped her arms around her middle. She'd panicked. It was silly and juvenile but the truth of the matter was she panicked about having Flynn stay the night. He made her feel safe and the sex was amazing but it was all so…much. It was like she was drowning in him. There was no escape from the tension between them. He was all-encompassing somehow and that scared the life out of her. The moment he'd left, she'd bitterly regretted kicking him out. The best course of action was to stay far, far away from him but, somehow, she just knew that wasn't going to be possible.

She glanced over as a flash went off. A crime scene tech had arrived. God, if she hadn't been caught by her oversize jacket, that could be her lying there dead right now instead of Calli. The whole thing was surreal. Two bodies in two days. She glanced at Susan. "Your presence here while a death occurred doesn't look good. You're going to have to be questioned like everyone else."

"Ya think?" Susan snarled.

Harper had had enough. She whirled on her boss and hissed through gritted teeth. "Don't you dare take this out on me. If you didn't have to screw anything that walks you wouldn't be in this mess and you wouldn't have to drag me in to fix it."

Susan's eyes widened. Then she frowned. "I'm going to let that go because you've had a hard time lately but don't—"

"Fuck right off," Harper snarled back barely keeping her voice and her temper in check. "Take your attitude and shove it. You screwed the pooch on this one. You need me to smooth it over so don't even try and play high and mighty with me. I know where all your skeletons are buried and I am fucking tired of carrying the shovel, so don't fucking push me."

Susan paled. She opened her mouth and then closed it again. She turned and stared at Jason and Clark in the foyer. "Are you going to help me?" she asked, her voice stilted.

"I'll do what I can but seriously, Susan, it's time to grow up. You're a sixty-three-year-old woman. You want to screw everything that moves, great, but do it on your own time. It's like you want to fuck things up. I'm tired of fixing your messes," she bit out. "We all are. Your entire office staff is done with your shit. Get yourself together and stop being stupid."

Susan's shoulders had stiffened and her face was now white. With her mouth pinched and her eyes wide, suddenly, she looked her age.

Harper sighed. *Shit. I shouldn't have said anything.* No that wasn't true. She shouldn't have said anything *here*. It all needed to be said and probably in nicer terms but well, too bad. The truth was out. If Susan wanted to get rid of her because of that, *c'est la vie.* She just couldn't bring herself to care.

Chief Clark came into the room and nodded at them. "Harper, Susan. This is a bad business."

"Chief Clark," Harper said.

Susan merely nodded.

Jason came over and stood beside his boss. "Mandy is almost here. I need to speak to the witnesses and start working a timeline." Just then the door opened, and Billy Lazlo entered shaking the water from his jacket in the foyer. "Jesus, Lazlo, not there," Jason barked.

Lazlo blinked, looked around and then immediately looked sheepish. Vincent grabbed him by the sleeve and led him around the corner.

Clark said, "Susan, why don't you and Harper head home?"

Clark didn't realize Susan was a witness or at the very least she was in the building. Harper tried to figure out a polite way of explaining this.

"Chief," Harper started, "Susan and I were here earlier to speak with Gina Ling. We were hoping you wouldn't mind me staying." There was no way to add that Jason needed to tell her everything without him losing his shit about it and she didn't blame him one bit.

Clark frowned, his big bushy eyebrows drawing together.

"There's no need for you two to stay. Answer all of Jason's questions and then you can go. I'll have someone call your office and update you later this morning."

This seemed to galvanize Susan. She straightened. "Alvin," she jerked her head to the side and walked across the room until she was closer to the dining room. She kept her voice low. "Rainy Day Club is a big donor to my campaign fund," Susan said. "I can't have them feeling mistreated or as if their concerns aren't being heard."

"Jesus, Susan. You can't expect me to alter an investigation because they're donors to your re-election campaign."

Susan's voice dropped further, and Harper could no longer make out anything she was saying.

"Eavesdropping isn't polite," Flynn said in a low voice. He seemed to materialize out of nowhere and was standing to Harper's left. He handed her a cup of tea. How the hell did he know? She raised an eyebrow at him as she accepted the cup.

He smiled at her making her heart rate tick up. So much for keeping her distance. "No, but it's saved my ass more times than I can count." Harper wrapped her hands around the mug as if it could warm the ice in her chest.

Beside her, Jason harrumphed loudly.

Flynn flashed a grin and this time his eyes positively sparkled.

Susan and Clark came back across the room to join them.

Clark said, "Jason, Harper is going to stay here with you. Make sure you loop her in on everything. With this tragedy, it's more important than ever for our two departments to work closely together."

Harper's mouth dropped open and she promptly closed it. She sought Susan's gaze, but the other woman's eyes danced away. Harper's stomach dropped. *What the hell did she just promise Clark?*

"Well, now that it's all settled, I am going to head out." Susan tried for breezy but sounded brittle. She turned and started out. "Oh," she said as she turned back to Harper, "and make sure you take notes. I want details on what is happening." With that, she started back toward the foyer.

"I'm afraid, Susan, that you're going to have to go out the kitchen door," the chief said. "This is still a crime scene. Before you go, did you hear or see anything?"

Susan's face went blank. "No, nothing."

A blind person could see she was lying. Harper's stomach dropped to her toes. What the hell did Susan know? She wanted to ask her boss more questions, but she couldn't do it in front of the chief.

Harper cleared her throat. "I think your car is out back anyway. Much faster and drier to go out that way. I'll walk you to the car."

"There's no need."

"It's dark out there and slippery." Harper put her tea down on a table, grabbed Susan's arm, and walked her boss out through the kitchen. Once they got outside, she turned to Susan. "What did you see?"

"Nothing. I—"

"This is not the time to lie. A woman is dead. *Two* women are dead. You were here. This is going to get ugly. Tell me now so I can do damage control. I will find a way to get the information to the police without involving you." She'd tell Flynn whatever it was and he'd help her with it. She was certain she could count on his discretion.

"Fine." They stood next to Susan's sports car. The rain had finally eased off to a drizzle. "I saw Calli earlier in the evening arguing with Gina. They were whispering so I couldn't make out what they said but Gina grabbed Calli by the arm and I can guarantee that she left marks."

"Did anyone else see?"

Susan refused to answer.

Harper caught her boss's gaze. "I don't care who you're fucking, but they are a witness and I need to know what the hell is going on."

"Fine," Susan said through clenched teeth. "I was with Richard."

"Lockerby?" Harper tried to keep the surprise out of her voice. Lockerby was a good-looking man and younger than Susan by fifteen or more years. He didn't strike Harper as the type to want to go out with an older woman.

"Yes."

Harper nodded. "Okay, then. I will do my best to clean this up and keep you as far from it as I can, but Susan, I was serious in there. Stop screwing around when you're on city business. Your sex life and Cedar Bluff business can't mix."

Susan's lips thinned into a belligerent line and her eyes snapped at Harper, but she said nothing. Turning, she got into her car and left in a shower of pebbles. Harper stood and watched the taillights fade.

"Learn anything good?" Flynn said coming to stand next to her.

"How much did you hear?"

Flynn smiled. She'd known he was there. She seemed to be able to feel his presence even when she couldn't see him. "Does it strike you as odd that Lockerby is sleeping with Susan?"

"Yes. He's up to something. I expect it's some business he wants to do here in town and he's going to need Susan's help to get something done. That's my guess anyway." Flynn touched his fingertips to the small of her back.

"You don't think it has anything to do with Calli or Astrid's deaths?"

Flynn shrugged. "Probably not."

Harper shivered.

"Let's get you back inside. But Harper, I need you to stay very close to me. I don't like you being here. It's obviously dangerous. Someone tried to push you down the stairs and they succeeded with Calli, so if you're here, you're doing what I say and not giving me a hard time or I will throw you out."

"Harper?" Jason called. "Are you coming in? Mandy is here."

"Yeah."

She started to move but Flynn caught her arm. "Harper." His voice was pitched low. It seemed to rumble out of his chest and she felt each syllable in hers. She swallowed. The electricity between them was still there, snapping and pinging. She was shocked no one else noticed. To her, it felt like the sky was alight with it.

"Yes, I'll do what you say. Despite what you think, I don't have a death wish," she said and then headed inside. She grabbed her tea from the table again and stood in the middle of the room, the reality of the situation sinking in.

She was going to have to stay in the house for a few days. Sure, Susan had said to stay and monitor the investigation. Make sure Jason treated the members with respect or whatever. But the subtext of her directive was *watch him like a hawk and report back if he screwed anything up*. If he offended the members of the Rainy Day Club, all the better as long as Harper was there to smooth everything over. The cops were bullies. They were bumbling. They were whatever Susan thought would make people dislike them. She and the chief were mortal enemies. Anything to make him look bad and her look good. Harper would have to stay and make sure everything was handled perfectly.

Flynn came up behind her. She turned to him. "I'm going to need an office or a place to work."

"Of course," he smiled. His eyes snapped at her, the promise of something dark and tantalizing in their depths. "Mrs. Carruthers will get you settled when you're ready. Then you and I can have a chat."

She wasn't getting off the hook and he wanted her to know it. *Fine.*

The chief looked over at them from the foyer. Flynn stepped forward with Harper. "Chief Clark, I'm Flynn O'Connor, one of the global security officers for the Rainy Day Club." He offered the top cop his hand.

"Mr. O'Connor," Clark said but he looked mildly confused. "Where's Ravi Shah?"

That was a good question. Harper glanced around. She could've sworn she'd seen Shah earlier. Where the hell did he go?

"Shah is currently checking our security video from our exterior cameras. He's already spoken with the night security guard at the gate and no one came by car. We're checking to see if they came by foot."

"I see. Are you taking over for Shah?" The chief still looked slightly confused.

"No. As part of the global team, I'm here to look after security for the Club as a whole. I'm in town for a site visit."

Clark nodded. "Got it. Perhaps we can sit down and have a chat in the next day or so."

"Anytime," Flynn agreed. He offered the chief a smile, but Harper was quite sure no one else noticed how the chilly smile didn't reach his eyes.

She side-stepped around Flynn and moved closer to Jason.

"Mandy," Harper said as the medical examiner looked up

from the body. "Sorry to meet you again under these circumstances.

"Harper. It is nice to see you and yes, the circumstances aren't so nice. Sad to see someone so young die."

Jason had his arms crossed over his chest as he stared at the body. "What can you tell me." He glanced at Harper. "Or should I say tell *us.*" His tone was snide. The chief shot him a hard look and Jason clamped his jaws shut.

Mandy looked up sharply, cocking an eyebrow at Jason. She glanced at Harper, who just gave a little shake of her head.

Mandy gave a single nod. The woman understood to let it go and Harper was grateful. Jason was pissed at her for having to stay. She didn't blame him. The last thing he needed was someone following his every move on this investigation. The thing was, he kept glancing over at Flynn and thunderclouds were building on his features. Was he pissed at her for staying, or at Flynn for making it happen? In the end it didn't matter, she decided. Jason was in a pissy mood and the rest of them were going to have to pay for it.

She closed her eyes for a second and tried to find her balance. The last couple of days had been hell and the taunting and threatening nature of the break-in the other night, she was just done. Pissed off royally. Honestly, she couldn't be blamed for snapping at Susan. She glanced outside. The horizon showed some lightening. Daylight was coming.

"Mandy?" Jason said again in a slightly grating voice.

"Sorry, Jason. I was just taking a look at a few things so I could answer your question more fully. These bruises on her face"—Mandy pointed to the skin around Calli's eyes—"were from earlier this evening. They were just starting to darken when she died. And her nose is broken. It was broken before the fall."

Jason ran a hand through his hair. "Can you determine a cause of death?"

"I can't say for certain until I get back to the lab. I'm not sure the fall killed her. I'm not seeing...I'll know more once I do a full autopsy."

Jason pushed a bit harder. "So do you think she fell and broke her neck?"

Mandy looked up and met Jason's gaze. "Anything I tell you right now would only be speculation." He stared at her and then gave a single nod.

"Okay, Mandy," the chief said. "Let us know when you know." He turned to Jason. "Let me know if you need anything else and keep me updated. I'm heading out. Send me any information on the woman so I can reach out to the NYPD, to make the death notification."

"Will do," Jason agreed as Chief Clark exited into the gray dawn.

Flynn touched her shoulder, and she looked up into his dark eyes. "Here," he said as he put a fresh cup of hot tea in her hands.

"Thanks," she whispered quietly.

"Harper!" Jason all but barked at her.

She jumped, almost spilling her tea. "What?" she said through clenched teeth.

"I'm going to start interviewing witnesses now. Mrs. Carruthers has us set up in a room off the kitchen." He nodded toward the other room.

"Okay." She glanced up at Flynn again. "Thanks for this."

"My pleasure." The deep timbre of his voice sent a ripple down her spine.

She moved in the direction Jason had disappeared to, feeling the weight of Flynn's gaze on her back. Damn, this was going to be hard. Flynn O'Connor completely threw her off her game. She sipped the tea he'd handed her. It was time to get serious.

As scary as it was to be at Everlasting Manor, it was also her chance to find out what the hell Astrid had been doing here. She'd keep her eyes and ears open. Maybe she could find someone here who knew Astrid or knew what her connection was to the house. She needed proof that the girl was here. Proof that the murderer was still under this roof. *With her.*

She entered the small sitting room and found an old wing-backed chair and settled into it. Jason was already seated on a wooden chair. A coffee table separated him from the sofa where Mrs. Carruthers sat. She had coffee in front of her and a cup in front of Jason.

"Mrs. Carruthers, your first name is Helen, correct?"

The elderly woman nodded.

"You live here at Everlasting Manor?" Jason continued.

"That is correct."

Jason had a large portfolio pad in his lap and was taking notes. "What exactly is your position here?"

The sound of footsteps reached her, but she didn't have to turn to know Flynn had entered the room. His scent washed over her, and an energy bounced from his body to hers. She couldn't help herself, she turned and glanced at him. He was leaning against the doorjamb, coffee cup in hand. Their gazes locked again and he offered her a small smile. Images of him naked filled her brain. Heat pooled between her legs.

Mrs. Carruthers cleared her throat. "I am the manager here. It's my job to make sure things run smoothly for our members."

"I see," Jason said but he was now staring at Harper, his eyes slightly narrowed.

Heat rushed up into her cheeks. She felt like she'd been

caught with her hand in the candy jar or something. She needed to get a hold of herself. Astrid needed her to focus.

Jason turned back to Mrs. Carruthers. "So, you brought in Calli to help with the party?"

"No. That was Gina Ling."

A frown marred Jason's features. "Gina brought her?"

Mrs. Carruthers sniffed. "Yes. Gina is the membership coordinator."

"I'm sorry, I seem to be confused. What is the difference between your position and hers?"

"I oversee everything operational. Gina makes sure the members are…entertained."

Harper felt a distinct chill in the air. Helen Carruthers did not like Gina one bit. There was some professional jealousy going on there for sure. But was it enough to make her kill? Harper couldn't picture it. And how could this older woman throw Calli down the stairs if she was already dead? Dead people weighed a lot. Or so she'd learned by watching true crime shows on cable. Did that mean there was a partner?

Jason turned toward Flynn. "Can you get Gina down here? I'm going to need Calli's contact information."

Flynn nodded and disappeared into the darkness of the house.

Jason continued, "Can you tell me your movements this evening?"

Drawing herself up to her full height in her seat until her back was ramrod straight, she asked, "My movements? That poor girl fell down those stairs. It's the only thing that makes any sense. Asking me for my movements as if she was murdered is just distasteful." She was positively indignant.

Jason's facade of calm was starting to crack, and Harper immediately felt for him. He was under a lot of pressure with

Astrid's murder. Adding another murder victim was just crazy.

"Mrs. Carruthers, Calli is dead. We don't know what happened but there is some evidence to suggest she was murdered. I apologize for the bald delivery, but it's the truth. I am trying to determine where everyone was last evening. That way I can discover who might have seen something useful. So please, your movements."

All the blood seemed to leave the older woman's face. She laced her hands together in her lap and stared down at them. Finally, she started. "We served dinner and had some unexpected guests." She glanced at Harper and sent Jason a pointed look. "Then I made sure that the staff had cleaned up properly and the kitchen was ready for breakfast in the morning.

"So the power went out at what time?"

"Dinner was over by nine. Clean-up was done by ten thirty. I did a walk-through of the house as I always do and then headed up to bed."

"And what time was that?" Jason asked, pen poised above the portfolio.

"I went to my room around ten-forty-five."

"The lights were out in the foyer," Flynn said from the doorway. He was back but no Gina. "What time do those go off?"

"They shouldn't go off, but we've been having some issues with that type of thing lately."

Jason shot a glare at Flynn but asked Mrs. Carruthers, "Issues?"

"Yes, someone keeps hitting the master switches."

"Explain."

She gave an exasperated sigh. "When the house was redone about twenty years ago, the owners had master switches installed. They are in the upstairs hallway. They control all the lights in certain sections of the house and not only the lights but the power to the outlets and such as well. I guess they didn't want to have to go to each individual room and turn everything off."

"Someone is turning off the master switches?"

She nodded. "It's happened a few times now. Those stairs are very steep and dangerous to go down in the dark. That poor girl," she sniffed. "I feel quite sure she must have fallen. I think your medical examiner must have made a mistake. The light in the foyer isn't great. I am sure when she can see better, she will tell you of her error."

Jason let that slide. "You said the lights were turned off. When did the power actually go out then? Was the power out when she fell or were the lights just turned off?" he asked.

"The power was off. I believe it must have happened sometime after midnight."

He took a sip of coffee and put his mug back down on the table. "How can you be sure there were no outside guests left in the building?"

She blinked. Her mouth worked and she pursed her lips, as if there was something on the tip of her tongue that she desperately wanted to say. Harper leaned forward, tension a live wire under her skin.

The other woman reached out and picked up her mug, taking a sip of coffee. She was stalling and everyone in the room knew it. Finally, she put the mug down again. "In my job, I must be discreet. If our members choose to have guests, that's up to them. We rarely have overnight unregistered guests, but it does happen."

"Was anyone here besides Susan Duggan?" Jason asked.

Harper knew his frustration. He was trying to get at the facts and this woman was stalling. Only she wasn't. She was doing her job as she saw it.

"Mrs. Carruthers." Flynn's voice cut through the dimness. "You need to tell them the truth." She looked over at him and her lips turned into a flat line. She was not pleased that he'd butted in, but it was more than that. There was an undercurrent between them. Something more to this than just the security guy telling her to cooperate. Whatever it was, the older lady resented the hell out of it. Her nostrils flared and Harper was pretty sure she heard the woman's teeth grind together.

Just then Gina appeared at the doorway. She ran a hand over Flynn's chest as she passed him. It was a sign of ownership. Were they lovers? That thought did not sit well. Not at all. Harper did not share. Ever.

Gina was beautiful even with the early hour. Perfectly put together. Harper instantly felt like a slob in her jeans and brown sweater. Gina was wearing tights with a short black mini skirt, a pair of black knee-high boots, and a black sweater that was a match for all her other black apparel. How long had it taken her to put together that look this early in the morning? On the other hand, maybe she'd put it together last night.

"Gina, sorry to disturb you," Jason said and rose from his chair.

"It's fine," she said in a throaty voice, and she touched his arm.

Flicking her long dark hair over her shoulder, she took a seat on the sofa, angling so her long legs were out in front of her and Jason's view of them was not blocked by the coffee table. Jason immediately obliged the display by taking a long look.

Harper wanted to roll her eyes. When she'd spoken to the woman earlier, her voice wasn't anything like that. She certainly knew how to work a crowd, of men, at least.

Mrs. Carruthers said nothing, but she met Harper's gaze

and Harper knew instantly she was trying not to roll her eyes as well. She hadn't understood the older woman until just that moment. Now it was all clear. Mrs. Carruthers was fighting for her livelihood and Gina was the interloper. But was that enough to kill for? Harper had the distinct impression that the answer to that was probably yes. But how did killing Calli help Carruthers get rid of Gina? She wasn't sure it did.

"Gina," Jason began, "do you have contact information for Calli? We need to reach out to her family."

"Of course," she said as she pulled her cell phone out of some pocket hidden in her skirt. Funny, Harper hadn't thought there was enough material in the skirt to make a pocket. It barely covered her ass.

Will wonders never cease?

What the hell was wrong with her? Why was she getting so catty? She took a sip of tea and tried to reset her thinking. She needed to do better. For Astrid. And now for Calli. How were those two young women connected and what the hell did it have to do with Everlasting Manor?

CHAPTER FIFTEEN

Flynn leaned against the wall and watched the show. Gina was superb. She was playing Jason like a fiddle. The smoky voice, the subtle eye contact, caressing her own legs to draw his attention toward them. She was a pro.

He froze for a second. That was it. She was a *pro*. Gina was an escort, or at least a former escort and now she was the madam for the Lock and Key Society. She was coming up in the world. What kind of a deal did she make with Archer? Was he paying her a salary? Probably, but if he had to guess, she was also raking in some kind of commission. Some percentage of what the girls and quite possibly boys, made.

Flynn's stomach curdled. He tried not to be judgmental. That was bullshit. He was very judgmental. He had to be. It was his job. He was brought in to be judge, jury and, on occasion, executioner for those who broke the rules.

If there was one thing he hated, it was the sex trade. Too often it led to human trafficking and he'd seen the outcome of that firsthand. Siobhan. He hadn't thought of her in a long time, but her life and death had changed him. Marked him. And now his animosity toward Gina blossomed. She was part of a growing problem, and he would like nothing more than to shut her down.

Mrs. Carruthers stood. "If you're finished with me, I'll go get things organized. The members will want their breakfasts."

Jason nodded but didn't take his eyes off Gina. "What time did you go up to your room?"

"Maybe eleven-ish?"

Jason wrote something in his book. "And when did you last see Calli?"

She cocked her head. "She and I walked up the stairs together, along with Payton. At the top of the first set of stairs, we separated. The girls have rooms in the new section toward the back of the house on that floor. I'm up one more and to the left."

Of course she was. Gina had a room where the members stayed. No employee treatment for her. He could almost admire her for getting what she wanted if she wasn't in the business of selling women for sex.

"I said good night to them both and then headed up to my room."

"Did anyone see you?" Jason asked.

She tilted her head once more. "No...I don't...Actually, Susan, the mayor. She saw me."

If he hadn't been so closely attuned to Harper, he might have missed her slight gasp.

"Susan?" Jason asked. "Where was she?"

Gina brushed her hair back off her shoulder. "She said she wasn't feeling well so I put her in a room down the hall from mine. I told her she could stay the night if she wanted and drive home in the morning."

"I see," Jason said as he made another note.

Flynn was pretty sure he'd just heard Harper's jaw pop. He

didn't blame her. While the mayor was getting laid, a girl was being murdered not too far away. That was not going to be good if it came out. He didn't think Susan Duggan was guilty of murder, but she was guilty of bad taste. She'd been screwing Richard while Flynn had been getting whacked over the head. And then screwing Richard again when Calli had been killed.

What he found most interesting, though, was Gina just lied to protect Susan. Did she think Susan would keep secret Gina's fight with Calli? Was it a pact they'd made out loud or just an assumption of some kind? And Susan had kept it. She'd only told Harper. Everyone was out to cover their own ass. Jason was never going to get these murders solved at this rate. No one was telling the truth.

"So, you didn't see Calli after that?"

Gina shook her head and then wiped a single tear off her cheek. Harper made a strangled sound and covered it with a cough. She wasn't buying this shit, either. He liked that. Sexy and smart was a killer combination for his libido. She could see through the bullshit. Good to know. He'd have to keep that in mind. He had some questions of his own for her later as well.

"Thank you, Gina. If I have any more questions, I'll come find you."

"Okay," she said as she stood.

Jason stood as well and watched her ass as she walked out of the room.

Harper got up. "I think I need some coffee. Anyone else?"

"I'll take a cup," Flynn said and handed her his mug.

Jason also nodded. Harper put her mug down and picked up the two of them again and left the room. Jason watched her ass as she left as well, which pissed Flynn off. He shifted to intercept Jason's gaze and Jason's face flushed red. *Busted, asshole*. Flynn didn't want anyone but him looking at Harper's ass or any other part of her.

"Do you have the video from the outside cameras?" Jason asked. His tone was aggressive as if he didn't like being caught out.

"I'll make sure you get a copy," Flynn said, keeping his voice neutral but he jammed his hands into his front pockets to avoid putting a fist into Jason's face.

"What about the inside of the house? Do you have any footage of the inside?"

"We do have footage of the foyer. We had a camera installed when all those break-ins were occurring last year." Shah had told him about the break-ins in passing yesterday and he used it because it sounded like a reasonable excuse to have a camera. He wouldn't give him anything, but Jason wasn't stupid. If he looked around the foyer at all, he'd see the camera. Fortunately, since the power was out, chances were excellent he wouldn't see any of the others. Archer made sure all the Society locations had cameras even though he told no one.

The sound of heavy footsteps reached them. "Um, Jason, can I talk to you for a minute?" Lazlo asked.

"Sure," Jason said and then glanced at Flynn. "I want a copy of the footage from the foyer as well."

"I'll see that you get it."

Harper walked back into the room and handed the men their mugs. Jason took his coffee and left the room.

She turned to Flynn. "I think the forensic guys are finished."

He nodded. He would have to find a way to get the report. Shouldn't be too hard. Worse comes to worse, he could get someone to hack into the computer system and get it. Not too hard but just another thing he added to his mental to-do list. "Where's your coffee?"

"I decided not to have any. I don't need any more caffeine." She ran a hand over her face and smothered a yawn. "Sorry."

"Not at all. Would you like me to get a room set up for you? You could take a nap?" Just the thought of her curled up in bed made blood rush to his groin. The only room he'd let her curl up in alone was his.

"I wish," she said. "I have to stay up and see what Jason wants to do. Then I'll need to send a few emails."

She stood in the middle of the room hugging herself, looking out the window at the watery sunshine. "They're connected. These two murders." It was a blunt statement. Harper raised her chin as if to challenge him, daring him to argue with her.

"Is that what you think, or do you have proof?" he asked.

"It's what I know. They were both murdered and they both had a connection to this house."

Flynn's gut knotted. "What connection?" he demanded.

"I don't know yet, but I intend to find out."

Jason returned. "Um, people are starting to get up. Lazlo is organizing some of the club members in the dining area and then we will interview them one by one. Do you want to join me?"

Harper let out a sigh. "Sure."

"Where is the coffee?" Peter Webber demanded as he stuck his head into the room.

"Presumably in the pot in the kitchen," Flynn responded.

Webber frowned and then his eyebrows went up. "Harper, what are you doing here?"

"Mr. Webber. I could ask you the same question. Long way from the bright lights of New York City."

"I came up to hunt and…things." He frowned. "What brings you here? I thought you went out west somewhere after that unfortunate incident."

"No, I came here. This is where I grew up."

"I see."

She lifted her chin and added, "I'm deputy mayor of Cedar Bluff."

Webber's eyes widened. "Well… nice to see you." He turned and left the room. Jason followed him out.

She started after him but Flynn laid a hand on her arm. "How do you know Webber?"

"He was close with my old boss at the Mayor's office."

Flynn's stomach knotted. "Who's your old boss?"

"William Findley."

That was an interesting turn of events. Will Findley was a member of the Society. "Listen, I have to do a few things." As much as it pained him to say the next sentence he knew it was necessary. "Do not leave Jason's side, okay?"

"What? What do you mean?" Her eyes narrowed slightly.

"I know you want to poke around the whole house but don't leave Jason. You can't be alone anywhere until I know what's going on. It's not safe."

She frowned.

"I will let you poke around to your heart's content later, but you're not going to do it without me until Jason leaves."

"You're going to help me?" There was that hope again. It was going to kill him in one way or another.

He nodded. "I want to find the person who killed your niece's friend and Calli just as much as you do." It was his job to protect the Society, and whoever was behind these murders was threatening everything.

"Do you believe me that the two deaths are related?"

He hesitated but finally gave a curt nod. Relief filled her eyes and her shoulders sagged slightly.

"Okay then. I'll let you know if I find out anything."

"What are you going to do?" she asked. Her eyes were watchful but there was hope in their depths.

Something in his chest twinged. He was, in the end, going to crush that hope but for now, he had to use it. It was his job. The Society had to come first. It didn't matter how sexy she was, or how smart, or how brave. She was, for all intents and purposes, the enemy at the gate. It was his job to keep her out.

He was striding across the salon when Payton careened around the corner. She was wearing a pair of light gray sweatpants and a pink crop top. Her eyes were red-rimmed, and her hands were shaking. "Do you know what happened to Calli? Am I in danger?"

"Why would you be in danger?" Did she know something?

"I-I... It's just that we were here doing the same thing and I...I got worried."

"Did you see anything?" Flynn asked.

She shook her head. "I was in bed sound asleep."

"Then I think you're fine. Try to relax. You'll be able to head home soon."

She sighed. "Not soon enough." She gave him a weak smile and then moved around him and continued toward the kitchen.

Flynn watched her go. The poor girl was terrified. This was why the Society running their own girls was a big mistake. He turned and headed for the basement. "You want to tell me what the hell you're doing? I've been covering for you all morning." Flynn crashed down in the guest chair across from Shah who was hunched over his desk.

Shah looked up. "I've been reviewing the video of the library from the time when Astrid went missing and reviewing all the video from last night."

Flynn rubbed his face. "So? Did you find anything?"

Shah remained silent but tapped on his keyboard. Then turned his laptop around so Flynn could see.

"Hey, Dad?" Donovan walked into the office.

Shah snapped the laptop closed. "What do you need?"

"Uh, I just wanted you to know that I don't have any classes until this afternoon so I'm going to finish up checking all the outside security cameras like you asked." Donovan's face looked a bit swollen and his red-rimmed eyes darted between his father and Flynn.

"You okay?" Flynn asked.

"Allergies," Donovan said and then sneezed. "Sorry."

Shah checked his watch. "Just make sure you eat something."

"Um, I wouldn't right now," Flynn offered. "Merritt and Lazlo are in the dining room interviewing members." He took his wallet out of his back pocket and pulled out a few bills. "Why don't you get pastries from that great place in town, the one on the main drag? Bring some back for your father and me."

Donovan's face lit up. "Can I Dad?"

Shah nodded and handed him a small black key fob. "See you in a bit. Don't eat everything on the way back."

Donovan grinned and waved then disappeared down the hallway.

"Sorry about that."

Flynn waved it off and then opened the laptop. He clicked on the *Play* arrow and the video began playing. A young girl, all dressed up, walked around the room looking at the books and admiring the shelves. Then she tried the door, and pulled more aggressively a few times, but it didn't open. She went to the windows and then the screen went black.

"Where's the rest of it?" Flynn demanded.

Shah shrugged. "I have no idea. Someone seems to have gone in and erased the rest. I think they tried to erase it all but I managed to find this bit in the trash."

"Who has access besides you?"

"No one. Or at least no one should. They're not even supposed to know the cameras are there." Shah leaned back in his chair. "Whoever erased it wasn't doing it on location, by the way. The system was accessed remotely."

"Fuck," Flynn snarled. "What you're telling me is it could be anyone?"

"Not anyone. Someone who is a kick-ass hacker or someone who is on the inside."

That thought stopped Flynn cold. Someone on the inside. "That would explain a whole lot when it came to the video."

"My thinking exactly. I've spent all morning trying to figure out how they got in and who it could be and all I can tell you is I'm pretty sure they have the passwords for the servers."

Flynn knew nothing about this stuff. "Who would have access to that?"

"You mean across the whole network?" Shah asked.

"Walk me through it," Flynn said as he steepled his fingers together.

"The Lock and Key Society runs its own network. We store some stuff virtually for each location and some we keep on servers. Video files are stored virtually." He held up his hands before Flynn could say anything. "Yeah, I know. It should all be kept physically on the servers but then Archer would have to physically go to every location if he wanted to view video footage. That's just not practical. We've made it as secure as electronically possible. And like I said, I don't think it was hacked. I think someone was given the passwords and had access."

Flynn shifted in his seat and then tapped his fingers under his chin. "So I'll ask again. Who would have access?"

"To the whole system?" He raised his eyebrows. "Maybe a handful of people. All of them are in New York. And they work closely with Archer."

Flynn stared blankly into space for a moment. That was not good news. He was going to have to tell Archer someone around him was betraying him. Heads would roll, possibly even literally. He let out a long breath. "Can you tell when this breach happened?"

"Right after Astrid went missing. It's not a recent thing."

Interesting. This whole puzzle was getting weirder and weirder. "Let's move to last night. Do we have any video of Calli's murder?"

Shah rubbed his head with both hands making his hair stand straight up. "At the risk of pissing you off and making you think I am entirely inept, the answer is no. Someone cut the power to the cameras around the stairs last night. All I could find is this." He turned his laptop back around and started typing. Then he spun it once again so Flynn could see the screen.

It was the hallway upstairs. Not the second floor though. Must be the third. There were people walking but it was so dark all he could make out were shapes moving. "Can't you get it any better than this?"

Shah shook his head. "The lights were off. The cameras still worked but with so little light they didn't get much." He leaned over and hit a few more buttons on the laptop. The video started over only this time there was sound. There were a few murmurs and then a woman giggled. *Calli.* The video ended. "Any idea who the man is?"

Shah shook his head. "That's what I've been trying to figure out. I tried the process of elimination but too many of the members were still floating around. I can't tell who went to their rooms and who didn't once the lights went out in the upstairs hallways."

Flynn played the video again, but it was no use. It just wasn't clear enough to see who the man was and he didn't speak loud enough to identify him by his voice. "Email it to me. I'll send it to someone who might be able to lighten it up some."

"Already done. Sent it to one of the Society's IT guys in New York. He said he'd see what he could do." Shah's forehead creased. "I can still give it to you if you want."

"No, that's fine. It's what I was going to do." Flynn rubbed the heel of his hands on his eyes. He was annoyed but more, he was frustrated. This whole thing was just fucking weird. "Did you see or hear anything useful?" Flynn felt obligated to ask.

"Not a thing. After we finished up, I grabbed some food and then went to bed. I came out when I heard the commotion."

This was not helpful. Flynn needed to formulate a game plan. That was the only way he was going to find out what the hell was going on.

"Do you know what Gina is doing?" He shot the question across the desk to see if Shah had any reaction. He needed to know if Shah was in on the secret or not.

His eyebrows drew downward in confusion. "Doing? You mean helping the members?"

"With the girls."

Shah's expression changed, became guarded. "Oh, that. Yes, I know."

"Thanks for sharing."

"I...I thought you must have known. You work with Archer."

Flynn let it slide. "Gina brought Calli here to work for the weekend. Had she done that before?"

"Yes, and she's brought other girls too." He grimaced. "I think it's a bad choice, just like throwing the party. And now the Halloween Extravaganza."

"What? I said no to that."

Shah snorted. "Gina and Mrs. Carruthers both said yes and as they run the location, they have final say or so they keep telling me. It's a done deal."

Flynn's blood pressure rocketed upward. He'd said no. It was a bad fucking idea. "Someone is dead. They can't be serious about continuing."

Shah shrugged. "I think it will depend on what the autopsy says. If she fell down the stairs, then I would imagine they'll go forward with it."

"Wonderful." Flynn wanted to punch something. "Someone is running around killing women and we have no video of it, nor do we have any idea who it is and no one has an alibi because everyone was tucked up in bed."

"That about sums it up."

It hit Flynn at that moment that his alibi was Eli Fisher. If that wasn't irony.

Donovan came sailing into the office. "Dad!" he said and then stopped short when he saw Flynn. He was visibly upset. He had the bags of pastries in his hands but his body was shaking making the bags rattle.

Shah was on his feet. "What is it? What's wrong?"

Donovan glanced at Flynn again and he stood up. "If it's personal I can go but if it has to do with what happened to Calli, I need to know."

The kid glanced at his father who gave him a nod. "Someone was in my room, er, your room." He swallowed hard. "I found some stuff."

"What kind of stuff?" Flynn asked.

The kid turned pale. "There's a bloody piece of cloth and some stuff…handcuffs and…things I don't even know what you do with." His eyes were huge, "but I know it can't be good."

Flynn's stomach hit the floor. "Wait, you have a room here too?"

Donovan shook his head. "Just for last night. It got late and the weather and Dad said I could stay too so Mrs. Carruthers gave me a room on the third floor but I was kind of…" his cheeks flushed. "I watched too many horror movies and I was…a bit freaked out so I asked if we could switch. I know my dad's room and with all of the haunting stuff, it's just…I knew that room was safe. I didn't know anything about the room on the third floor. So Dad and I switched. I slept in his room, and he slept in the one Mrs. Carruthers made up for me."

"Tell me from the beginning what happened," Shah said. He pointed to a second guest chair and they all sat down again.

Donovan sat but his legs bounced and he couldn't keep his hands still. "So, I went into town like you said and got the pastries." He glanced down at the bags that were still in his lap and then put them on the desk. "Anyway, when I got back, I needed to take a leak, so I went up to your room. I was coming out of the bathroom when I saw the cloth sticking out from underneath your bed. I didn't think. I just bent down and picked it up and that's when I saw the blood. I was completely freaked. Then I looked around and saw someone had put some weird shit—sorry, Dad—in the room. A set of handcuffs. And some crazy-looking stuff. They were hidden under the bed. I called you but you didn't answer your cell. So I came down here to get you."

"I'm so sorry, son. Are you okay?" Shah was first and foremost a father.

Flynn however was not. "You're sure you've never seen the stuff before?"

Donovan nodded.

"Did you meet up with Calli last night? Maybe you thought it would be fun to have sex with her?"

The kid looked so stricken that Flynn had to try hard not to laugh. A virgin. Good for him.

"N-no w-way. She's sort of scary. I mean she was." He immediately looked stricken again. "I'm sorry Dad, I know I'm not supposed to speak ill of the dead."

"It's okay son, we know what you mean."

A sudden thought hit Flynn. "What are the detectives doing?"

"Merritt?" Shah asked. "He was interviewing people."

"What about the other one?"

Donovan said, "Detective Lazlo was organizing a search of people's rooms when I got back with the pastries. Or at least those who will let them which seems to be pretty much everyone. Mrs. Carruthers said it was a cursory search. She said it was one of those things that they were going to have to do and if they got a warrant then they would tear the place apart. She advised everyone to let the detective search their rooms."

Shit! Flynn was on his feet immediately with Shah only a fraction of a second behind.

"Stay here," Shah directed to Donovan. Flynn was out the door with Shah hot on his heels. "We need to get to the stuff before Lazlo."

Flynn cursed as they came out into the hallway. They took the first set of stairs to the main floor two at a time. "Slow down. People will notice if we rush." They immediately changed their gait. "I think we'll need to check all the windows and doors. Do a systematic check," Flynn said.

Shah looked at him like he was crazy and then immediately smoothed over his features. "Yes, I agree."

Two women Flynn hadn't seen before were coming down the stairs.

Shah smiled at them. "Good morning." They responded in kind and kept going.

Once they hit the landing, they went down the hall and turned right and then took the left into the newer section where Shah's room was just a few doors down from Flynn's. As they turned the corner they came to a halt. Lazlo, Jason, and Harper were standing in the middle of the hallway.

"I hear you're conducting a search," Flynn stated. "A heads up might have been nice."

Jason gave him a tight smile. "I asked for permission from the club members as I interviewed them and they said yes."

Flynn kept his temper in check. So that was how it was going to be. *Big mistake.*

"I see." He glanced at Lazlo who gave him a blank stare just for a second before his expression went soft and he looked like a big kid again. There was definitely something going on with Lazlo. He was not what he seemed.

"So, did you find anything?" Shah asked.

"Not so far," Jason admitted. "We still have a few rooms left on this floor and some on the next."

"Oh, yes?" Shah asked.

"We would like to search yours, Flynn's, Mrs. Carruthers and Gina's on this hallway."

Jason gestured toward Flynn's door. "If you wouldn't mind."

Flynn smiled coldly. "But I would. And so would Shah, Mrs. Carruthers, and Gina. You will not be searching those rooms."

Jason's eyes narrowed. "Why? Do you have something to hide?"

"No." Flynn stood there with his arms folded across his chest.

Jason rolled up onto the balls of his feet. "I thought you wanted this investigation to go forward. We can't solve this poor girl's murder without cooperation."

"So you got the autopsy back then?" Flynn asked.

Jason blinked. "No, but we're proceeding on the assumption—"

"Not good enough. You've been abusing our cooperation. Now it's over." Flynn wasn't budging an inch.

"You know I can get a warrant to search the premises."

Flynn snorted. "You couldn't come close and you know it. You don't even know if it is murder at this point and, even if you did, you don't know what you're looking for, do you?"

Jason tried to play it off. "That's not true. We—"

"You do have the cause of death then?" Shah asked.

"Well no," Jason admitted, "but—"

"This is all a fishing expedition, and it ends here," Flynn growled.

He felt the weight of Harper's stare but ignored it. He had to take a stand or Donovan was going to wind up leaving here in cuffs.

Jason tried another tack. "So maybe you won't mind answering some questions then. You're the chief of security," he said to Shah. "Where were you when Calli went down the stairs?"

Flynn cut Shah off before he could open his mouth. "He's not talking without his lawyer present. None of us are."

"A wise choice," a voice behind them said.

Turning, Flynn realized it was Lockerby.

"And you are?" Jason asked.

"Richard Lockerby. I am a member here, and also an attorney."

"Then maybe you can help out," said Lazlo.

Lockerby glanced at him. "No. I specialize in corporate law, but Mr. O'Connor is correct. I think you will find those remaining guests you have not interviewed yet will not do so unless they have a lawyer present."

Jason's face was starting to flush. "Look," he snarled but Harper put her hand on his arm.

"That is, of course, your right. We just want to get to the bottom of what happened. I know for myself and Susan, we want guests of the manor to feel comfortable. If you would like, I'm sure we can find a lawyer for you, Mr. Lockerby."

"Let me chat with my lawyer in New York and see what he comes up with. If he has no suggestions, then I will take you up on your kind offer." Lockerby offered Harper a smile.

"Great. When is that going to happen?" Jason demanded.

"Monday at the earliest. My lawyer is in Tahoe for the weekend."

"Wonderful," Jason growled. "Then I guess we're done here for now. But we'll be back." He gestured to Lazlo and the two men turned and went back down the hallway.

"Mr. Shah, I was wondering if I might have a word?" Lockerby asked.

"Of course." He and Lockerby started down the hallway.

"You could have helped him out," Harper said accusingly to Flynn.

"Yes, I could have but I'm not here to make his life easier. I have a job to do. I have to protect the members of the club. My duty is to them. Not to Jason, or to the dead girl. That's just reality." He took her arm and dragged her toward the library.

Harper's face lost some of its color. "I see."

Flynn's gut rolled. He hated disappointing this woman and he didn't even know her.

Yeah, reality sucked.

CHAPTER SIXTEEN

Harper stared out the window in the library at the watery sunshine, as behind her Flynn shut and locked the door. High clouds dulled the sun's glow. At least it wasn't raining. She let out a breath and tried to get her emotions under control. She was annoyed with Flynn. She'd expected more from him.

"Surely helping Jason was the decent thing to do."

"Yes, but I'm not decent."

She whirled around and looked at him. He wasn't smiling. Was he serious?

He walked over to stand beside her. "My job is to keep this place and the members secure. Obviously, I failed at that. I cannot fail again. Making Jason's job easier goes against the interests of the club."

She licked her suddenly dry lips. It was hard to concentrate when he was this close. Those dark eyes just seemed to suck her in and then she lost all focus. Stepping back, she bumped into the windowsill. "I thought you were going to help me find out who killed Astrid? You said these two deaths were related."

"I will still help you, but I will not help Jason." He brushed a stray hair out of her eyes and tucked it behind her ear. That gesture seemed absurdly intimate. She wanted to back up but she was already against the window. She didn't want him to know how badly he was affecting her so she tried to casually turn away but he blocked her exit.

"Did Jason learn anything in the interviews?"

She wished he would back up or she could escape past his big, beautiful body. "Why should I tell you?"

Heat came off him in waves and landed point-blank on her chest. Her nipples were getting hard. *Ridiculous. Grow up.* She'd been yelling at Susan for behaving like an oversexed teenager and here she was doing the same thing. She wanted him again no matter how much she tried to deny it.

"Because you want my help," he said and then propped one forearm on the window next to her head, "Harper." His rumbling voice caused a needy vibration between her legs. He ran a finger down her cheek. "You need to decide if you want to know who killed Astrid or if you want to *prove* who killed Astrid. I can help you with one but I can't help you with the other."

Heat pooled between her legs as she tried to remind herself to behave like an adult. Astrid. *Focus on her.*

She cleared her throat. "I don't understand."

His voice was soft and sent shivers across her skin. "Jason needs to follow the rules and find proof. I just need to find answers. You need to decide what you want to find."

She took a deep breath. *Big mistake.* His scent swirled about her. A mix of citrus and something darker, but wholly masculine. It made her think of having sex with Flynn which in turn made heat creep up her neck into her cheeks. He was right, of course. Jason would do things by the book and that may or may not lead to the truth. She had no doubt that Flynn would get to the truth, but he may not get justice.

"I can live with just knowing who did it. That's a start. We can build on it. Find proof later." It came out quickly as one run-on sentence. She hated that she rambled when she got nervous.

"What did he find out from all those interviews?" he asked as he traced her jawline, his touch feather-light.

She swallowed. "Nothing interesting. No one has an alibi. They were all in bed alone." As she said it she had a mental image of Flynn in bed, naked and alone. She sucked in a breath.

Flynn seemed to be able to read her mind because he slanted his mouth across hers, capturing her lips, opening them with his tongue. She leaned into him and wrapped her arms around his neck. It felt so fucking amazing, so…right. He slid his hands down and cupped her ass, pulling her against his erection. Heat pooled between her legs, and she deepened the kiss, sinking her fingers into his hair.

There was another sound. Flynn broke off the kiss and looked at the wall. The hair on Harper's arms stood up. A book fell off the shelf behind the desk, and Harper jumped. Maybe there really was a ghost and they didn't like people making out in their library. She was completely creeped out.

Flynn walked over and stared at the shelf the book had fallen from. She immediately felt the loss of his body next to hers. He put his hand on the back of the shelf and then shifted the books on it all around.

"What is it?" she asked her heart pounding against her rib cage.

"I'm not sure," Flynn said. "But whatever it was, is gone." He bent down and picked up the book, placing it back on the shelf. Turning he moved around to the front of the desk and rested his butt against it, crossing his legs out in front of him.

She was immediately disappointed that he wasn't coming back over to pick up where they left off.

"Tell me about Astrid's murder," he said. "I want to know details. I understand she was found recently but had been missing for a while."

"Three months." Three torturously long months. "She told her father she had plans to go out with friends. They were celebrating before going off to college in the fall. She was dressed up which Paul, her father, thought was weird, and he'd asked her about it. She said they'd all wanted to dress up and go out to dinner. He just figured it was kids having fun until she didn't come home."

"What was she wearing?" Flynn asked.

"A little black dress. She and my niece had gone to the mall and bought it the day before. Astrid told my niece that she had a secret date and didn't want to tell her father about it. She said she would tell Audrey all about it after the date, but of course, she never came home again. I have a theory about that."

"What's your theory?" he asked.

"I think that Astrid knew Audrey wouldn't approve of whoever she was seeing so she didn't want to tell her until… something happened. Until they were official or until…her stomach turned at the next thought. "Until they were serious."

"You mean until she'd slept with him," Flynn clarified.

She nodded her assent.

Flynn rested his hands on the edge of the desk. "Who would your niece not approve of?"

"An older man. I floated the idea to Jason and George Crawley and Lazlo last night over dinner but they didn't say much. Flynn, I know it. Like, I know it in here." She put her fist over her heart. "She was seeing an older man."

"Where did she meet this older man?"

She shook her head. "I have no idea. School possibly, but a better guess would be The Clam Shack. It's an upscale restaurant in town. Astrid worked there when they needed extra help for functions and stuff."

Flynn nodded absently. He was staring at the wall opposite him as if not really seeing it.

"What are you thinking?" she asked.

"Nothing good." He straightened. "I don't like you being here. It's not safe."

"As opposed to my place where someone broke in and threatened me? That's safer." She folded her arms over her chest and shrugged. "There's safety in numbers. I figure I'm safer here than at home. There are more people around. There's you." She immediately stopped talking. She hadn't meant to say that last bit. It just slipped out.

"Me. You think you're safe with me?" He walked across the room to stand inches from her. "Do I seem safe to you?" he growled as he backed her up against the window once again.

She licked her dry lips. "I... you seem..." scary as hell. The ferocity in his gaze was frightening but also...exciting. There was something about Flynn O'Connor that made her blood rush and desire pool between her thighs. "Safe might not be the word."

"Uh-huh," he said as he put an arm on either side of her head.

"Maybe protective. I feel like you would protect me. That you would stop others from hurting me." Her breath was coming faster now. "I don't know why I feel that way, I just do. It's weird and..."

"And what?" He demanded his voice deceptively soft.

"Sexy as hell." There, she'd said it. She was an adult, and she could admit to feeling adult things.

He lowered his lips until they were a hair's width away from hers. "Harper," he breathed.

The door to the library burst open behind them and Flynn whirled around placing his body between her and the door. There! She knew it. He would protect her.

"Sorry, I didn't realize anyone was in here," Gina said as she stood in the doorway.

Harper peeked around Flynn's shoulder. She wanted to talk to Gina. There were questions that needed to be asked by someone who didn't fall for her little act.

She moved out from behind Flynn. "Gina I have a couple of questions if you have a minute."

Gina narrowed her eyes at Harper. "No sorry I don't. Flynn, I need to speak with you." She glanced at Harper. "Alone."

Flynn studied her for a second and then turned to Harper. "Go down to the salon. I'll be down in a minute."

She opened her mouth to protest but he simply cocked an eyebrow and said in a quiet voice. "Do you want my help or not?"

Glaring at him, she shut her mouth and then made her way across the library. She passed Gina and went out into the hallway. She might have been dismissed but that didn't mean she had to go where he said. Instead, she went up to the third floor. It had the same setup as the second floor only it looked more updated. Better carpet and newer drapes on the windows in the hallway. She tried a couple of the doorknobs on the main landing but found them locked.

She wandered over to the window and looked down at the driveway and the ocean beyond. The water looked gray and angry. She knew exactly how it felt. Pissed off seemed to be her default state these days. Her cell phone went off in her pocket. She pulled it out and looked at the screen.

She sighed as she answered. "Hello, Susan."

"Harper, what's going on? I told you I wanted updates."

Susan was probably doing her best to keep her temper in check.

Harper's fingers tightened on the phone. "There's nothing to update you with. Jason still doesn't have the autopsy back and although he questioned many of the guests, he didn't turn up one witness." She dropped her voice. "You're the only one who saw anything. Do you remember any part of the exchange between Gina and Calli?"

Susan stayed quiet for a moment. "They were arguing about something."

"So you said."

"No, I mean they were vehemently arguing about some *thing*. Gina accused Calli of taking something but she denied it. Gina told Calli she was jeopardizing everything, and she needed to give it back pronto or it wouldn't look good for her. It was a serious threat. At least Calli took it that way. She turned pale. And that's it. That's all I know."

Harper was at a loss. What could Calli have? If only Gina would talk to her. No, if only Flynn would let her be in the room while he spoke to Gina. That's when they'd find out the truth. Gina might not take Harper seriously, but she'd listen to Flynn. He wasn't the kind of guy that could be ignored.

"Thanks for telling me, Susan. I'm working on finding a few things out. I'll update you if anything comes of it."

"See that you do," she said and then hung up.

Harper was about to put the phone back in her pocket when another call came through. "Dad," she said as she answered. "How are you?"

"Doin' fine, Sunshine. How are you? Your mother said you called."

She had a sudden longing to go home and sleep in her parent's house. "I'm okay. How's the roof?"

"Fine. Not a big deal."

"Glad to hear it," she said.

"So what's up? Your mother said you wanted to chat with me."

She looked all around and made sure she was alone. "Dad, do you remember working on Everlasting Manor when I was a kid?"

"Sure do. It was one of my first jobs when I went out on my own and started my own construction company." He chuckled. "In those days I'd do anything and everything."

"Do you remember the green paint you used in the Manor and then let me paint one wall in my room with?"

"It was a deep green. I remember it. Your mother didn't want to let you do it, but I convinced her it was better than the black you wanted."

Harper bit back a smile. Her mother had told her the same thing only she said she had to convince him to let Harper use the paint. "How many rooms did you use the green paint in up at the Manor?"

He chuckled again. "Do you know how many years ago that was? You expect me to remember that? What's this all about?"

She let out a sigh. It had been worth a try. "It's not important, Dad, just an idea I had." As an afterthought, she asked, "Do you remember anything interesting about the Manor?"

"That place was in dire need of fixing back then. It had good bones but had been left to wrack and ruin. I always thought it was such a blessing when old Peter Farnsworth bought it. He was keen to bring it back to its former glory. We did a lot of work on it. It needed a lot of electrical if I remember correctly. At least those tunnels made that easy to do."

Harper's breath froze. Tunnels? Fine sweat broke out

across her upper lip. "Tunnels?'" she squeaked. "What tunnels?"

"Well, I guess you'd call them more secret passages although the one in the basement would qualify for a tunnel."

"Dad, what are you talking about?"

"Well now, Sunshine, you can't tell anyone. I promised Peter I wouldn't tell his secret."

"Peter Farnsworth has been dead for twenty years. I doubt he'd care now."

Her father sighed. "I guess you have a point. Still don't go spreading it around."

"Spreading what around?" her voice rose in frustration, but she caught herself and lowered it again. "Fine," she agreed, "I won't tell the whole world." She couldn't say she wouldn't tell anyone because she knew she'd tell Flynn.

"Well now, apparently back when the front part of the house was built in the late eighteen hundreds...or was it the early nineteen hundreds?"

She gritted her teeth and prayed for patience.

"Anyway, the original owner was a bit of a smuggler. He used to bring in booze among other things. He'd bring it in by boat. When he built the house, he dug a tunnel to bring in the stuff from the boats to the house and then he had secret staircases and rooms put in so he and his friends could drink. Peter found them and wanted to keep the secret so I promised him I would. He used them to play pranks on his friends when he first got the house but then he had a stroke and lost the ability to speak. I don't think anyone else ever knew about the secret passageways and rooms."

Harper's knees went weak. Secret passageways, tunnels for smuggling, rooms hidden in the walls... No wonder people thought Everlasting Manor was haunted. She needed to check them out.

"Thanks for telling me. I won't spread it around."

"Okay, love. I've got to go. You be careful. A nor'easter is coming in the next few days. Make sure you're prepared."

"Will do," she said, anxious to get off the call. "Wait! Dad, do you remember how to access the passageways?"

"Well now...it seems to me there's a door in the basement, in the unfinished area. . . Also, there's one in the kitchen if I remember correctly."

"Thanks, Dad. Love you."

"Love you too, Sunshine." With that, her father was gone.

Harper's hands shook as she put the phone back in her pocket. This had to be it. Astrid must have been here in the passageways and in the secret room. That's why no one saw her. She needed to find Flynn right away. They needed to search the house.

She went back to the staircase and descended to the second floor. Flynn wasn't in the library. She continued down to the main floor and stuck her head around the corner but no Flynn. She really should go look in the dining room and the kitchen but the basement was calling. Maybe she could just go down and check it out. The kitchen had too many people but the basement would be empty.

She rounded the staircase and headed down. It was stupid to go alone. She knew she was that character in the horror movies who does the stupid thing that makes everyone yell at the screen. But she also had a powerful curiosity and maybe she was just a teensy bit pissed that Flynn dismissed her so quickly. She'd just take a quick peek. What could go wrong?

CHAPTER SEVENTEEN

"What is so important that you dragged me all the way out here?" Flynn asked as he adjusted his collar against the wind.

Gina had led him to the top of the bluff just down from the house. Standing with this woman he cataloged that his senses were on full alert. He didn't like being this far away from Harper.

"I needed to speak to you alone." Gina tucked her hands under her arms.

"And you couldn't do that in the house?" He studied her.

He didn't trust her as far as *she* could throw *him*. He could throw her much further than she could imagine. He glanced around again to make sure no one was nearby. The thought that this could be an ambush hit him right away and he was as prepared as he could be. The lack of a weapon bothered him but until now, he hadn't thought running around the manor with a gun would be a good idea. He'd definitely changed his mind on that and would rectify the situation as soon as he got back inside the house.

Gina looked around again.

"Spit it out, Gina. I haven't got all day."

"Fine," she said as she tucked her hair behind her ears. "You know that Calli worked for me."

"As an escort."

Her eyes narrowed. "You don't like that."

"No. I don't." He crossed his arms over his chest. The wind was fierce and his jacket wasn't cutting it.

She sniffed. "Archer sees it differently."

"I doubt that, but we're not here to discuss the merits of you supplying your own girls. You're going to tell me whatever it is you want to tell me, and I'm going to go back inside and get warm."

"Fine. I lied to the cops."

"No shit."

She shot him a look. "I lied to them about Calli and Mrs. Carruthers backed me up."

"What are you talking about?"

"I had Payton switch rooms with Calli so the cops searched her room instead of Calli's. I had her switch their clothes but that was it."

"Why the fuck would you do that?" Flynn just couldn't see the upside of doing that.

"Because Calli was the thief. She stole the necklace and that's not all. She stole quite a few pieces of jewelry along with credit card numbers and anything else she could get her hands on. I only found out because I saw her do it at the party."

"You saw her steal the necklace?"

"Well, she was next to Mrs. Addison one minute and then she was gone along with the necklace. I put two and two together. So, I had the girls switch rooms for the police search. Calli doesn't have any family and I compensated Payton in order to replace all the stuff they'd confiscated."

"I'm still not following you."

"I didn't want the cops to find the jewelry. They'd think it was a motive for murder. Calli was a drinker. She fell down the stairs. If they found the jewelry, it would just complicate things. Plus, it might call attention to the Society, and no one wants that. I found most of the things she stole but I know she took a pair of earrings and a few other things I couldn't find those. Making the girls switch rooms ensured the cops didn't find them either."

"What things?"

Gina looked at him blankly. "What do you mean?"

"Don't play innocent with me, Gina. I won't fall for your bullshit act. What did Calli have on you that you didn't want the cops to find?"

Gina glared at him and then she shifted her weight from foot to foot.

"Spit it the fuck out," he growled. "I don't have time for your shit."

"Fine! She had pictures."

Flynn wanted to strangle her. Instead, he cocked an eyebrow and waited her out.

"Me and several Society members naked engaging in certain acts that would make us all look bad."

The picture became crystal clear. "You didn't want the cops to find the pictures because you would be a suspect."

She nodded.

"Who else was in the pictures?" He had a pretty good idea, but he needed her to say it.

"Peter Webber and Steven Bryson."

Frozen, Flynn stared at her. He didn't know a thing about Bryson's kinks, but he was guessing the pictures were bad if Gina went to such lengths to hide the truth. Really fucking bad. Webber's involvement surprised him, though. Not that he'd participate, but that Gina would. He must have paid very well. "She blackmailed you to get work?"

"Yes."

"Why are you telling me now?" Then he got it. "Because you need help returning the stuff and finding the pictures. You've turned the place upside down and you can't come up with them."

She gave a nod, misery written all over her face.

"Did you kill Calli?"

She shook her head.

He wasn't sure if he believed her. Of all the stupid shit. This was why running their own girls was a big fucking mistake. Because they did crap like this. He looked out at the ocean. Ghosts suddenly looked so much better than dealing with this fucked up situation. "I will do what I can to find the pictures, but you better be telling me the whole truth. If I find out you lied, things will go downhill fast."

She said nothing just turned and walked back toward the manor. Flynn let out a breath and took the cell out of his pocket. "Archer."

"Where the hell are you? You sound like you're in a windstorm."

"Something like that."

"What's going on with the murdered girl investigation?"

Flynn didn't know where to start. "A lot," he said finally. "But for the moment, the two most important things are someone seems to be able to get into the security system and delete video footage. Shah thinks they have the passwords, meaning it's someone on the inside."

Maybe it was the wind distorting his hearing, but Archer's voice was fully neutral when he said, "And the second thing?"

His response threw him off completely.

"Flynn? What's the second thing?" Archer said.

"The dead girl was stealing from members."

"Fuck," Archer said. "Do we have the items she stole?"

"Gina says she has everything but a set of earrings and some pictures. The pictures might present a problem."

"Do I want to know what the pictures are of?" Archer's voice was weary now.

"Gina, Peter Webber, and Steven Bryson performing some twisted sex acts."

"For fuck's sake. Does no one obey the rules?" Archer roared. "No cameras. How many fucking times do I have to say it?"

Archer paused, and Flynn could just about hear the wheels turning. Since he agreed completely with the man's rancor, he held his peace.

Finally, Archer grunted. "I suppose they were taken at Everlasting Manor, and if the pictures are found people will know the location. Jesus, this is why there are rules. If those pictures are discovered, some intrepid reporter will just keep digging until they discover the Society. Find the pictures, Flynn. That's priority."

"I'll do my best, but, Archer, I can't promise anything. This is fucked up six ways to Sunday. Hard to make any headway."

"Just get it fucking done." Archer dropped the call.

Easy for him to say. Flynn headed back inside to look for Harper.

She wasn't in the salon. "Why am I not surprised?" Flynn muttered to himself as his gut tightened. This woman was going to be the death of him. If she wasn't so damn curious, and smart, and spirited, it would be better. But he had to admit, those were the things that made her so attractive. He liked her nerve and her intelligence. The fact that she was so damned sexy was just icing on the cake.

He made his way to his room and got his gun, tucking it in the waistband of his jeans underneath his sweater. Leaving Harper unprotected was not an option anymore. He left his room, stumbled on the stairs, and grabbed the banister as it sunk in that somewhere in the last few days—day, actually—that he'd unconsciously moved Harper from hot sex partner to something more meaningful. That wasn't good. Meaningful brought problems and vulnerabilities. As a monster slayer, having vulnerabilities was fucking stupid.

It seemed more expedient to find Harper by looking at the security feeds, so he went into the video room and looked at the feeds from the cameras in the house. Nothing. Did she leave? No, because he would've seen her car go. Where the hell was she? His gut tightened and adrenaline surged in his bloodstream.

He rewound the video to when he was in the library with her. She left and went upstairs to the third floor because of course she did. Why listen to him? While she had many traits he admired, it appeared she lacked common sense. Another feed caught her chatting on the phone, and a short time later she went down to the unfinished section of the basement.

"Fuck," he snarled and lit out of the video room like it was on fire. He flew down the hall and entered the unfinished section within seconds.

If anyone hurt Harper, he'd kill them. It wasn't a question or an idle threat.

"Harper?" he called out as he strode down the cement-lined hallway. No response. "Harper?" he called again.

He made his way down to the electrical panel area but found the area empty. He turned and retraced his steps along the wall until he came to the part of the hallway where the overhead vent was. If she was down here and hurt... He pulled his gun out from under his sweater and moved forward slowly.

The sound of someone shuffling reached him. He slowed his pace and lifted the muzzle of his gun. A few feet later Harper came into view. She stood in front of the wall running her fingers over it. He glanced around, saw she was alone and tucked his gun back under his sweater.

"What the hell are you doing?" he asked as he leaned against the wall, Goddamn, why were his knees wobbling like jelly?

"Ahh!" she yelled spinning around. "You scared the hell out of me!"

He stared at her. "Is there a reason you couldn't stay in the salon?"

"I spoke to my father and he told me—"

"I thought we agreed you were going to do what I said. That it was dangerous for you, and you were going to stay in the public spaces. You told me you weren't going to wander off on your own. Why couldn't you fucking obey my order?"

She reared back as if he'd slapped her.

Then her eyes narrowed, and she jammed her hands on her hips. "You know what? I'm getting damn tired of this troglodyte attitude of yours. I get it. You're the big strong man, out to protect me. And yes, I do need help but there's no need to be so overbearing and dramatic. I'm not a child and I don't need you hovering over me like I am one."

He took a step forward and then another until he was well into her personal space. "You want to be here? You'll listen to me. That was the deal. You want to go do your own thing, then I will turf you so fast it will make your head spin."

She glared at him. "I did listen to you. I just didn't agree."

"Don't fucking split hairs with me. Two people are dead and I'm trying to keep you from being the third."

"You don't have to tell me people are dead. I'm aware and I seem to be the only one doing anything about it," she snarled back. "Now, do you want to know what I found out or do you want to stand there like a caveman and pound your chest some more?"

He grabbed her around the waist and pulled her to him, kissing her hard on the mouth. Her arms went around his neck, and she kissed him back just as hard. Teeth clashed together, lips were bitten. He sunk one hand into her hair and used the other to bring her hips closer to his. She ground against him.

God, he loved that she matched him. Not afraid to stand up to him and she didn't take shit off him. It was the sexiest thing ever but, dammit she needed to listen to him.

He broke off the kiss and told her as much. "Honey, I can't keep you safe if you don't listen to me. I don't want you to get hurt but I can't be everywhere all at once. Can you work with me? Please?"

She was breathing heavily just like he was. Her chest, rising and falling against his chest was tantalizing. If they didn't move apart, he'd take her right here.

"I get what you're saying but I need you to ease up a bit," she said stepping back from him. "I don't do well with over-bearing."

He gritted his teeth but said nothing. After silently counting to ten, he said, "What did you find out?" *Chicken shit.* Taking the easy road and picking a safer topic than her recklessness.

"I talked to my dad. I think I told you that he did construction up here when he first started his company. Anyway, he told me that, get this…" she leaned forward and dropped her voice. "There are secret passages in the house."

Flynn stared at her. "Seriously?"

She nodded. "He said there is an entrance down here and one in the kitchen. And supposedly, there is a tunnel up from the beach as well."

Like tumblers for a lock, so many things clicked in place

in Flynn's mind. In a flash, it all made sense. "You're trying to find the entrance?" He stared at the wall ahead of them.

"Yes, but I'm not having any luck." She turned to face the wall again. "I've tried everything I can think of, but it all seems solid."

"That's because you're looking in the wrong place." He grabbed her hand and then tugged her further along the hallway until they came to the spot where someone had hit him over the head. He turned and they went until they hit the back wall in the small room.

"How do you know it's here?" she asked.

"Because someone came out of nowhere and clobbered me. They didn't get by me, and they weren't in here when I looked so—"

"They must have come through the passage," she finished.

He went to the wall and stared. Solid concrete construction, and seamless as well. So where was the entrance? He ran his hands over one side of the wall and Harper did the same on the other.

"There's nothing here," Harper huffed as she stepped back.

Flynn had to agree with her. They were missing something. He turned and looked at the hallway they'd come down. Had they missed an opening? If there was, the debris that lined the hallway would have made it impossible to sneak out of the passage and get behind Flynn. Too much stuff to move.

"Let's go try the kitchen," Harper said and started down the hallway.

Flynn grabbed her hand. "It's too early to try the kitchen. At four in the afternoon, the staff will be getting ready for dinner."

"So, what do we do now?" She was practically hopping

up and down with energy but he knew once the adrenaline rush was over, she'd crash.

"We go get some tea and go to my room. I want to check on a couple of things and make some phone calls. You can relax and I can keep an eye on you."

She opened her mouth ostensibly to protest and then she yawned.

"Fine," she mumbled, "but I need a snack, too."

He smiled. "I think I can cover that." He took her hand and started down the hallway. "Is it okay if I lead or is that too troglodytic for you?"

She rolled her eyes and stuck her tongue out at him.

An hour later, and with a full stomach, Harper was sound asleep on his bed. She ate a sandwich and a bag of chips along with her tea. He liked a woman who liked good food. All of the salad pickers drove him crazy. Nibbling on lettuce to keep their figure. Not worth it.

He slid out of the room but not before he triple-checked to be sure the walls of his room were way too thin to hide any passageways behind them. He moved along the hallway until he was standing around the corner from the library. He could still see his door and he could see anyone coming up the stairs. It wasn't ideal but he wasn't taking any chances.

"Flynn, this is becoming a regular thing." Archer's voice was tight. "Tell me no one else is dead."

"Not yet, but not for lack of trying."

"What the fuck is going on there? Did you find the pictures?"

"I haven't even started looking for the pictures yet." There was silence on the other end of the phone. "Before you get your balls in a twist," Flynn said, "I doubt the pictures are here and that's why I haven't started looking for them. Calli must have been clever to get pictures of Webber, Bryson, and Gina in the first place. If she's as smart as I believe, she wouldn't bring the pictures to Maine. I think they're probably in her apartment. Send Rush to check it out. He'll find them."

There was another silence but this one wasn't so fraught with tension. "I guess that makes sense."

"There's something going on up here but it ain't supernatural. I'm hoping to figure it all out but...if things go like I think they will, there will be repercussions. I may need a cleaning crew."

"Noted," Archer said. "Give me a heads up beforehand so I can review and make sure the punishment suits the crime."

"Will do." He hung up. It was still a tangled mess but if the secret passages did exist, it changed a lot of things. No one's alibi would hold, not that anyone had one besides him and Fisher. It was a damn shame it wasn't Fisher. But it also gave a window into how Astrid moved around the house without being seen. Only someone who knew about the passages could have killed her.

He also was certain Gina had lied to him. Along with Mrs. Carruthers. There were a lot of action items necessary to sort this out. First, though he had to figure out what to do with Harper. He stared at his door. No time like the present.

He slipped back into his room as quietly as possible, but it was wasted effort. She was already awake and sitting in one of the wingback chairs.

"Did you go searching without me?" she demanded.

"No. I watched you sleep and then made a call."

"Oh," she said but he wasn't sure she believed him.

He sat down in a second wingback chair. "We need to figure out a couple of things."

"Like?" she asked.

"Who left you the candle and the note?"

She shrugged. "I have no idea."

"I do." He met her gaze. "Think about it for a minute."

Frowning, she said, "I've thought about it a lot and I don't see..." her voice faded. She cocked her head. "But I just can't believe he would do that."

"Why? You said yourself it wasn't particularly threatening. Just something to scare you. And if you were scared, who did he expect you to call?"

"Him." Her eyes flashed. "That fucker!" She pulled out her phone, but Flynn took it from her. "Hey!"

"We have no proof that Jason broke in."

"But he was the only person I mentioned the paint to. The only one who would know I was poking around in the investigation. And," she held up a finger, "he was the only one with access to my door to unlock it. He commented about the chairs on my deck while I was pouring him tea. He could've easily unlocked it then."

Flynn had come to that conclusion a while ago. "The thing is, I think he did it to scare you into calling him." That rankled. Flynn wanted to kill him for scaring Harper. "It was innocuous in the grand scheme of things. He wanted you to stay the hell out of his investigation and call him so he could protect you." If it were up to Flynn, Jason Merritt would pay a hefty price for that but retribution on the fucker wasn't his call, and any action he took could make things more difficult.

"You don't think he was the one that tried to push me down the stairs, do you?"

Flynn shook his head. "Not likely. I think whoever was in the passageway by the library overheard us talking and wanted you to stop looking into things so they tried to push you down the stairs. I don't think it would've killed you. Just put you out of commission a bit."

"But it killed Calli."

He shook his head again. "Calli was dead before she went down the stairs. I'm pretty sure someone beat her to death and then threw her body down the stairs to make it look like she fell."

"Why do that?"

"Calli made some serious enemies."

Harper's eyes narrowed. "You know something."

He didn't deny it.

"You have to tell me."

This was the moment that he knew was coming but didn't want to face. The moment where he had to put the Society first over Harper. The moment when she suddenly understood how this was going to go.

"I can't tell you. There are things I can't share. It goes with the job."

She sighed and he thought she would argue with him, but she remained silent.

"What did Webber mean when he said about you leaving the mayor's office?" His question could be considered prying, but he was working on a need-to-know basis.

Harper studied him for a minute. "I was Will's assistant but I was dating another assistant at the time, Kenny Jacobs. The unions threatened to strike and Will made a quiet deal behind the scenes to grease the wheels to avert the labor dispute. Kenny told a reporter all about the secret deal and they quoted it as a source in the Mayor's office. When the article came out, the world assumed it was me. I bore the brunt of all the mistrust and the antagonism. Kenny even played like he couldn't believe I'd done it.

"Asshole," Flynn muttered.

She nodded. "Yup, but Will knew the truth. He also knew his days were numbered so he gave me a glowing reference and I got out of there as quickly as possible. Now Will is on a bunch of boards and is pretty much retired with a golden parachute and Kenny works for the borough president in Staten Island."

The list of people he wanted to kill on Harper's behalf was growing exponentially. "I'm sorry you had to go through that."

She shrugged. "It was all for the best, in the end. I saw who Kenny truly was so, I didn't marry him. He just became my biggest mistake. I came home to Maine, and got a great job, which means I get to spend time with my friends and family. It was a win for me."

"You're very tough. It took guts and courage to survive that kind of shitstorm." He meant every word. Harper was the whole package. Too bad it wasn't a package he would get to keep.

"Your turn," she said.

He cocked an eyebrow. "To do what?"

"Tell me about your biggest mistake."

Flynn leaned back in the chair and straightened his legs out in front of him, crossing them at the ankles. "I've made a lot of mistakes. Not sure one qualifies as the biggest over any of the others."

She met his gaze. "Pick one."

He could tell her about running with the gangs, about joining the army to get away from them and becoming a sniper which led him to realize he was good at killing, not something he wanted her to know. He could tell her about the stealing and drugs he did in his youth. Instead, he thought if he was going to share a big mistake it had to be one that mattered.

"Her name was Siobhan. We grew up together in the same neighborhood in Queens. I'd had a crush on her for years. She had red hair and blue eyes and a razor-sharp tongue. We both ended up hanging out with the group of kids that parents always called the 'bad lot.'" He chuckled before going on. "It was a gang and eventually Siobhan and I turned to each other as a way to keep safe. Any port in a storm. We dated through our late teen years. Siobhan was tough and smart, but she was also erratic and had a wicked temper.

"I decided that I'd had enough of gang life, of that neighborhood and I wanted out. I asked her to come with me. Told her we'd just go and make our life somewhere else." He still remembered the look on her face. "She laughed. Said people like us don't get out. I told her I was going; she could come along or stay, it was up to her. She picked staying."

He lost himself in the memory of her laughing at him. Calling him stupid for thinking he could get out.

Harper shifted in her chair, a sympathetic look in her eyes.

Flynn sighed. "She told the head of the gang, a guy named Colin, that I had delusions of grandeur, and I thought I was getting out. Colin had his boys jump me to teach me a lesson."

The next bit was going to be tough for her to hear but she had to know who the real Flynn O'Connor was. Chances were good it would be enough to end this thing between them and he needed it to be over, but he wasn't sure he had the strength to do it himself.

"I killed the two kids who jumped me. And then I killed Colin."

Harper's eyes widened. Her knuckles turned white on the arms of the chair, but she said nothing and showed no other reaction.

"Siobhan stood there and watched. She didn't help me, she didn't run. Just stood there and watched the whole thing. When it was over she tried to hug me. Told me she loved me. I turned my back on her and left. Joined the army the next day and got out.

"I came back a few years later, home for a visit. Ran into her at a party. She was hanging off some asshole gang leader.

He was playing cards with his cronies. Whoever won the pot got to screw Siobhan. That game happened every weekend. She'd become just another commodity for him to bet. I tried to get her to leave but she just laughed. Said I ruined her life. It was all my fault. The next time I came home, she was dead."

CHAPTER EIGHTEEN

Harper didn't know what to say. She knew there was a darkness in the man across from her, but she'd never dreamed he'd be a killer. No, that wasn't true. On some level she knew he was a killer, but she just didn't want to admit it. The world he'd lived in…probably lived in still…was so far removed from hers. But if she'd learned anything in the last few days, she'd learned that life was fragile and no one was safe from violence.

"I'm so sorry, Flynn." She couldn't think of anything else to say. There were no platitudes for this kind of situation. She understood, though, why he was so protective. He didn't protect Siobhan and now she was dead. That's how he saw it because that was a typical male thought process. "It wasn't your fault and there was nothing you could've done to change things."

"How would you know that? You weren't there."

"You know what? Men rarely give women credit for making their own decisions and making their own mistakes. It's always 'it was my fault she didn't get to work, it was my fault that she two-timed me.' Like we don't have a mind of our own. Let me tell you something, Siobhan made her choices for whatever reasons, and she had to live with the consequences. Tuck your fragile male ego in your pocket and realize it was all on her and had nothing to do with you. You weren't the center of her world. So, stop carrying any responsibility."

He stared at her.

"Yeah, I know. Shocking. But I'm telling you now, Siobhan's choices were all about her, not you." She stood up and moved until their knees touched. "Just like my choices are about me. And right now, I'm choosing to have sex with you." She straddled his legs and sat down on his lap. "I'm sure you told me that story to scare me off. To prove what a bad guy you are. That could be true. But what I do know about you is this: You have your own code and you follow it. That's more than most people have. I admire it. It's also sexy as hell because I know you'll protect me even if you're a wee bit troglodytic when you do it. So, are you going to sit there and pout or are you going to make me scream your name when I come?"

A smile tugged at the corners of his lips and then they claimed hers. She clasped her arms around his neck as she deepened the kiss, pressing herself against him and rolling her hips. As he scooped her up, she wrapped her thighs around his waist. He carried her to the bed, laid her down, and then covered her body with his own. Her hands caressed the hard ridges of his chest through his sweater, and it sent fire through her veins. His erection was rock hard, and she was desperate to have him inside her.

He pulled up her sweater and bra, exposing one breast for him to suckle. He devoured her nipple with his mouth as desire took complete control of them both.

"Flynn," she breathed.

He planted soft kisses along the side of her neck. She let out a moan and grabbed his sweater. Lifting on one hand, he pulled the garment off with the other, dropping it to the floor before he lowered his weight onto her once again. She reveled in it.

His lips searched hers while she traced circles around his chest with her fingertips. He pulled back from her and helped to remove her sweater as she shivered beneath him.

"Are you cold?" he asked.

"Not at all," she replied breathlessly.

He unclasped her bra and pulled it free. When he brushed his tongue over one of her nipples she moaned. "God, that feels so incredible," she whispered into his ear.

She reached for his belt buckle, but he stopped her, grasping both of her wrists in one hand and holding them above her head. He took control of the kiss again, their tongues dancing with desire. Then he moved slowly down from her lips to her neck and then to each of her nipples, tugging lightly at them until she gasped for air.

She tried to free herself from his grip, but he held on tight, whispering, "Stop fighting me or I'll go all caveman on you, and you won't like it."

"Who says?"

He nipped her breast and she yelped. He pulled away again and then rolled her onto her belly. Holding her hands above her head, he kissed her neck and pressed his hard-on against her curvy backside. It was so damn hot. Heat coursed through her. She moaned his name.

He reached his hand around to find the apex of her legs and then massaged her through the jeans.

"Take them off," she demanded and pushed her hips upward.

Flynn undid the button and the fly. Harper lifted her hips higher, and he stripped the jeans down her legs. Then he kissed her neck as he worked his fingers inside her thong. He rubbed her clit gently. She was wet with anticipation, pushing back and forth as his fingers moved at a leisurely pace.

"Faster," she ordered, and he increased his speed.

Under him, she writhed until he finally plunged his fingers inside of her, which elicited a yelp of pleasure from her lips.

He turned her over again and took off her underwear. She loved his alpha male streak when it came to sex. It made her want him desperately.

Flynn pressed his body completely against hers, trapping her against the bed as he kissed her again. The feeling of his skin against hers ignited an uncontrollable need. When he touched the hot center between her legs, she moved fiercely under his touches. He kissed her neck while flicking his fingers against her clit. He made his way down her body until he was kneeling on the floor, positioned above the apex of her legs.

He blew on her heated center while she dug her fingers into his scalp. His grip on her ass kept her still as he increased the intensity of his tongue. Then slowly, he eased one finger inside while continuing to swirl his tongue around her clit.

Her hands moved to caress his hair as she lifted her hips to meet his mouth. She got closer and closer to the edge until finally, he nipped her clitoris with his teeth, which sent a jolt through her body.

His name slipped from her lips as she reached her climax.

"Flynn, I want you inside me," Harper demanded. She wanted to feel him. To taste him. He started to kiss her, but she backed off. "Take off your jeans now." She helped him out of the rest of his clothing and then pushed him gently until he was lying on his back on the bed.

She straddled him then, determined to enjoy this time with him for as long as she could, she kissed him deeply. Then she traveled her lips down his neck to his chest. With her teeth, she teased his nipples, and he groaned. He tried to grab her ass, but she squirmed away from him.

"Harper." His low voice rumbled from his chest and spread shivers across her body.

She touched the hard planes of his abdomen, running her fingers over the tight, thick muscles. He was so damn beautiful. She wanted to burn his image into her memory.

She toyed with his nipples, licking and pinching, and then trailed lower until she hovered her mouth over his cock. She ran her tongue across the tip before making slow circles around the crown, first one way and then the other. Gradually, she drew him deeper into her mouth as she sucked and twisted.

Flynn growled her name; his deep voice sent shivers down her spine. She wanted him inside of her, but first she yearned to hear him say her name again. His hips began to move, and she responded with her tongue.

"Harper, you're killing me."

She stopped and looked up, staring into his eyes before ordering, "Don't come yet."

Then she smiled wickedly before returning to her previous position. The fact that he wanted her so badly made desire course through her body. She was already soaking wet with anticipation. When she started to ease herself over him, he grabbed her hips and pulled her down hard.

She gasped as she stretched to accommodate his girth. "You need to wait."

"Fuck waiting." He began moving his hips underneath her. She moaned and arched to take him in fully. She matched his rhythm and urged him to go faster.

"Jesus, Flynn. You feel so damn good inside me. Faster," she demanded again. He obliged, holding her hips as she rode him.

"Harper," he said through gritted teeth. She knew he was on the verge of coming but so was she. She ground her clit over his pubic bone and keened as sensation roared through her. She arched, her hips bucking as she came. A few strokes later, he careened over the edge with her.

Exhausted, sated, but still wanting more, she flopped down onto his chest. Her body trembled from the intense, earth-shattering orgasm. But a hollow feeling was already building in her chest. This bliss wasn't made to last. Their worlds were too different. They were too far apart for it to work. She knew instinctively all they had was right now and even that was slipping away.

Flynn quietly slid out of bed. Harper pretended she was asleep and hoped he wouldn't notice.

He pulled on his jeans and black sweater. The gun he'd left on the bedside table rattled against the wood when he picked it up and then removed something else from the drawer. Curiosity made her want to figure out was he'd grabbed, but she didn't dare open her eyes to check.

He slid quietly out of the room closing the door behind him.

Harper gave him a few minutes then she sat up and rubbed her face. He was going to do his thing, and she was going to do hers. She slid from the bed. The truth of the matter was, she liked Flynn, probably way more than she should. If circumstances were different, they might even have a chance for something long-term. But he'd head back to New York, or wherever, eventually and she'd be staying in Maine. They wanted two separate things in life.

She pulled on her jeans and searched for the green cashmere sweater he'd tossed away in his rush to get her naked. She was still grinning about their haste as she quietly padded out of the room. He would be livid at her for skulking around on her own but well, too fucking bad. This was life. She couldn't live it for him. She had to make her own choices. Finding the secret passages was going to help her find out who killed Astrid.

She crept down to the basement and entered the unfinished section. She went back to where she and Flynn had searched earlier. He seemed so sure it was there. She stared at the blank wall, but she still couldn't see anything that was remotely door-like.

She turned and leaned her back on the wall. Where else could it be? She stared but nothing jumped out at her. Finally, she started forward but tripped over a box on her left. It was pushed out ever so slightly. As she moved to push it back, she noticed the floor next to it had marks on it. Squatting for a closer look she saw a small black pebble looking thing. She pressed it and the side wall of the small room swung inward revealing a staircase.

Harper grinned. "Thanks, Dad," she muttered and then stood.

She went through the doorway and looked around for some kind of latch on the inside but saw nothing. She could wait or she could go explore. There was no question. She started up the stairs and when she hit the third step the door swung quietly closed. She tromped on the step again but the door didn't open. She took another look around for a secret button but there was nothing.

Nowhere to go but up. Giving a small shrug, she started to climb the stairs again. If worse came to worse, she could scream and hopefully someone would hear her. They might have to break through a wall to get to her but at least she wasn't permanently trapped here. Or so she told herself.

CHAPTER NINETEEN

The sound of soft footsteps broke the silence he'd waited in. A figure entered the kitchen area and hurried directly to the pantry. Opening the door, the person slid inside and closed the door after them. Flynn quietly made his way over to the pantry door and waited until he heard the sound he knew was coming. He jerked open the pantry door, and flicked on the light switch.

"If it isn't the ghost of Everlasting Manor, in the flesh."

Mrs. Carruthers whirled around and stared at him open mouthed. A gaping wall in the pantry exposed a staircase. "I — How—"

"How did I know it was you sneaking around trying to scare people?"

She snapped her lips together and glared at him.

"Because no one else has anything to gain by driving people out of here. The 'regular' members, as you think of them, all know the stories of this place and don't mind at all. But the New Yorkers, and the not-so-nice members, hate it. You figured you could get your domain back if you could drive the new people and, most importantly, Gina out."

She crossed her arms over her chest. "I'm not saying anything."

He leaned forward menacingly. "You don't have to. I have you dead to rights. You know the best thing about being one of the enforcers of the Lock and Key Society? We're not big on needing proof."

Her face paled.

"I would suggest you answer all my questions in *excruciating* detail. What happens to you will depend on your answers."

"But I haven't...that is, it was harmless."

"Not quite," Flynn closed the pantry door. "Did you steal all the stuff that's gone missing, apart from Mrs. Addison's necklace?"

"I only took small stuff and I still have it. I was going to start returning it randomly around the Manor but then…"

"Then someone stole the necklace and someone else killed Calli."

She nodded. "I didn't do either of those things."

"No, you didn't but you made it all possible because you used these passageways and other people found out about them."

Her face completely blanched then. "I didn't tell anyone."

"Maybe not, but you're not as stealthy as you think. Your snide comments to people gave you away. You commented about me eating chicken, but I was alone in here and the house was full of guests. How could you know it was me? You couldn't have… Unless you were watching and the only way I wouldn't have seen you is if you were hiding in here. Others will have put two and two together as well. And now people are dead."

As if the wind had gone out of her sails, she sagged against the shelves. "I had no idea. I would never."

"And somehow, here we are. Show me how you open and close the door here. Where are the other entrances?"

"There's one in the basement in the unfinished section and there's one in the main floor billiard room next to the storage room."

She turned toward the shelves and lifted her arm to move stuff out of the way. Her scent wafted over to Flynn and recognition set in. "You fucking hit me on the head in the basement."

Mrs. Carruthers looked at him and there were tears in her eyes, along with defiance. She sniffed and the tears disappeared. "Yes, I was. I came out to make sure it was the storm and not something that I had done that caused the power to go off a second time and you were there. I couldn't escape without you seeing me."

"So you whacked me on the head. The fact that you've resented the hell out of me since I arrived had nothing to do with it, right?"

She kept her mouth shut. But it was too late as far as Flynn was concerned. Any sympathy he might have had for her evaporated. She could have killed him with that blow if it had more force behind it. She wasn't some misguided old lady. No, her bitterness and fear had overtaken her common sense and she'd gone for it. Now she would pay.

"Show me."

She turned back to the shelf and moved a pickle jar out of the way. Then she pressed on a small patch on the wall. It looked like a smudge mark. The back wall of the pantry swung closed. She hit it again and it swung back open.

"Is there anything I need to know about these passages? Any kind of traps or weak spots?"

She shook her head once.

"If I find out you've lied to me, it will only be worse for you."

She twined her fingers together at her waist and nodded.

"Go to your room and stay there until I say otherwise. Do not talk to anyone. Am I making myself clear?"

She gritted her teeth but gave him a single nod. He opened the door for her and she pushed by him. He watched her walk out of the kitchen, back ramrod straight, head held high. He closed the pantry door and pulled out his cell. "Karl? You've got about ten minutes before she leaves. Twenty at most. She won't dawdle." He dropped the call.

Helen Carruthers had a choice. She could stay in her room and wait like he'd told her to do at which point Archer would come up with some punishment for her. They couldn't fire her exactly, that's not how the Society worked. She betrayed the members by harassing them and stealing from them. She couldn't be allowed to just retire peacefully to the countryside because they had no guarantee that she wouldn't open her mouth. But her crimes weren't serious enough that she should suffer the ultimate fate. Chances were good, Archer would send her somewhere like Outer Mongolia and she would live out her days quietly, which was what she'd been trying to do here. So not so bad.

If, on the other hand, she ran, something Flynn believed extremely likely, then Karl would pick her up and deliver her to the jet where she would be flown to meet Archer in person. Flynn had no idea what that outcome would be, and he sure as hell wasn't going to ask. He was grateful it wasn't his decision to make.

Flynn pulled out his gun and then a small flashlight from his jeans pocket. Then he hit the switch and turned off the lights in the pantry. He stepped through the door and started up the stairs. When he got to the third one, the door behind him swung closed.

He kept his flashlight and his gun raised. Mrs. Carruthers was another person he wouldn't trust as far as she could throw him. Who knew what lurked up here? He moved cautiously and as quietly as possible. Reaching the top of the staircase a dim passageway stretched out before him.

The walls were exposed studs and old school lath and plaster. The floor was made of wide, rough planks. The passageway was just slightly wider than the width of Flynn's shoulders. Dim single bulbs dangled from the ceiling at long intervals, doing little to light the way.

The sound of snoring reached Flynn as he moved cautiously along the passageway. He was inside the wall of the house in the older section that contained all the bedrooms. He admired the ingenuity of how they built the passageways. Essentially, the hidden corridor ran the length of the building with bedrooms on each side. It was the wall everyone's headboard was on. That meant whoever was in here could listen to anyone at any time.

More snoring and then voices. He looked around and spied holes in the walls. Small but enough to see through. He glanced through one hole to see the two women he and Shah had passed on the stairs playing cards.

As he made his way down the passageway, two things became obvious to him. One, these passageways were used regularly by more than just Mrs. Carruthers because the footsteps in the dust in certain places were of different sizes. Two, they gave whoever was inside them full access to almost every room in the building. Calling up the floor plans in his head, the only rooms that these tunnels didn't access were the employee rooms in the new wing on the second and presumably the third floor.

The sound of footsteps halted him. Someone was coming toward him. He moved slowly, keeping his gun up but put his penlight back in his pocket. In close quarters like this the element of surprise was vital. The passageway turned in front of him. He waited at the corner. As the steps came closer, he braced himself.

He moved swiftly around the corner and came face to face with Harper. She opened her mouth to scream, and he slapped his hand over her lips. She stared at him as he cursed under his breath.

"What the hell are you doing here," he hissed quietly.

She tried to speak but he still had his hand over her mouth. He removed it and she whispered, "Same as you, I'm guessing."

He wanted to demand she leave but he knew she wouldn't and if he took her out of here without letting her explore, she'd just come back on her own which was worse.

"The door in the basement?" he asked in a whisper.

She nodded. "Looks like Everlasting Manor's ghost is someone wandering around in here."

"Mrs. Carruthers."

"No!" she said a little too loudly. He clamped a hand back over her mouth. They both froze. Her eyes got big but a minute later they relaxed again. "Sorry. I just wasn't expecting that."

He looked behind her. "Is that directly up from the basement? Were there any other hallways off this one?"

She shook her head. "Nope. This is it."

"Okay." He stared at her. "We'll keep going this way." He pointed to her hallway since his intersected it. "But do not make any sound and for once in your life, do what I say."

"I'll try. I make no promises." She gave him an impish grin.

He wanted to turn her around and spank her. Take her out of there, straight back to his bedroom and keep her busy all night long. A sharp tug strained below his belt. But this was work and it had to come first.

"Follow me." He moved quietly along the passageway. More snoring, a few people on their phones from the sounds of things and then voices. A few of them were together in one room but the sound was weird. It wasn't as distorted as the other sounds.

He stopped. There was a room up ahead. He could make out a doorway. Of course there'd be secret room, because why the hell not?

He glanced through the hole in the wall next to him. They were not far from the library. The secret room must fall behind the broom closet and share a wall with the library. That made all kinds of sense.

He turned and gestured to Harper to be silent. She nodded. They moved a bit closer.

"The deal looks good, Davis." Eli Fisher's voice came down the hallway at him. "I spoke with some contractors and if we break ground early next year, they say phase one can be completed within twelve months."

Why was he not surprised Fisher and Austin Davis were involved in whatever this shit was? His nerves were taut. He regretted telling Archer to not send anyone else. Back-up might be good right now.

"That is good news." Davis's voice sounded tinny, like it was coming through a speaker. Made sense, because the man wasn't physically present at the manor. "But it's all for naught if we don't get the approval. How is that going?"

Another voice cut through the air. "I believe quite well."

Bryson. The third musketeer. *Should've guessed.*

Bryson continued. "He seems to be working his magic. The mayor is certainly enjoying his attention. We're thinking this can be wrapped up shortly."

Flynn glanced back at Harper and raised his eyebrows. What was this about? She shook her head slightly as if to say she didn't know but then her eyes got wide for a moment. She closed them and mouthed a curse word. He'd have to ask her later what all this was about.

"How do we know for sure she won't change her mind?" Davis demanded. "We're looking at six months out from the time we buy the property to the time we can break ground. How do we know she won't change her mind and not give us the variances and the zoning changes we need? Plus, she's just one vote. What about the town council? They would have to be onside to change the zoning."

Harper bit her lip. Worry had etched fine lines on her face. He could read her mind. What stupid shit had her boss dragged her into now? He didn't know yet what this was all about, but it was starting to take shape in his mind.

"It's all in hand. Certain steps are being taken to ensure the mayor's cooperation. She'll bring the others around. And if there are any holdouts we'll fix the situation."

"What about the other mess?" Davis inquired. "The murder of the young girl and the one that went down the stairs? What's happening there?"

Harper tensed beside him. He found her hand and squeezed it.

"Also well in hand," Fisher replied.

"Is it?" Davis demanded. "Gina, I didn't put you there to make trouble. I'm quite concerned about all this. The girl was supposed to be a dry run and it did not turn out well."

"That's not my fault." Gina had been silent until now, but she was quick to deny his words. "We couldn't test the tunnel from the beach because of the storm. The water was too high. We brought her in and had her here to test the room. It was fine but then she had to use the restroom, something we didn't consider and so we had her wait in the library until it was free. Dumb bitch panicked when she discovered the door was locked. She freaked out and had to be subdued."

Davis growled, "My sources tell me she was beaten to death."

"That's on him," Gina huffed. "That wasn't the plan, and he knew it. We had a buyer lined up and we were ready to ship her out, but he got carried away. If you have an issue, talk to him."

Flynn's stomach hit the floor watching Harper's face blanch as she realized they were talking about Astrid. She swayed slightly. He put his arm around her and gestured for her to go but she shook her head. He wanted to kill these people for the pain they were putting Harper through. And then he'd resurrect them and fucking kill them all over again for trafficking women. That's what they were talking about, human trafficking. Nothing more than a bag of limp dicks, the lot of them. Adrenaline spiked in his bloodstream, making his rapid heartbeat thump in his ears. He wanted to storm in and kill them all. He took a deep breath and then a second one. It took him a few moments to calm down and focus again.

Fisher spoke up. "Don't worry about the murdered girl. We have someone in the police department. He is going to take care of everything for us."

Flynn glanced at Harper. *Jason*, she mouthed the name. The bastard had broken into Harper's place so Flynn didn't know why he was so surprised that Jason was that bent. Maybe he was losing his touch. He hadn't had that read off Jason at all.

"At least," Bryson said, "we know that the system works in theory. The bathroom thing has to be worked into the plans along with soundproofing but other than that, it's quite solid. We will have to shore up the tunnel in spots just to be on the safe side and depending on the cargo we're bringing in we might have to be cognizant of the fact certain things might have to be brought in smaller amounts. Otherwise, I think it will work beautifully." The sound of ice cubes rattling in a glass preceded a *thunk* that Flynn recognized immediately.

"Jesus, be careful. That makes a loud thump in the library," Fisher admonished.

"No one is in the library so it doesn't matter," Bryson said.

"Steve, just be more careful," said Gina.

"Well, the plans are impressive," Davis started. "The development looks amazing. The pool and tennis courts will be popular along with the inside pickleball courts. I am quite sure we can convince Will Findley with all this detail. Probably a few of the other members too."

"Agreed," said Bryson. "We will have to explain about how we're going to keep the members separate from the outsiders that buy into the development. That's going to be a thing with some of the members."

"Yes," Fisher said, "but I think we can reassure them that activities will continue as normal, and we can encourage certain new people to join the Lock and Key Society. Those who are less desirable, we can keep separate."

"The only real problem is Archer Gray," Bryson pointed out. "He'll go ape shit if he finds out about this."

Flynn's heart rate ticked up. He needed to get Harper out of there immediately if they were going to discuss the Society, but he also needed to hear what the response was about Archer. If trouble was brewing, he needed to warn his boss. Turning, he gestured to Harper to leave. She shook her head. He glared and gestured again but she crossed her arms over her chest and stood resolute. *Fuck. Fuck. Fuck.*

"That problem will be resolved in the not-too-distant future," Davis stated. "I have plans in place to replace Archer Gray as the head of the Society."

"And not a moment too soon," Fisher said. "Well, if there's nothing else then I think we can adjourn the meeting. I will follow up about the zoning etc. and Gina, you follow up with the police. Davis, we'll keep you updated."

Flynn turned toward Harper and turned her around. He made her as move quickly as possible without making a sound back down the passage. When they got to the fork, she turned to go back toward the kitchen, but he shook his head and made her go back the way she'd come.

They got to the stairs going down before Harper turned to him and said, "I don't know how to open this door."

He brought out his penlight and flicked it on. Then he scanned the area around the door. Finally, he located a button on the side of the door frame and hit it. The door opened and they emerged into the basement.

Harper stepped on the black button and closed the door behind them and then turned her back and leaned on the wall.

"Are you okay?" Flynn asked. He leaned his shoulder on the wall next to her.

"No," she said in a wavering voice. "I'm not."

There was nothing he could do that was going to make this better. "I'm sorry you had to hear all that."

She crossed her arms over her chest and looked at him. "I'm not. I wanted to know what happened and now I do. Except I don't know who did it. Do you?"

He had a theory he wasn't ready to share. "No."

"We need to talk to Gina. She knows everything."

Flynn waited a beat. She was upset and he needed her to stay calm but there was no way in hell he was going to allow her to talk to Gina. Gina was his problem and then she was going to be Archer's problem to solve. Instead, he tried to point her in another direction. "Knowing Jason is bent doesn't help much. There's no way to prove it."

She nodded. "That was a surprise. I just didn't peg him for it, but I supposed I should have after he broke into my place."

"Let's get you back upstairs. You've got to be exhausted." He needed her locked in somewhere so he could call Archer. They needed to deal with all this pronto.

She raised an eyebrow at him. "What do you mean?"

He stared at her. "You need some sleep."

"After what we just heard? You're crazy. We need to call the police. Those people were talking about trafficking girls. Are we supposed to just let that go?"

"*You* need to let it go. I will take care of it. All of it. You need to stay as far away from all this as possible."

"That's just insane. We need to tell the police what's going on."

He had to make her see reason. Maybe if he appealed to her ambition because appealing to her safety hadn't worked. "Listen, we have no proof and telling the police won't change anything. Hell, did you hear them? Your boss is probably already compromised, as is the police department. I'm asking you to stay as far away from this as possible because if it all blows up someone is going to have to take the reins of the local government. Your boss's days are numbered. And so are the police chief's."

The appeal seemed to drive home the reality of the situation for her. She rubbed her face with her hands. "What do we do then?"

"*We* don't do anything. I'll take it from here."

She straightened. "That's not acceptable. Astrid and Calli deserve justice."

"And they'll get it, but you can't be a part of that. It's too dangerous both physically and career-wise." If she only knew how dangerous it was for her. If anyone ever found out that she heard anything about the Society then it could be the end for her. His heart crashed against his ribcage at that thought.

She stared at him, then let out a sigh. "I'm not shocked to find out that my former boss, Will Findley is involved with these guys. He was always shady. I knew at the time he was up to all kinds of shit. Backroom deals were just the tip of the iceberg. The fact that the Lock and Key Society is involved in this doesn't surprise me either."

He started to reply, but then froze. Did she just... What the fuck did she know? And how did she find out? He forced air back into his lungs and tried to figure out what to say.

"Do you know about them? The Rainy Day Club reminds me a bit of them except you guys are more public. There's nothing public about the Lock and Key."

Wait...she hadn't connected him with the Society yet. "What's the Lock and Key Society?" He kept his voice as neutral as possible.

"It's this secret society that a lot of the top-tier people in New York and around the world belong to. Supposedly you can get anything you want or experience anything you can think of if you're a member. Apparently, Will was, and still is, a member. He used to talk about it in hushed tones with Webber, but we all knew about it. His hushed tones weren't so hushed when he was drinking. I never knew if it was real or something he made up, but it sounds like it's real and it's involved in some nasty business."

She ran her hands through her hair. "We have to do something about all this. Who do we tell?"

Flynn said nothing. She was going in circles trying to absorb the situation and deal with the shock.

"I need to talk to Susan and tell her what the hell is going on here. She's being used. And as horrible as she can be at times, she's a damn good mayor. I'd hate to see her do something stupid to wreck her political career."

"It's probably too late for that. As I said…you don't want to be anywhere near this. You need to take a breath. We can go up to my room or, if you want, I can take you home and stay with you. I think we need to take a step back and assess before we do anything. I don't want to make a mistake that could jeopardize things."

She stared at him and then gave a small shrug. "I want to go to my place but I…" she licked her lips. "I just need to be alone."

The pain that shot through his chest was unexpected. He rubbed the area above his heart but said nothing. Instead, he just nodded. "Being alone is not a great idea. Can you stay with a friend or go see your parents?"

"Yeah, I could do that. I can go see my folks. They won't question me too closely. I can just say I can't sleep and needed to be with family." She glanced at her wrist. "It's just gone one a.m. I better get a move on. My dad will still be up." She pulled her phone out and sent him a text. She got an immediate response. "Okay, I'm good to go."

He walked her out of the basement and through the building to her SUV parked outside. "Text me when you get there so I know you made it safely."

"I will."

She was so pale and looked so worn out that it broke him somehow. He wanted to hold her close and tell her it would all be okay but he could tell her walls were already up. She didn't hug him or kiss him or give any indication they were anything more than acquaintances. Smart girl. If only he could do the same. He stood back and watched her drive away. A feeling of dread washed over him, leaving him a bit queasy and clammy. It was the same reaction he'd had many times when he was in the gang or when he was in serious trouble in Iraq. His body was telling him this was far from resolved and if he wasn't careful, it wouldn't end well for him or Harper.

CHAPTER TWENTY

F lynn pulled out his phone. Karl had sent several texts. Carruthers had run and he'd scooped her up. She was on a plane on her way to see Archer. He sent a text to Karl asking if he was around and if could he make sure Harper made it to her parents' place. He responded immediately and said he would text when she made it and then hang out for a while to see if she stayed there. Karl was a good man who knew his shit. Flynn idly wondered if he wanted to leave Maine. There were lots of good positions for someone like Karl.

He started back inside and then thought the better of it. Turning, he went to his rental and drove into town. He sat on Main Street outside the Coffee Cake and made the call he'd been dreading.

"Mrs. Carruthers is due to land shortly. What do you need?" Archer's voice was icy.

"Mrs. Carruthers is the least of your problems." Flynn went on to explain everything he'd heard omitting the detail that Harper had been with him. No need to drag her into this. "Davis seems to have something big planned for you.

He told them that you wouldn't be the head of the Society in the not-so-distant future."

Archer was silent for a moment. "I've heard rumors of this before, small whiffs of it here and there. I knew there was something more than ghosts going on in Maine. I sent you to see if you could get a line on it without me telling you what it was."

"Are you serious? You don't trust me to do my job?" Flynn was more than insulted. He was seriously pissed off.

"You misunderstand. It's not you that I don't trust. I hear things all day every day. Most of it is bullshit but some"—he sighed—"some is real. If you discovered this on your own, I know it's real. I don't trust myself. When you're at the top, you start to see conspiracies everywhere."

Somewhat mollified, Flynn asked, "How do you want to handle all this?"

"Unfortunately, Fisher and Davis have not done anything at this point that is actionable. I would be inclined to let this play out but I'm not sure how much longer I can control the outcome. I'll handle things on this end and kill their real estate deal. They'll have to start all over somewhere else, which will buy time.

"Gina is yours. She's a disaster. Make it look like an accident if you can. Suicide would be a good option as well. Nothing to raise suspicions. And we need to know who the silent partner is. Find out. We need to deal with him."

For a brief moment, Flynn said nothing. Normally this part didn't bother him and he didn't feel any sympathy for Gina, but this time there was hesitation. Harper. She was making him hesitate. Not good. He needed to destroy what he felt for her because his job and his life depended on him not hesitating. Not ever.

Flynn cleared his throat. "There's one other thing." He proceeded to fill Archer in on another score.

"Okay. I'll have Ryker deal with that. You should know, I have help for you in the area. I sent someone up a while ago to keep an eye on things as rumors began to swirl. Say the word and he will come out of hiding."

"Okay. I'll let you know."

"How is Harper?"

That caught Flynn completely off guard. How did Archer know, or a better question was, what did he know? "She's at her parents' place. I think she'll be fine. I'm trying to keep her controlled, but she's a wild card."

"See that she doesn't get in the way," Archer said and then he was gone.

Flynn let out a breath he'd been holding. Rush had said Archer knew far more about he and Kat than he'd realized. The man had eyes everywhere or maybe he had the sixth sense and a crystal ball. However he knew, his last words had been a warning. And he wasn't just talking about her physically getting in the way. She was in his way mentally and he needed to stop that from happening. Distractions in his line of work could get him killed. Or worse, get her killed and he wasn't about to let that happen.

Harper curled up on her side and tried to get some sleep, but the effort was useless. The conversation they'd overheard played again and again in her head. She should call the police but Flynn was right, who could she trust? Now that she was sure Jason had broken into her place, did that confirm that he was crooked? Or was Chief Clark on their payroll? He'd certainly done a quick about-face after Susan spoke to him. Had she promised him something or had she informed him they were on the same side?

And what about the mayor? Was she willingly going to

go along with whatever zoning changes they wanted? Was she being blackmailed? It could be either or a combination of both. Susan had her issues but until now, Harper thought she was doing a good job. Was there more to it?

Everything swirled around and around in her head. And then there was Flynn. What the hell had she been thinking? He told her he was a killer and she'd eagerly hopped into bed with him. Should she be worried about her safety? Some instinct made her believe Flynn wouldn't hurt her. He would protect her as much as he could, but he couldn't be with her all the time. Had she put her parents in danger by running home to them? Anxiety was a dreadful bedfellow. She rolled to her back and butted her head against her pillows.

She heaved a gigantic sigh as the litany of unanswerable questions continued. That was the Lock and Key Society. The more she thought about it, the more the Rainy Day Club seemed similar. Was the Rainy Day Club just a front for the Lock and Key? That was a very scary thought. That meant that Flynn worked for the Society.

There'd been rumors about the Lock and Key Society for years. But one night when her boss had gotten blackout drunk, he'd confessed to being a member, saying that all the stuff that went on there scared him sometimes.

Flynn had told her to sit tight and let him handle Gina. But she had to believe Gina was the key. She knew who killed Astrid. Was it the same person who'd killed Calli? Harper had an idea of who it might be, but she needed confirmation. And then what? If she couldn't trust the police then who could she trust to help her? Which brought her full circle back to Flynn.

Several sleepless hours later, Harper rolled out of bed. The air was crisp as the sun came up over the ocean.

"Coffee?" her mother asked as Harper walked into the kitchen.

"Please." She sank down on a stool at the kitchen island.

"Not much sleep, huh?"

"No." Harper rubbed her face with both hands.

Her mother put the mug of coffee down in front of her. "What's keeping you up? Is it Astrid's death? The police are investigating. They'll figure it out."

Harper grunted. "Maybe."

"What's really bugging you?" her mother asked as she poured herself a cup of coffee and sat next to Harper.

"Do you ever wonder if you've made the right decision?"

Her mother laughed. "All the time. Should we have pot roast or lamb? What vegetables should we have? Maybe the mushrooms would've been better than the peas."

"Seriously, Mom."

Her mother smiled. "Darling girl, if you didn't wonder if you made the right choices sometimes then you wouldn't be human. But why don't you tell me which choices you're questioning?"

Harper shrugged. "I'm second-guessing my decision to come back here to Cedar Bluff. All the stuff I went through in New York, it's not that different from what's going on here. I still work for an ambitious, hard-driving politician whom I'm constantly cleaning up after. I still work too much, without getting credit for my hard work. What's changed?"

"Your family and friends are near. You live in an amazing condo that I know you love. You are appreciated much more than you think by everyone in town. They know what you do and how you take care of so many things behind the scenes. I don't think you're giving yourself enough credit."

"Maybe."

"Is it Astrid's death that has you discombobulated?" Her mother put an arm around Harper's shoulders. "I know it must have been very upsetting for you to see her like that."

"Her death has thrown me, but that's not it. I think I'm just tired of the politics of everything. There are so many lies and half-truths. People angling to get more power. Cedar Bluff is a small town and yet you have Jed playing hardball and not allowing us to hold the Halloween Extravaganza in the square without all kinds of silly rules because he's angry at Susan. She insulted him and bent his ego.

"And Susan is always throwing Chief Clark under the bus because she needs someone to blame for the escalating crime rate and anything else she can pin on him. And he's always trying to do the same to her. It's like kids on the playground, I swear. I'm... I'm just sick of it all."

"Is there something else you would like to do?" her mother asked.

Harper took a sip of her coffee. "I have no idea and I think that's the problem." She tapped her fingertip on the warm ceramic.

"Mornin', Sunshine." Her father blustered into the kitchen. "Look who I found lurking outside." He moved out of the way and Jason was standing in the doorway.

"Hey, Harper. I just wanted to check on you. I swung by your place and you weren't there so I thought I would stop here."

Her mother greeted Jason with a smile. "Come in. Can I get you some coffee? I was just about to start making breakfast. I'm a bit slow this morning. You'll stay and have bacon and eggs with us, won't you?"

"That would be great, Mrs. Edwards."

"Connie, please. You're not in high school anymore."

Harper's skin chilled. Here he was, playing nice with her parents when he wasn't nice at all. She wanted him out of her parents' house and out of their lives altogether. Fuck this Mr. Roger's *it's a beautiful day in the neighborhood* bullshit.

Her mother set the coffee down on the island and waved Jason over to a stool.

Harper stood up. "Why don't Jason and I go have our coffee in the sunroom? It's a beautiful view from there and we'll be out of your way."

Her mother smiled. "That sounds like a great idea." She gave Harper a look that said she knew something was up.

Grabbing her coffee cup and wrapping her sweater more tightly around her pajamas, Harper led Jason through the house to the sunroom. They sat in the side-by-side rocking chairs that faced out toward the water. The view over the ocean was amazing and she used admiring it as an excuse to get herself together.

"How are you doing? Yesterday was a lot on top of… everything else."

"Yes, it was," she agreed.

"I'm sorry if I was a bit of a jerk. The stress of having two homicides was getting to me, I guess."

Harper made a noncommittal noise as she pondered how to best confront him. *Fuck it.* She was done with playing nice. "Why did you break into my home?"

Jason froze, his coffee cup halfway to his mouth. "I don't know what you're talking about," he said as he lowered his cup again.

"Fuck all the way off, Jason. I'm done with your bullshit. You broke into my place. It could only have been you. You unlocked the door when you stopped by and returned later, coming in that way to leave me the candle and the note while I was sleeping."

He stared at her and then his brows drew down and his lips thinned out. "When did this happen? Someone threatened you? Why didn't you tell me? We need to file a report so I can assign you some protection."

"Enough! I want the truth." Her heart pounded as she tried to keep her temper in check.

He frowned. Pretend hurt darkened his brown eyes. "I don't know what to tell you, Harper. It wasn't me." He shook his head. "And I'm a bit insulted that you would think I would do such a thing."

Was she wrong about Jason? Had she just forgotten to lock the door and someone broke in? She stared at him.

"Seriously, Harper. I would never do that to you. I'm a cop. It's frowned upon for us to break into people's houses." He offered her a small smile. "Tell me what happened."

She took a deep breath. Maybe she was wrong. "Someone broke in and left a candle burning in my living room with a note telling me to keep out of investigating Astrid's death."

"Do you still have the note? We could dust it for prints."

"I'm not sure." She rubbed her forehead with her free hand. "I can't remember what I did with it, to be honest."

Jason squeezed her arm. "You've been through a lot. Don't worry, I'll take care of it. Of you." He amended. "Do you still have the lavender candle? Maybe there are prints on that."

She froze. Adrenaline rushed through her body. "I never mentioned the type of candle." She stared at him. "It *was* you. You broke into my home, and you lied to me." She stood. "Get the hell out of this house and away from me."

He jumped up too. "Harper, I just wanted to keep you safe," he said as he reached out to touch her.

She backed up. "Get out, Jason. Now. Stay the fuck away from me."

He took a step forward.

"I don't think you want to do that," Flynn said from the doorway to the sunroom. The gun in his right hand was pointed at the floor, but the menace was clear. "Harper asked you to leave, so you're going to go."

Jason's face changed. Gone was the folksy, caring expression. His eyes hardened and his lips curled into a snarl. "Who the fuck are you to tell me what to do? Do you even have a license to carry that? I could arrest you right now. As a matter of fact, you're under arrest, Flynn O'Connor." Jason started forward.

Flynn raised the gun. "I have a license and I wasn't the perp who broke into her condo. You have nothing to arrest me for. Come a step closer to me or to Harper and I will shoot you dead where you stand. I will be perfectly justified because Harper is terrified of you. You should go now. Before I change my mind and kill you just because you scared her."

Jason looked at the gun and then back at Flynn. Hatred mottled his face. He turned and stormed out of the side door. Flynn was immediately at Harper's side and put his arm around her while watching Jason go. "You okay?"

She leaned against him, taking in the warmth and strength of his body. Her knees were weak and relief at seeing him flooded through her, making it hard to stand. "W-what are you doing here?"

"I came to check on you."

"How did you get in here? My parents—"

"Are very nice people who let in a stranger because Bob Ross told them I was throwing pebbles at your window. He gave me his stamp of approval." Flynn grinned. "Your father was good enough to take that into consideration. He likes Bob. Your mother didn't like the look on your face when Jason arrived."

God, if he just told her he'd reversed the tide, she couldn't be more shocked.

"Let's get you more coffee," he said tucking his gun back in his waistband and adjusting his sweater and jacket over it.

They walked back into the kitchen. "Breakfast is ready.

Would you like to stay, Flynn?" her mother asked. "There's plenty. Where's Jason?"

"I'd love breakfast, ma'am."

"Jason left." The four of them sat down at the kitchen table. Harper took a bite of her bacon and then put it back on her plate. "There's something I need to tell you about Jason."

An hour later she was walking Flynn out to his SUV. "Thank you for saving me."

"For the record, I don't think he was going to hurt you, but I do think he has major issues."

She shuddered. "I don't care what he was going to do, I'm just glad you were there to stop it. You heard my parents; they want me to report what happened. What do you think?"

Flynn leaned against his vehicle. "I think that's a wise move. It gets him out of the investigation though and leaves it in the hands of the other two. But if he's crooked, like we think, that can only improve things."

She nodded. "I know. I'm just worried. Lazlo and George Crawley don't exactly inspire confidence."

"There are other options."

"What do you mean?" she asked.

Flynn's cell went off. "I have to take this." He straightened and then leaned down and kissed her thoroughly. "Think about reporting Jason. Go to work. You should be safe there. Stay in contact with me throughout the day and don't go anywhere alone."

She nodded. "I'll think about it and you're right I should go to work."

He kissed her on her forehead. "I'll stop by and see you later." Then he got in his vehicle and drove away. Harper watched him go. She needed to get to work. There was so much to do for the Halloween Extravaganza, but she couldn't seem to move. Flynn had rescued her yet again. He seemed to know when she needed help. She'd left the Manor thinking a relationship with him was out of the question. That they'd never work. She had been clear on that. He was dark and wild and could never live the life she wanted. Long distance relationships didn't work either.

Now she wasn't so sure. Nothing had changed except she didn't want to be without him. And that was a scary thought.

"Harper?" her mother's voice reached her. "It's Susan. Some crisis at work."

Harper waved and started toward the house. Was this just a regular crisis? Or was this something more massive? Something like someone blackmailing Susan to get what they wanted. And if that was the case, what the hell were they going to do about it?

CHAPTER TWENTY-ONE

"Archer," Flynn said as he drove away from Harper. She was framed in his rear-view mirror, watching him leave. A shiver went across his skin and his shoulders tightened. Unease settled over him.

"Where are we on this? Have you spoken to Gina?"

"No."

"Why?" Archer demanded.

Flynn spoke through clenched teeth. "Because she's disappeared."

Archer cursed. "When?"

"Sometime after I got off the phone with you and I went to look for her. Her stuff is still in her room but it's hard to tell if anything is missing. The members are just getting up about now. The kitchen staff will do their normal routine and make sure everything is taken care of. I've alerted Shah to start reviewing the video feeds to see if we can find her or determine when she left."

"I don't fucking care about the kitchen staff. We need—"

"Fisher and his crew need to think everything is normal or we'll spook them," he ground out.

"We cannot touch Fisher and Davis. You need to let that go or I will have to replace you." Archer's voice was frosty.

It was a threat. Replace meant he would send someone up to deal with the crisis and then Flynn, whether it happened in a week or a month, would be taken out. *I'd like to see you try.* Archer might be all-powerful in his world, but he didn't know jack shit about the world Flynn grew up in, the world his family was still a part of. That world was his escape plan when the day came, and he knew it would come. Nothing was forever.

"Let's set the record straight. I want Fisher. I want him dead. But I'm not fucking stupid, and you declared him off-limits so he's off limits," Flynn snarled. "His partners aren't. One of them killed Astrid Windsor, and, most probably, Calli. Gina knew about it and probably helped. She's an employee and should have reported it but didn't. I'm sure she's skimming on whatever deal you made with her, not to mention she's one of Davis's people. All of which means *she* is not off limits. If we spook Fisher or Davis or any of them, then we lose her for sure. Right now, all I know is she's not in the Manor. At least not in the regular rooms. I have no idea if she's locked in some secret room. That place is huge and I haven't been through all the secret passages yet."

Archer was silent for a moment. "I apologize. I shouldn't have jumped to conclusions."

Flynn was nonplussed. He didn't know what to say. Archer Gray never apologized. What the fuck was going on?

"You should know I trust you implicitly. My comment was out of line. I am frustrated. My hands are tied by the rules and my adversaries are not under similar restriction. Things not going my way makes me mean."

Jesus. Someone was getting to Archer? Did hell freeze over? Was it the end of days?

"Understandable," Flynn replied. What else could he

say? Archer held on a lot longer than he would've. He would've taken Fisher out at the house in New Orleans when they'd discovered him with all those underage girls. Fuck the rules.

"What is your plan?" Archer asked.

"Find Gina. Use whatever means necessary to get her to talk. I told Shah to tell everyone that they aren't allowed to leave due to the in-house investigation until the end of the week. There will be a few grumblings, but it buys me probably twenty-four hours before they start to lose their shit and we have to let them go."

"Okay. I'm sure I'll get a few calls."

Flynn had a thought. "Put the jet on standby and have it ready to go at the airport. When I find Gina, after I speak to her, it's best if she's gone immediately. Then she'll have no chance to speak to her cronies."

"I already sent it back to Maine."

"Do you have someone to take over the Manor? With Carruthers and Gina gone, Shah can manage it for a bit but not long term."

"For your information and in case anyone should ask, Mrs. Carruthers is now installed as the manager of an inn we own in Finland. Just above the Arctic Circle. The Everlasting Manor will be closing its doors next month. The property will be sold to The Sunny Travel consortium and will open up as a five-star hotel in the late spring after some much-needed renovations."

"Seriously?" Flynn asked. "The Society has something called the Sunny Travel Consortium? Is that like the Rainy Day Club? What's with the weather fixation?"

"We also have the Snowy Foundation which runs retreats."

"No fuckin' way."

"Yes fuckin' way," Archer retorted in a much more

relaxed voice. "Without boring you, these entities help allow the Society to exist. The money has to move somehow."

"Huh. I guess I never thought about that."

Archer responded, "No one ever does. Keep me updated." And he was gone.

One of these days, the man would say goodbye before he hung up, and that's the day Flynn would know the world was ending.

Flynn pulled up to the gate and put his window down. "Hey, Karl."

"Flynn," the older man said as he stepped out of the guard house. "No one has come or gone since you left. I'm expecting a bunch of deliveries in the next hour to set up for the Halloween thing. I have extra guys posted around the property. They are sub-contractors so they don't know details, but they know to watch out for anyone trying to sneak on or off the property."

"Good. And thanks for the backup." He still hated that the grounds would be open to an outside event. The one bright spot there was Harper would be near enough for him to keep an eye on.

Karl cleared his throat. "If I've overstepped, let me know but I also have a guy watching Harper. He stayed in front of her folks' house all night and didn't like what he saw when Merritt left this morning so I had someone else come on shift when he went off."

Flynn's shoulders tightened. "What did he do?"

Karl shrugged. "He took off like a bat out of hell but didn't turn on his lights and there was no radio call. My friend is an ex-cop with a police band radio in his car. He's heard a rumor or two about Merritt. None of it good. The guy's a stalker but apparently no one complains because he's a cop."

"Shit." Flynn wanted to turn the BMW around, find

Merritt and pummel the asshole into the ground. "Okay, thanks. I appreciate you taking the initiative. Let me know if anything pops."

"Will do," Karl said and stepped back from the vehicle.

Flynn cruised up to the Manor and parked off to the side in the front. No Mrs. Carruthers to complain. Above the Arctic Circle. He grinned wryly. Wonder how she likes that? He took the steps two at a time and walked into the foyer to find Shah standing there looking frazzled.

Flynn's stomach lurched. "What is it? What's happened now?"

"We can't find Payton. She's not in her room and no one has seen her."

CHAPTER TWENTY-TWO

"Your lack of a Halloween costume is not a crisis." Harper sighed and wondered if she should make some tea. Her nerves were jangling from way too much caffeine this morning. She glanced at her watch. It was later than she thought. Already after eleven.

Susan glared at her across the desk. "I must look fabulous. My costume has to be a statement. People will see me. I'm the mayor. They expect something next level from me."

People didn't give a shit what she wore. That was the truth. Only Susan gave a crap about it. "Go as a witch."

"A witch?" Susan sniffed. "No."

"I'm sure Arnold down at the Little Theatre will have some terrific outfits. No one else would have anything as realistic. Call him and ask."

"He gave away my original costume. Why would I call him?"

Harper was rapidly losing patience. "Because he will feel guilty and want to help you and because he owns the only costume shop in town."

Susan harumphed. "I was going as Wonder Woman. A witch seems so…ordinary."

Of course she would pick Wonder Woman. Harper got up from the guest chair in Susan's office and stated out the door.

"Where are you going?" Susan bellowed.

"To make tea." *And get the hell away from you.*

Harper went into the little office kitchen, filled the kettle, and plugged it in. She was still off-kilter from this morning's run-in with Jason. Coming to work seemed like the best thing, but now she wasn't sure. She couldn't concentrate. She wanted to confront Gina. Find out who was responsible for Astrid's death.

She also wanted to confront Susan and find out what someone had on her that could coerce her to change zoning laws. The problem was Susan probably wouldn't know at this point. If someone was blackmailing her Susan would be pissed off and yelling about everything. She'd be in a rage even if she didn't say why. She was just ticked off at this point, so chances were excellent that no one said anything to her yet. Should she tell Susan what was coming?

She made her tea and went back into Susan's office. She was going over details for the Halloween event at the Manor with Brenda Holmes.

Brenda was cautioning the mayor on her address to open the Extravaganza. "You will be giving your remarks around six p.m. That kicks off things for the kids. I've written them out. I know you like to go off-script but whatever you do, keep it short and sweet. The families are there to have fun and if you speak for any more than two minutes the kids will get antsy and then the parents will get mad and the whole thing will be a public relations bust."

Susan stuck out her hand. "Give me your remarks. I'll keep it short."

"Brenda, can you give us a second?" Harper stood by the door, tea in hand.

She glanced at Susan, who was studying Harper.

"Go ahead," Susan said. "Check and see how things are going up at the Manor."

Brenda got up and left the office, shooting Harper a questioning look on her way out the door. Harper closed it after the woman, and then went and sat in the seat she'd just vacated.

She set her mug down on the desk. "We have to talk."

"I gathered that," Susan said wryly. "What's up?"

"I heard a rumor."

Susan snorted. "By now you should know better than to believe anything you hear."

Harper ignored the outburst. "This is about a group building some kind of community on the bluff by Everlasting Manor." She stared at Susan.

Susan waved her hand. "There are always rumors," she said dismissively but there was no force behind her words and she hadn't outright said no.

"In order to build on that ground, zoning laws would have to change. There would be an outcry in the community because it would limit beach access to the bluffs. The wildlife supporters would be incensed. This would be a major fight, and not one to be undertaken lightly. You could lose the next election."

Susan balked. "That's not necessarily true. You can't know for sure."

"I'm from Cedar Bluff, and I know these people. The voters will hate it, and you know it. You got elected the first time because you promised to bring in business but do it in a way that supports what's already here. No rezoning or overdevelopment. You put the wildlife protection order in place. And so far, you've stuck to that. Your supporters are happy. They'll flip on you if you roll over on that promise."

Susan pursed her lips and glared at Harper, but then seemed to relent. She pushed some papers around her desk and then slumped in her chair. "You're right. I know it. The voters wouldn't go for it. As much as the deal appeals to me for all kinds of reasons, including a sharp increase in the general funds based on the taxes the developers would have to pay, there would be no way to convince people it's a good idea."

This next part was the delicate bit. Harper bit her lip. "Along with that rumor, I heard something else. Someone earnestly wants to get this deal done. They are willing to go to great lengths to do it."

"Yes, they are very keen on it."

"I've heard they might try blackmail. Is there anything that they might have on you to force you to make the deal happen?"

Susan scoffed. "They're hardly likely to try blackmail. That's ridiculous. That is a silly rumor."

"It's really not a rumor." Harper pushed, "Is there anything they could blackmail you with?"

"What do you mean it's not a rumor?"

"I overheard it being discussed as an option if you didn't cooperate. Tell me there's nothing they can hold over you."

"There's nothing. I haven't done any business with them and all of my deals have been above board." Susan's tone was indignant.

"What about personally?" Harper hated to have to push this, but she didn't have a choice. As much as she thought Susan was short-sighted for all the sleeping around she did, that was her business. As a grown-ass adult, she didn't need anyone's approval. Susan started to protest. Harper cut her off. "No pictures? No incriminating letters or the like?

"Absolutely not." Susan was firm.

Some of the nagging pressure in Harper's chest eased. Maybe Susan wasn't as naïve in this area as she'd feared. "You're sure? No one could have taken any video or pictures secretly, maybe even while you were asleep?"

"No, I don't…" her voice petered out and all the color drained out of her face.

"What? What is it?"

"I— I usually bring men back to my place. I like to control the environment. I can kick them out when I want…" She stared sightlessly at her desk. When she met Harper's gaze again, her eyes were bleak. "Last night, he insisted we go to this hotel. The Ocean Walk Inn. I thought it was odd but went along with it. He insisted on… other things too. They were…" she stopped speaking altogether. Her skin had gone gray and she'd aged twenty years. "Oh God. Harper, what am I going to do?"

The door behind them burst open and Brenda hurried in. "Sorry, but we have an emergency. All of the stuff is being delivered to the Manor and there's no one there to help the delivery people."

"What about Mrs. Carruthers or Gina?" Harper asked.

"That's what I'm telling you. No one knows where they are."

Susan stared at Harper. "I need you to go there and see to this. You too, Brenda. This has to go well. You two need to pull this off. Take whoever else you need. We'll deal with the other stuff later. I think it won't happen today, so we have some time."

Harper stood. "Okay, but let me know if it changes. Don't do anything rash either. We'll figure this out."

Susan nodded but Harper knew she wasn't listening. This was turning into a nightmare. She could only hope Susan wouldn't do anything stupid. She couldn't protect her boss if the lady killed someone. There were limits to what she could solve.

Thirty minutes later, Harper pulled up to the gate. "Hi. It's Karl, right?"

The guard nodded.

"I hear we have a crisis brewing. I'm here to get things sorted. Can you let me in?"

He offered her a smile. "Of course. And good luck to you. You're gonna need it."

Harper tried to smile but failed as she pulled away from the gate. She was pissed that she hadn't been able to continue her conversation with Susan. She needed the name of the man in question. He was the one who held all the answers.

She pulled off and parked near Flynn's SUV. Relief breezed through her just knowing he was here. It was a comfort to her to know he was close by. The knots in her stomach eased slightly. Crazy how only having known him a few days, she found strength in his presence. She longed to go inside and find him and then throw herself into his arms for a big hug. Hell, she wanted to take him upstairs and spend the rest of the day in bed with him but a hug would be a good start.

Unfortunately, seven people were standing by the edge of the driveway all waiting for her to sort everything out. A hug would have to wait. Disappointment rocked through her as she waded into the crowd. "One at a time," she said and turned to a man holding a clipboard.

CHAPTER TWENTY-THREE

"And you're sure Payton left last night?" Flynn asked Shah.

"Yeah, around nine p.m. She went out through the back door. The same one Astrid came in. She got into a car and drove off. No one has seen her since. The members are worried. She had an appointment to play golf with some of the ladies today."

"Where's Gina?" Flynn asked.

"That's the other thing. No one has seen her, either." Shah shook his head. "I haven't located any video of her leaving so she's got to be here somewhere. But I have no clue where.

Flynn had an idea or two but as long as Shah was monitoring the exits, then Gina could wait. He needed to concentrate on Payton. It was far more likely that she was in danger than Gina. "Put up Payton's car on the camera. Get the plates." He glanced around the foyer, but they were alone. He dropped his voice anyway. "Call the guys in New York. Have them see if they can hack into the GPS on the car or into any traffic cameras that are around. Do the same with her cell. See if they can hack that. We need to find her ASAP."

Shah nodded. "What are you going to do?"

"I'm going to find Gina." He strode toward the kitchen at a fast clip. Making sure no one was around, he slipped into the pantry and then into the secret passage. He moved quietly, keeping his gun out in front of him. Gina had to be desperate at this point if she'd gone into hiding. That meant something had changed. She'd been confident last night but today she was missing. Either someone had taken her out and her body was stuffed somewhere or, more likely, something had happened to Payton and Gina was cutting her losses to be sure she wasn't next.

He reached the passageway outside of the small room and listened. No sound. He was pretty sure the room was empty. He moved quietly up to the doorway and took a quick peek. Unoccupied. He moved into the secret room and looked around. It was tight, no bigger than ten feet by ten feet. The walls were green. The same shade as the library. A table with four chairs was positioned in the middle of the room. A portable cart nearby had doors. He was sure if he opened it, he would see liquor. This was a meeting room.

Maybe this was where Astrid got the paint chips on her. He hadn't found the spot in the library, and he didn't see one where the paint was missing. His cell went off and he quickly silenced it. He moved swiftly over to the small holes in the wall and looked through but the library was empty. He declined the call. Archer wouldn't like that but he'd have to wait a minute until Flynn got back outside.

Retracing his steps, Flynn headed toward the tunnel that opened in the basement. He came out in the unfinished section but again, no sign of Gina. Where the hell was she? His phone went off again. He answered this time. "Archer."

"We've got Payton. She's at something called the Ocean Walk Inn. Go see her. I want updates."

"On my way." Flynn hung up and left the unfinished section to go into the security offices. "Shah," he said. The other man looked up from his laptop. "I need you to sit in front of the monitors and let me know if Gina surfaces. I've got a lead on Payton."

Shah stood. "I'll do it from the live feed in the other room."

"Let me know if you see Gina or anything else that's interesting," Flynn called over his shoulder on his way out the door.

He took the stairs two at a time. Maybe Payton was just scared and in hiding. That would be the best-case scenario. Unfortunately, the best-case scenario rarely happened in his line of work.

CHAPTER TWENTY-FOUR

Harper scanned her surroundings. Everything had come together. Crisis averted. Just another day in her work life. Tents were being erected and participating merchants were starting to set up their displays. If everything else hadn't happened, she would be overjoyed with this event. A chance for the kids to come out and celebrate Halloween in a safe space with their parents where everyone could enjoy themselves. And since Halloween wasn't until Friday night, it was a chance for parents to let the little ones enjoy themselves without being too scared and still be home to hand out candy to the older ones.

But with Astrid's murder and Calli's death, there was just too much going on in her mind. They were in the home stretch of the setup and she needed to focus. She should be done in another hour and then she was going to find Gina and get to the truth.

"Ms. Edwards," a voice said over her shoulder.

She turned. "Hi, Lazlo. What are you doing here?"

"Detective Merritt asked me to tell you that the autopsy report on Calli finally came back."

Harper's shoulders tightened. She looked all around but Jason wasn't anywhere in sight. She breathed a sigh of relief.

"He's back at the office," Lazlo supplied.

She shielded her eyes from the bright sunshine that finally decided to show itself. "What does the report say?"

"Ms. Gant died from a broken neck."

"Was it from the fall or from…something else."

A muscle jumped in Billy Lazlo's jaw. "Someone deliberately broke it, ma'am."

"Shit," Harper mumbled and closed her eyes. She swayed slightly.

"Are you okay?"

She opened her eyes again and met his gaze. "I'm fine." She looked around at all the work being done. "Let's not tell anyone, okay? No need to spoil everyone's hard work. The people of Cedar Bluff need a chance to celebrate without this cloud hanging over them."

He glanced around. "I can see that, ma'am. I won't say anything."

She reached out and touched his arm. "Thanks, Billy." Then she strode off in the direction of the Manor. She needed a moment to collect herself. This had to stop happening. These women dying. They needed to put a stop to it. Now. She squared her shoulders as she walked into the kitchen. It was time to find Gina.

CHAPTER TWENTY-FIVE

Flynn entered the Ocean Walk Inn and asked at the desk for Payton's room. The girl behind the counter gave him a small smile as she apologized to him. "I'm afraid we're not allowed to give out guest's room numbers."

"I understand. Could you call her room for me?"

The woman went to her computer and tapped away. Then she frowned. "We don't have anyone here by that name." She smiled again, showing off her white teeth. She was a cute little thing with dark hair and dark eyes. Too bad she wasn't going to be helpful. He could tell by looking at her neat and wrinkle-free white blouse and navy pants with a razor-sharp crease she was not a person who bent the rules.

"Thanks, anyway. Is it okay if I go sit in the bar?" he gestured off to the left.

"Of course. Their special today is a black magic margarita. You won't be sorry you tried it."

Without comment, he ventured into the bar area and grabbed a stool right in front of the bartender. Here he would have more luck. The guy had a scruffy beard, and his eyes were bloodshot. He looked hung over. His white shirt wasn't nearly as clean and probably had never met an iron.

"Hey," Flynn said.

"What can I get for you?"

Flynn pulled out a wad of cash and peeled off a hundred. "I need the name of a woman who's staying here. She's thin, blond, about twenty. She would've come in later last night."

"Sorry, dude. Can't help you."

Flynn peeled off another hundred. "I feel like you can. I'm not here to hurt her. I think she needs help. I want to make sure she's okay."

The bartender stared at him, as he screwed his lips up and blew out.

"Could you call her and tell her Flynn O'Connor is here. See if she wants to talk to me."

The guy stared a second longer and then went to the phone. He placed the call and spoke in a low voice. When he was finished, he came back and said, "She'd rather not at the moment."

Flynn nodded. He dropped the money on the bar and walked out. He turned immediately to his left and took the stairs two at a time. The bartender had dialed room twenty-three.

The room was tucked in the corner off the main hallway. He knocked on the door and waited. There was no response. "Payton," he said, "I need to talk to you. I'm here to help."

The sound of footsteps and then the door's chain rattling. The door opened but she stood behind it, using it like a barrier. *To what?*

He put his hand on the butt of his gun and slid inside. The door closed behind him and he turned to see Payton had been beaten to a pulp, barely able to stand up.

He immediately reached out to her and helped her to a chair by the window. "Jesus. I won't bother to ask if you're okay. You're not." He picked up his cell and placed a call. "I've got Payton. She needs care. Send someone from the medical center at the Boston location to come get her."

Archer swore. "How bad?"

"Brutal," Flynn said and hung up.

"We're going to bring people up to get you and take you to Boston for treatment."

She just stared at him.

He sat down on the foot of the bed. "Can you tell me what happened?"

She licked her lips and winced as she shifted in the chair. "Will I be in trouble?" she asked.

Her voice was quiet and raspy. He glanced at the bruises circling her throat. Someone had choked her hard enough to leave finger marks. Flynn was surprised she was still alive. And he wanted to kill whoever had done this. But it wasn't against the rules. Bile rose in his throat as he answered. "You're not in trouble. Just tell me what happened."

She nodded and then closed her eyes for a second. Opening them again, she fixed her gaze on Flynn. "He asked me to help him with a project. Said it would be safer for me away from the Manor after what happened to Calli." She swallowed. "I was scared. I thought I could be next. I didn't realize...Anyway, I agreed. He told me to meet him at this hotel. I thought he wanted a night of fun but that wasn't what he was after at all."

Flynn frowned. He didn't want to interrupt her and break the flow of the story, but he had questions. "So, he didn't want to have sex?"

"He did. Just not with me."

Flynn was confused but decided keeping silent might be better than peppering her with questions. Hopefully, she would explain it.

"I got here and texted him. He told me to come up to

this room. He'd left the key in the door. I came up and then a few minutes later, he showed up. He said he needed me to take some video and pictures. I thought it was a bit weird but whatever. Everyone's got a thing, you know? Anyway, I thought he meant of him but he said no. He handed me a cell and said when he texted me on it to come next door to room twenty-four." She pointed toward the connecting door. "He said he'd open it from the other side. Then he left."

Wincing, she readjusted in the chair. Broken ribs for sure, and possibly some broken fingers by the swelling in her hands but Flynn said nothing. Help was on the way. It was the best he could do for the moment.

"I sat down and waited but then he came back in. He said he was having problems. The woman he was here with didn't excite him and he had to get it up so could I help?" Tears sprang into her eyes. "That's sort of my job, so I agreed." He came over and gave me a cloth and told me to bite down. Then he told me I couldn't make any sound as he put on some gloves."

Flynn's stomach churned. He didn't want to hear this next part. He knew what was coming and it made him physically ill.

"He punched me really hard in the stomach. I dropped to my knees. He pulled me up by the hair and did it again into my ribs. Then he did it twice more. Then he left. I stayed on the floor. It hurt so much. Then I got the text. He opened the door and motioned me in. I didn't want to get up but I couldn't argue with him. I thought he would hurt me again. I got up and went into the other room.

"That mayor lady was tied to the bed. She was wearing a blindfold and she was naked. He kept talking to her, flirting with her as I took pictures. Then he went silent, and I filmed a video." Once I was done, he shooed me out of the room again. He came in behind me and closed the door then he pulled up my skirt and slapped my ass. He said I'd done a great job and if I waited for him, we'd go back to the Manor together. I wanted to leave but my ribs hurt, so I wasn't sure I could drive.

"He came back about an hour later and…" her voice faltered. "And did this." She gestured to herself. "The sicko gets off on the hitting. Anyway, he finished up and then went back into the room next door. He said to stay here if I knew what was good for me and he'd come pay for everything later."

She bit her lip as tears fell down her cheeks. "I wanted to leave but I can barely stand up. I've been terrified all day that he'd be back."

He'd make sure the asshole who did this suffered as much as Payton had. He'd take his time and inflict the maximum pain. Fuck the rules. He pulled out his phone. "Karl? I need another favor. You have someone who can sit on a hotel? I need a woman kept safe."

"I can call a buddy. I have the Halloween thing going on here. Which hotel?"

Flynn gave him the name of the hotel and the room number. "Medical is on the way from Boston."

"It's like that, is it?"

"Yeah," Flynn said. "Tell him to stay until they get here but do not under any circumstances let anyone else in."

"Got it," Karl agreed. "He should be there in about a half an hour."

"Great. Thanks." Flynn hung up. "I've got someone coming to watch over you until medical arrives. I will stay until he gets here. Payton, I am so sorry this happened to you. I will make the man pay, I promise." He knew he was asking a lot, but he had to know. "Who did this to you?"

She nodded and gave him the name. It was not a surprise. Flynn ground his teeth. He wanted this fucker badly. He needed to get back to the Manor as soon as possible but he wouldn't leave Payton on her own. If taking down this asshole was what caused him to have to pull the ripcord and disappear then he was fucking fine with that. It would be worth it.

CHAPTER TWENTY-SIX

Harper's arms crossed over her chest as she stared through the salon's French doors toward the area where the tents were set up. She'd searched the house, but Gina was nowhere to be found. She'd even asked Karl at the gate if Gina had left but he said she hadn't. That meant she needed to search the secret passages. Part of her wanted to wait for Flynn. She wanted his strength and his protection. She always felt better when he was around. Harper knew she was going to have to face what that meant at some point, but not right now.

"Ms. Edwards," a voice called. She turned to see a group of men sitting around a table sipping drinks. "Do come join us."

One of these men was about to blackmail Susan. The others were involved in human trafficking and God knew what else. She had no interest in talking to them but as Flynn had pointed out a few times, it was better to not let them know what she knew.

"Gentlemen, what are you up to on this fine day?"

"The sunshine is glorious," the man who'd called her over said. Fisher, if she remembered correctly.

"I don't think we've been properly introduced," Harper said and then offered her hand. "Harper Edwards."

Fisher laughed. "Of course, we all know who you are." He took her hand. "Eli Fisher." Then he went around the table to his left. "Steven Bryson, Peter Webber, and Richard Lockerby.

"Nice to meet you all. I hope you will join us this evening for our Halloween event."

"Wouldn't miss it," Fisher said.

She smiled. "Then I guess I will see you there." Turning on her heel, she headed toward the staircase into the basement. Two minutes later she was making her way quietly up the secret staircase. *Here goes nothing.*

Harper's heart hammered against her rib cage as she went to the room they'd heard the small group meeting and was disappointed to find it empty. She went back to where Flynn had scared the life out of her but there was nothing in that direction except another exit. Standing at the intersection of the two hallways, she leaned against one of the beams and tried to picture it in her head. Were there any other spaces or passageways?

She headed back to the meeting room, but this time she bypassed the doorway. It looked like a dead end but when she got closer to the end of the corridor she realized another staircase was tucked into the shadows in the corner.

Did she venture up on her own? Maybe now was the time to call Flynn. Astrid and Calli were both dead. She could be risking her life. On the other hand, they deserved answers and since she was the only one on the scene at the moment, it fell to her to get them. A fine sheen of sweat broke out on her upper body as she climbed the narrow staircase, going as quietly as possible.

It didn't take long to reach the top. Her head poked up over the low wall to the right of the staircase. This must be the attic. The roof slanted steeply on each side but the walls were green. The same hue as in the library and under Astrid's fingernails.

Harper's breathing quickened. She peered around. The single large room had a couple of double beds that were little more mattresses on the floor, with a table with four chairs in the middle. Dust motes danced in the beam of sunlight streaming in from a small window at the far end of the room. The only window, Harper noted.

She climbed the rest of the staircase and entered the attic space looking for any signs that Astrid had been there. She walked to the window. There were scratches in the frame. Nausea twisted in Harper's stomach. This is where they held her. Poor Astrid. At least she left something of herself behind. There would be DNA in the scratches on the wall. That should be enough to prove she'd been here and held against her will. Now, maybe she could figure out who had held Astrid and then killed her.

Turning, Harper stopped dead. Gina had snuck up behind her and was holding a gun pointed right at her belly. "How did you get up here?" she demanded.

The urge to scream and run right through the woman was almost irresistible. Blood hammered away through her veins. Her hands started to shake. She took a trembling breath and then said, "The same way you did. Why are you hiding, Gina?"

Gina's eyes darted all around. "Who says I'm hiding?"

"No one can find you and we've been looking. I'd call that hiding. Why? What are you so afraid of?" Harper glanced at the gun and willed her hands to stop shaking.

Gina pressed her lips together and shook her head.

Harper pressed on. "Is it Fisher? Or Davis? Are you afraid they'll kill you because you fucked up with Astrid and Calli?"

She snorted. "Fisher and Davis like me. They need me. I'm good at what I do. I know how to wrangle the girls. I'm not worried about them."

"Who are you worried about then?"

Gina just glared at her.

Harper decided to try a different tact. "What happened to Calli? I get the feeling that wasn't planned."

"Stupid, stupid girl thought she could blackmail me."

Blackmail? "What did she have on you?"

Gina clamped her mouth shut.

"But you didn't kill her."

"All she had to do was tell us where the pictures were, that was it, but she refused. Stupid girl."

"Someone killed her. Before she went down the stairs. The autopsy is in. She was dead when you threw her body over the railing. You even screamed to make it seem real but the medical examiner said she died by a broken neck not caused by the fall."

"He got frustrated. Lost his temper." She rubbed her temple.

"Headache?"

Gina frowned. "Men just suck. If he'd just kept his temper in check then we wouldn't be in this mess. He got mad with Astrid, too. She was the perfect test of our whole plan, and he got pissed off with her. Stupid. And then you!" She gestured with the gun and Harper's breath froze. "You just had to bring the cops here. I tried pushing you down the stairs to shut you up, but you refused to fall. It's all your fault I'm in this mess."

Bitch. This woman had tried to kill her! She wanted to scream and rage at Gina, but she knew it wouldn't get her anywhere. "It was his fault. All that planning you did, and he messed it up. That's a tough one to swallow."

"Are you trying to be my friend now?" Gina waved the gun again with a demented chuckle.

"Just trying to find out the whole plan for Astrid." She told the truth. Gina was too smart to believe her lies.

"Astrid wanted to have fun. To stay at the Manor for the summer and experience life. That's what she said. He saw her at The Clam Shack and was smitten. Chose her to be our guinea pig. I told him a local girl was not a good choice, but the stubborn man wouldn't listen. So she came here and then got upset. He lost his temper and killed her. She was supposed to go out through the tunnel to the boat waiting on the beach, but the storm fucked all that up. She was here too long and started to panic."

"So... Astrid panicked and he killed her. Calli tried to blackmail you and him and he killed her? Is that what happened? Who is it? Who is *he*?"

"I thought you'd never ask," a voice said as it came out of the shadows. Harper hadn't heard him coming up the stairs. He came out from behind Gina. Harper's mouth went dry. Richard Lockerby was also holding a gun.

"Yes, it's me. And yes, I have a temper. It did get the better of me a few times lately but I'm trying to keep it under control." He glanced at Gina. Her eyes were wide and her hand shook.

"Get over there with Harper." He gestured with the gun. "Oh, and you can leave your gun on the floor.

Gina bent down slowly and dropped the gun. Then she walked over to stand beside Harper. Her whole body shook.

"In my defense, things did not go smoothly, and I hate when that happens, don't I, Gina?" The other woman nodded. "Like last night for instance. Gina was supposed to help me with something but I couldn't find her, so I had to ask Payton. Poor girl had no idea what she was getting into. She's still alive by the way, Gina. Couldn't kill her yet. Too many bodies. But I have plans for her. She's too hurt to leave the hotel. I'll get her later."

He waved his gun again, finger wrapped around the trigger.

Harper prayed the safety was on.

Lockerby sighed dramatically. "But you, you were supposed to help me. I don't like being let down." His eyes went flat and Harper's knees wobbled.

She deeply regretted not waiting for Flynn. *Flynn* she thought, *where are you?*

CHAPTER TWENTY-SEVEN

Worried, Flynn surveyed all the tents, then asked a young woman with a clipboard, "Have you seen Harper?"

The woman frowned. "No, and I am going to kill her when I find her for leaving me to deal with all of this by myself."

His gut tightened. "Is Susan here?"

"She's on her way and she's livid. She can't reach Harper either."

Flynn turned and headed for the house. Harper was missing. Not good. Every nerve in his body jangled, knowing she was in trouble. He didn't need the gift of knowing inherited from his parents to realize that. No doubts she'd gotten fed up with waiting and just barreled on ahead with her own agenda. And now she was missing. Icy fingers clutched at his heart.

"O'Connor."

Someone called his name. He ignored it. Harper was more important than anything else.

"O'Connor," the call came again. Louder this time.

He wanted to keep going but he felt someone coming up beside him. He stopped abruptly and turned. George Crawley was huffing from trying to catch up to him. Beside him stood Billy Lazlo.

"What do you need?" he demanded.

"We want to talk to Harper. Have you seen her?"

His radar pinged erratically. Trouble. "What do you want to speak to Harper about?"

"A woman is making some claims about Jason Merritt and we understand Harper might be able to shed some light on it."

This was not the time. "I just got here myself. I have no idea where she is. If I see her, I'll let you know."

He turned and went through the French doors into the salon. Fisher and his cronies were sitting at a table having a cocktail. He nodded to them but kept moving down to the basement and into Shah's office.

"Gina hasn't shown up yet."

Flynn sat down. "I need to find Harper. When was the last time you saw her?"

Shah frowned. "A while ago. She was walking all over the house searching for Gina."

Closing his eyes, Flynn willed his heart rate down and took some deep breaths to try and clear his head. She was looking for Gina. She must have gone into the secret passages. The kitchen was busy with party prep. She must have entered the tunnels through the basement. He'd like to know when but if he asked Shah to pull up that camera then he'd have to explain and he didn't have time for that.

Shah was way ahead of him. "This is the last time she was on camera. She's heading into the unfinished section of the basement. What the hell?" He looked at Flynn.

"Thanks," he said and got up. He started out of the office.

"Do you need some help?" Shah was standing now too.

"You got a gun?" Flynn asked.

Shah paled. "I can get one out of the gun locker if you want, but why do I need a gun?"

"Do it and stay by your phone. I'll call or text if I need help. Watch the cameras. If anything weird happens, I'll need your help."

"What do you mean by weird?" Shah asked but Flynn was already on his way down the hallway.

Two minutes later, he stood in front of the door to the secret passages. Nothing happened when he tapped the button with his foot. "What the fuck?" Flynn tried again but it didn't work. He bent down and tried the button again but nothing. He put his hand on the wall and there was a slight vibration but then it stopped. He looked down and noticed dust bunnies floating across the floor. He put his fingers down by the bottom of the wall. A cool breeze went over them.

What the fuck was going on?

CHAPTER TWENTY-EIGHT

"Now I am going to get you both to go down the stairs. We can't stay up here. First though, I want you two to take this rope," he tossed them a piece of rope that was several feet long. "And tie your hands together with it. Gina, you know what I mean."

Gina took the rope and gestured to Harper to put her arms out in front of her. She did so reluctantly. Gina looped the rope around her wrists and made some fancy knot. Then she took the other end and handed it to Harper. "Take it and loop it around my wrists."

Harper did as she was told but when it came to knot-tying, she was hopeless. Lockerby came over and rested the gun on the windowsill as he knotted the rope around Gina's wrists.

He retrieved the gun and stepped back. "This is how this is going to go. You are going to go down the stairs. Gina first. You're going to do exactly as I say, and if you try to run or escape I will shoot Harper. Gina, you will never be able to drag her and get away. Harper, the same goes for you. If you try anything, I'll shoot Gina and you will have to drag her body. Does everyone understand?"

Both women nodded but stayed silent. Harper had no clue what the hell Gina was thinking but her own mind was frantically searching for some sort of plan. Any kind of plan that didn't involve her dying.

"Why did you kill Astrid?" she asked. "And why did you bury her on the bluffs?"

Lockerby lined them up and then nudged Gina. "Walk slowly." He glanced at Harper. "In point of fact, I did not kill Astrid. Someone else did that and then buried her. I'd have just tossed her body into the ocean and let the fishes feed on her corpse."

They'd arrived at the top of the stairs. Gina took the first step down and then the second which made her pull on the rope and Harper stumbled down the stairs, hitting Gina in the back and knocking her down the next two steps into the wall on the landing with Harper directly behind her.

Lockerby cackled. "Now you know how hard this is. Don't do anything stupid. Walk slowly."

Gina righted herself and then moved, taking the next set of steps one at a time. Harper kept her balance this time. They made it safely to the bottom. *If Lockerby didn't kill Astrid, who did?*

"So you just had your fun with Astrid and then someone else killed her?" she asked, her voice soft.

"That sums it up nicely."

They moved quietly along the hallway. Harper wanted to scream and shout and kick the walls but she knew Lockerby would probably shoot her before anyone came to her rescue. And there was Gina to think about. As much as she loathed the woman, she did not want Lockerby to kill her.

"Go straight," Lockerby said when they came to the intersection between passages.

They were going to the basement door. Maybe she could attract some attention when they left the unfinished part. Surely someone would see them, wouldn't they?

They got to the top of the stairs when Lockerby told them to stop. "Up against the wall," he ordered and then proceeded to move past them. He tweaked Harper's breast painfully on the way by.

She hated this man with every fiber of her being. Adrenaline poured anew into her. She wanted to vomit. He did the same to Gina. Gina looked away and met Harper's gaze. In this, she was a victim, too. That thought came out of left field, but Harper knew it to be true. Whatever Gina was doing, she felt she had no choice. However she got involved, she was not here by choice. It didn't excuse anything, but it sure gave Harper more context.

Lockerby went down to the second to last step and leaned over to the side wall. He touched the far side of the door frame and after a quiet click, a second door swung open, blocking the first one. The smell of saltwater hung in the air and the sound of waves reached Harper. He was taking them through the tunnel to the beach.

Fear sweat broke out across her body. This was not good. The beach was secluded. In order to see anyone by the rocks, the person needed to be standing on the edge of the bluff. With all the cars and commotion of the event, everyone would be looking the other way toward the tents. They weren't even letting cars up the driveway. They were parking down by the trees and having people walk across the open lawn to the tent area. It was a never-ending nightmare.

"Move," Lockerby said and waved his gun at them. Gina stumbled forward. Harper waited a beat and then followed along. They got to the bottom of the stairs. Lockerby stood in the doorway. Gina hugged the opposite wall trying to get past without touching him. He laughed as she shrank by. "There was a time when you wanted my touch."

"Don't kid yourself," Harper said without thinking her words through. "She was paid to make you happy."

Lockerby glared at her. She tried to move by him, but he pinned her to the wall and pressed his body into hers.

He put his face right next to hers and whispered, "Be careful, honey. You don't want to make me angry. It will be much worse for you." Then he bit her ear.

She pushed at his chest trying to get him off her. The hallway was too narrow to get any leverage. She tried to knee him in the balls but that didn't work either.

He grabbed her by the hair and yanked her head back. "You want to be feisty? Then you and me are going to have some fun." He shoved her forward and she banged into Gina. The two started walking again.

This part of the passage was solid rock, damp, and smelled of mold. The single hanging bulbs did little to illuminate the surroundings. The path was dark, dank and slippery. Gina's feet skidded out from under her and she ended up on her ass. Harper managed to catch herself and just leaned down to help Gina up as best she could.

"Almost there," Lockerby chortled.

A slight bend in the tunnel meant Harper couldn't see the water but the sound of waves crashing was getting louder, as was the smell of the salt and seaweed. As they moved around the bend and the beach came into view, Harper's heart sank. They weren't on the beach. The water came right into the tunnel. A small motorboat was tied up to a ring fixed in the rock. They were beyond a jut out in the bluff, so no one would be able to see them from the Manor, even if they were on the bank. They'd have to walk almost over to the next property.

Gina halted at the edge of the water. She would have to

jump the rock slab on the side of the tunnel to get to the boat if she didn't wade through the water. Lockerby came up behind her. "Move," he said.

"I can't. Not with my hands tied. I can't jump to the side. I'll have to go through the water."

Lockerby came up next to her and put the gun to her head. "I don't care if you're going to get wet. Move!"

Gina let out a strangled sob and started into the water. Harper reached out and pulled her back. She turned on Lockerby.

She was done with this. "Listen, asshole. If she goes through the water there's no way for either of us to get into the boat. Our hands are tied and the water is at least to my waist. It will be higher on her," Harper snarled.

Lockerby glared at her. He raised his gun in his hand and started to bring it down toward Harper's face. She tried to twist away.

Someone behind them yelled. "Freeze!"

Lockerby whirled around and lost his footing on the mossy stones. Harper tried to lunge toward him to knock him further off balance, but Gina's weight brought her up short and she barely managed to stay on her feet.

"I said freeze. The next person that moves gets a bullet to the head." George Crawley stepped out of the shadows.

Harper sagged with relief. "Oh, thank God. George, arrest Lockerby. He killed Astrid."

Lockerby smiled slowly at her. "Like I said before, I did not kill Astrid." He gestured with his gun toward George. "He did."

CHAPTER TWENTY-NINE

With his hand on the wall, Flynn felt the vibration once again. He'd thought he heard voices but couldn't be sure. He put his fingers on the floor and the breeze was gone. He pulled out his gun and hit the button one more time. The wall swung open. He went up the stairs to the third step and waited for it to close again. He was about to keep going up when he noticed a wet mark on the floor. A splash of water that was spread in an arc.

He came back down and examined the floor. There were faint grooves cut into the rough pavement. He touched the wall adjacent to the wet mark. Could this be a door, too?

Running his fingers over the surface, he looked for some way to open it. It took him a few minutes until he finally stumbled onto the button on the other door jamb. He hit it and the door swung inward blocking the other door. Ah, that's why it wouldn't open.

Flynn put his gun up and walked slowly into the other tunnel. The smell of seawater hit his nose along with the sound of the surf. He walked a few steps and then the sound of voices reached him. He inched his way carefully to the slight bend in the tunnel. Years of training had him plastered against the wall, and wishing he had a periscope mirror. He settled for a quick look-see around the corner.

Lockerby was there with Gina and Harper. His knees gave a momentary wobble and he darted back out of sight. He leaned against the stone wall of the tunnel. She wasn't out of the woods but at least she was alive. There was another voice. It was familiar, but he couldn't place it. Not with the sound of the waves nearly drowning it out. He crouched low and snuck another quick peek. Harper and Gina were tied together which made things more difficult. Lockerby was standing slightly to one side which was better, but the other man remained hidden in the shadows.

He stayed low and tried to hear what was being said but it was no use. He needed to get closer but the light was in his eyes. If he went in, he'd be blinded for a few seconds and that could be deadly. He was just going to have to stay low and risk it. Not the best plan but Harper's life was at stake. He needed to get her out of there.

Harper was dumbfounded. "You killed Astrid? Why, George?" She just couldn't get her brain around it.

"Because he'd beaten her so badly, she would never be the same. It was a mercy killing. She'd suffered massive blows to the head. If she survived, she'd have been a vegetable. There was no way she'd want to live like that. It would kill Paul. Her father is a good man. He didn't need to go through that."

"Why didn't you give him the choice? You could've taken her to a hospital. She might have pulled through. You don't know what might have happened."

George said, "I've been at this a long time. I know what

the chances were that she'd survive and I'm telling you she was better off." He gestured with his gun toward Lockerby. "He's an animal."

She agreed with him on that score but still couldn't get her brain wrapped around the rest. "Why were you involved with these people in the first place?"

Lockerby grinned. "Why don't you tell her about that, Crawley?"

"I made a mistake, Harper. And they offered help, but it came with a price. I've been paying for a while now."

"That's why the investigations into the robberies and everything else have been so slow. You were doing it for them."

George sighed and then nodded.

"We own his ass," Lockerby gloated as he turned toward Harper. "Now get *your* ass in the boat."

She looked at George. Was he going to help her?

He had a hangdog look on his face as he shook his head. "Sorry, Harper. Nothing I can do."

"Is the entire police force corrupt?" she snarled.

Gina stared at her. "What the fuck does that matter? Just get into the damn boat."

Harper frowned. Why would Gina want to get into the boat? She looked down where Gina was standing in the water. Her feet had to be frozen. The North Atlantic at the end of October was icy.

"Jason been stalking you?" George asked.

Harper turned back to him. "What? Yes. He has."

"That boy has a problem. Known about it for a while."

"But you didn't do anything. That makes you an asshole." Harper snarled. "Why turn him in when he turned a blind eye toward what you were doing."

"Enough," Lockerby yelled. "It's time to go. Get in the fucking boat."

Gina turned and walked over toward the side of the tunnel where the elevated flat rocks were, dragging Harper into the water with her. She clamored up onto the rocks and half-dragged, half-helped Harper up as well. Lockerby was about to jump to the rocks when Flynn came up behind him and put a gun to his head. "Freeze, Asshole."

Harper had never been so happy to see someone in her whole life. Her knees weakened and she sagged against the cave wall in relief. Gina turned and stared at her. "What are you happy about? He's one of them."

"One of them? What do you mean? He's not part of Fisher's group."

"No, but he's part of the Society. He's one of their enforcers."

Society? Enforcers? What was she talking about?

"Put it down, Lockerby. You too, Crawley."

"Shoot him," Lockerby demanded. "Shoot him, Crawley."

Flynn pushed the gun harder into the side of Lockerby's skull. "He's not going to shoot me. This is his chance to get rid of you. I'm not the cops. Gina's right. I'm with the Society and you've broken the rules. You're not allowed to kill someone on the premises. The penalty is death." After listening to what Crawley said Lockerby had done to Astrid, Flynn had no qualms about taking the man out.

"Kill him, Crawley. It's not just me. Fisher and Davis have the information too. You won't be free if I die."

George raised his gun. "Man's got a point."

"So what? You're going to kill all of us? You going to try and bury us too? Isn't that how you got your hernia in the first place?" Crawley was off his rocker if he thought he could manage all that.

Flynn glanced at Harper. Her mouth was hanging open and her eyes were wide. Now she knew the truth. It killed him that she had learned of his role, but it was better this way. It didn't matter that his heart physically cracked in his chest. This was who he was, and the sooner she understood that the better for the both of them.

Harper stared at him and then started to cough. Bending over, she slipped and fell into the cold water, dragging Gina with her. They both went under and came back up thrashing, trying to get their footing. Flynn wanted to jump in to get her but he didn't dare take his focus off Lockerby. The water was only waist deep. She just needed to get to her feet. His heart was pounding in his chest watching her and then there was movement out of the corner of his eye. Crawley was raising his gun.

The sound of the gunshot was deafening in the enclosed space. Harper and Gina froze. She looked at Flynn. He was still standing there. He hadn't fired. Did George Crawley shoot him? Was Flynn okay? She fell to her knees in the water and dragged herself back. She pulled Gina along with her trying to get to him. He had to be okay. If Flynn was hurt, or worse…

There was a sound and she spun to the right. George was staring down at the growing stain on his shirt. He'd dropped his gun and slid down the wall. Flynn nodded toward the doorway. "Thanks."

"No problem. Sorry I was a bit late. Hard as hell to find this place," Billy Lazlo said as he walked through the water coming deeper into the cave.

Harper stared. Gina was shivering beside her. They needed to get out of the water.

Flynn turned to Lockerby. "Now we have to deal with you." He still had the gun to the man's head.

"You've got nothing on me. I didn't kill Astrid. You can't prove I did. Gina don't say a thing. They can't prove anything."

Flynn looked at him. "Do you honestly think we're going to hand you over to the cops?"

Confusion lit Lockerby's face. "But he's a cop. He shot Crawley to protect you."

Lazlo snorted. "I'm not a fucking cop. Well, I guess I am. But I'm also Society." He pulled himself out of the water next to Crawley and then squatted down and checked for a pulse. He looked up at Flynn. "He's dead."

Flynn nodded. "As I said, you broke the rules. The punishment is death." He pulled the trigger and Lockerby dropped to the ground. Half in and half out of the water.

Harper's whole world flipped on its axis. She gasped for breath and flailed for something to hold on to. Flynn waded into the water and pulled her and Gina out. He untied her hands and put his arm around her. "I'll take Harper back to the house. There's a cleanup crew on the way."

"Got it. I'll keep this one here with me." Lazlo nodded toward Gina, who was shivering with her hands still tied.

Flynn walked with Harper back through the tunnel. She wanted to yell at Flynn, to rage at him for lying to her, for killing Lockerby in front of her. For leaving her all alone with him. But she could barely stand. She was freezing and in shock. He opened the door and sat her on the steps until the door to the tunnel closed.

"When we go out there, not a word to anyone. No one will ask you any questions. You can never speak about any of this to anyone. If you do, I won't be able to protect you."

She stared at him. She couldn't think. Couldn't speak. How could he tell her this stuff now?

"I'm going to take you back to your condo. You weren't feeling well and went to lie down in one of the rooms upstairs. I took you home. Do you understand?

No. She didn't understand. She didn't understand a damn thing. But she just stayed silent. He turned and opened the door. Shah was standing on the other side, gun in hand. "I need a blanket," Flynn said.

Shah took one look at Harper and sprinted away. He was back before they'd cleared the unfinished area, with a thick, woolen blanket.

"I'm going to take her home. Hold things down here. Let me know if there are any issues."

Shah nodded. "Understood."

Flynn wrapped Harper in the blanket and then tucked her under his arm. He guided her upstairs, out the door, and into his rental. Twenty minutes later he walked her into her condo. "I'll stay here until you're settled. You're safe."

She nodded and started walking toward the stairs. It was so fucking overwhelming she didn't know what to do or what to think. She went up the stairs and straight into her bathroom. She turned on her shower and peeled off her wet clothes. Once under the hot spray, she stared sightlessly at the wall. She stayed that way for a long time. Finally, as the water temp cooled off, she washed her hair and the rest of her. Her hands had stopped shaking and her teeth finally quit chattering. Rinsing off for a final time, she turned off the water and climbed out of her shower. A hot cup of tea had been left on the counter.

Harper stared at it and then promptly burst into tears.

CHAPTER THIRTY

"I spoke with Lazlo. The cleaners arrived. Everything has been handled," Flynn said as he drove back toward Everlasting Manor. "He's bringing Gina down to you. Or he'll do whatever you decide is necessary."

"Yes, I spoke with him," Archer said.

"You might have given me the heads up about him." Flynn was ticked off that Archer hadn't trusted him enough to tell him the truth about the young cop. Although, if truth be told, he should have realized it at the very beginning. He had the look of a killer. *Takes one to know one.*

"You're pissed. I get that, but the whole point of men like Lazlo is to blend in and be support if needed. I sent him there months ago to get a bead on what was going on. I knew Fisher and Davis were up to something. Lazlo's job was to find out what without them knowing. If I told you about him, it could have blown his cover."

"Thanks for the vote of confidence," Flynn snarled.

"Flynn, there are things going on that are extreme, even for the Society. I don't have all the pieces of the puzzle...yet. I will not do anything to jeopardize the chances of me finding out what's going on. Live with that or get the fuck out."

Flynn still was pissed, but frankly, it was less at Archer and more at himself. The whole situation made him want to vomit. Maybe he should do as Archer had suggested. Although it wasn't that easy. Archer's version of getting the fuck out usually ended up six feet under in some unmarked grave. It might be time to pull the pin. Get as far from the Society as he could. And as far from Harper as physically possible. The look on her face after he shot Lockerby slayed him. The horror at what he'd done. He could have gotten her out of there and let Lazlo do the deed, but she needed to know the truth. There was no future for them if she didn't understand who he really was. Now, there was just zero future for them.

"How is Harper?"

"She'll be okay. It will take her a while to get over it but she'll come around."

Archer's voice changed. "We have a problem. Harper knows about us now. We can't let that stand."

"I've got news for you; Harper knew about us before. She knew all about the Society from her ex-boss William Findley. Apparently, the man gets blackout drunk and tells anyone who will listen about the Lock and Key Society."

Archer swore. "I'll take appropriate action with Mr. Findley. However, that doesn't solve our Harper problem."

Flynn's pulse pounded in his ears. Adrenaline shot into his veins. "We don't have a Harper problem. I just told you. She already knew about the Society and she won't say anything."

"It's not that simple."

"It is that fucking simple. Harper Edwards is not a threat," he growled.

"I understand you care for her, but we have rules. You

need to follow them. Harper can't know about the Society and not be a member or an employee. Out of respect for you, I will offer her membership or a job. I'll give you a few days to get it sorted but I need an answer by the end of the week." Archer clicked off the call.

Flynn slammed his hand on the steering wheel. How the fuck was he going to get Harper to have anything to do with the Society? He had no fucking clue. He'd thought Harper was safe. That he could survive because he knew she was safe now. He'd thought this nightmare was over, but it had gone from bad to a hell of a lot worse.

CHAPTER THIRTY-ONE

Harper sat on her deck wrapped in a thick blanket and stared out at the waves. It was Friday morning and she should have been back at work, but she'd told Susan she still had a cold and she didn't want to bring it to the office.

The local newspaper was on the table beside her being held in place by her mug of tea. The headline screamed "Death of a Local Hero." It was a story about how George Crawley had died in a car crash on his way home from the Halloween Extravaganza. The press speculated he'd had a heart attack brought on by his excessive weight, and poor eating habits, along with the extra stress of his recent surgery.

"Would you like some of Kim's coffee?"

She jumped to her feet and whirled around. Flynn stood in the middle of her living room. "You could've knocked.

"I did. For the last couple of days. You won't answer. I thought it best to just come in."

"Well, you can just leave again." She wrapped herself in the blanket and sat down again.

Flynn came out and put the coffee on the table next to her. Then leaned against the railing blocking her view of the water. He was wearing a pair of faded jeans and a navy sweater, and he looked so damn good she wanted to jump into his arms. She hated him for it since she was wearing sweats and hadn't brushed her hair in a couple of days. She hated herself more for noticing how good he looked and smelled. Life was just not fair.

"How did you manage it?" She pointed to the paper. "Crawley died in a car accident? Seriously?"

Flynn just stared at her.

"And I supposed the bit about Jason taking a job with the Boston Police Department was you guys, too?"

Again, he said nothing.

"They're bringing a retired detective back to run the department until they can find some new people. I suppose Billy Lazlo will leave too sometime soon. Was that even his real name?"

Flynn sipped his coffee.

"Paul will never know that the man who killed Astrid is dead. He'll never have that peace of mind. How can you live with that?" she demanded. "I just don't get it."

"You through?" he asked. "I can't discuss any of this stuff, not on your balcony. You wanna go inside so I can tell you some things."

She glared at him but jumped up and marched into her house. He grabbed her tea and came in behind her. He set the mug on the small dining table and then closed the doors.

"First, I don't know how they made Crawley's death look like a heart attack caused a car accident. It's not my department. Second; yes, Jason's going to Boston was me. I have someone who will keep an eye on him there and if he steps out of line, there will be consequences. He is aware of that. I assume Lazlo will leave in a month or two and I have no idea if Lazlo is his real name, but I highly doubt it."

"As to Paul knowing the truth, in a few months when

things die down, he will receive a phone call. The person will tell him that Astrid got mixed up in something that she shouldn't have, through no fault of her own. He'll be told that the person responsible is dead and he'll be told that there is a scholarship fund being set up in her name at the university she was going to attend. He will be given a number to call should he ever need help with anything. He will be told that his family is owed a debt that cannot be paid but that we will try should he ever call. It is the best we can do."

Harper stared at him. It wasn't a trial or a guilty verdict, but it was better than nothing. She ran her hands over her face. "I just don't… I can't process it all."

"I know. It will take a while."

She crossed her arms over her chest. "When do you leave town?"

"Tonight. The Rainy Day Club is closing. The official press release goes something like, "After the death of Calli Gant, the Rainy Day Society had thought it best to close Everlasting Manor for a while." It will never reopen. It will be sold.

"So that's it, huh? Everything wrapped up in a neat little bow?"

"There's one thing left to deal with," Flynn said.

"What could that possibly be?" she demanded.

"You."

Her heart thudded against her ribcage and fear tingled down her spine. Was Flynn here to kill her?

Flynn stared at her, trying to gauge her reaction. She looked exhausted with the dark circles under her eyes and her hair a mess. She also looked so damned beautiful and vulnerable he just wanted to pull her into his lap and tell her everything would be okay.

She blinked and backed up. Her eyes widened and her gaze started pinging all around the room searching for something...a weapon maybe? Did she think he was here to hurt her?

He spread his hands wide, palm out. "I'm not here to hurt you," he said.

Just having to say those words cut him. That she would think he could do that to her. It answered every question he had about the state of their relationship. They didn't have one. It was as if someone hit him in the chest with a two-by-four. He sat down hard on one of the counter stools. A few days ago they'd had sex on that counter. Now she thought he was going to kill her. The whiplash was incredible, and it wasn't something he was going to recover from anytime soon.

She stared at him through narrowed eyes. "Then what do you mean that you have to deal with me?"

"Do you think I could hurt you?" He shouldn't have asked the question, but it just slipped out.

She paused. "Ye... I just don't know."

He swallowed the rising nausea. Maybe that was fair, but it fucking hurt. He cleared his throat. "You know about the Society. We have rules about that. So, I have been authorized to offer you membership with us, or, if you prefer, a job with us."

She reared back. "What do you mean you've been authorized? And why the fuck would I want to be a member or work with you? I don't want any association with you."

The kicks just kept coming. He gritted his teeth. "You're not understanding. You have to pick one of those two things. If you chose option three, which is to ignore both offers, then I will stay and protect you for as long as I can, but the

Society will send someone and eventually, they will kill me and then you. That's the truth."

She stared at him. "You're serious."

"Hell yes, I'm serious. If you want to refuse the offers then I will do my best to protect you for as long as possible, but a time will come when they kill me to get to you. That's just a fact."

"You'd do that for me?"

He nodded. He'd go to the end of the earth for her.

"How long do I have to decide?"

"You have until five p.m. if you want. I would highly advise you to choose membership and move on with your life. Membership does not require anything from you. You just say yes and that's it. You do not have to ever visit a location, nor do you have to speak to anyone who is involved with the Society. It's just a way to ensure your silence. If you do talk about the Society with anyone outside, it is punishable by death in extreme circumstances."

"Is there anything that isn't punishable by death?" she asked with a sneer.

"Very little. Harper, join the Society and keep your mouth shut. That's all you have to do. You'll never see me or anyone else from Lock and Key ever again." *Just do it*. He pulled the papers out of his pocket. "Sign it, Harper. It's the easiest way out." He needed her to sign it so he knew she'd be safe. He couldn't stand the thought she might be in danger. She wasn't the only one in the room not sleeping.

She bit her lip. Then she nodded. He handed her the paper, and she picked up a pen from the counter and signed her name. She handed the papers back to him. "Now what?"

"Now you never have to see me again." He stood. His chest hurt and he rubbed it. "Take care of yourself, Harper. If you ever get into any kind of trouble, call me. Otherwise, have a nice life." He turned and headed for the door. He desperately wanted her to call out to him, to stop him from leaving, But he heard nothing but silence. Emotion rampaged through him as he opened the door and then closed it behind him, leaving his heart behind.

CHAPTER THIRTY-TWO

Harper stared out her office window at the square below. The spring sunshine glistened off the dew on the flowers. It was a glorious day and she should be happy. Work was going well. Since the whole debacle with the almost blackmail, Susan had calmed down. She was doing an exceptional job as mayor and even getting along with Chief Clark. Everything was cruising along nicely. So why was she so damned depressed?

She let the sun warm her face in the hopes that the heat would warm her insides, but she knew it wouldn't. She was hollow. That's what it was. Like there was a great gaping hole in the middle of her chest that had turned to ice and nothing she did could warm it.

"Harper, do you have the file on the new jetty?" Susan asked as she walked into the office.

"Um, yes. Here." She swiveled her chair and handed the folder to Susan.

The other woman stared at her. "You know ever since that cold you had at Halloween, you haven't been yourself. I have a friend that's a specialist down in New York City. I want you to go see her."

Harper smiled at her boss. "I don't need a specialist, but thanks."

Susan shrugged and started out of the office. "Don't forget we have a three-thirty with Jed about the Spring Fling."

"I'll be there," Harper called. She stared at the door Susan just had just gone through. *New York City*. She hadn't been to New York in an age. Maybe it would be fun to go. She bit her lip. The truth was she wanted to see Flynn and maybe if she went to New York she could bump into him. *Grow up*, she told herself firmly. In a city of millions of people, the likelihood of her running into Flynn was astronomical.

But if she went to a Society location she'd have a better chance. Did she want to do that? Could she accept who Flynn truly was? It was the question she'd wrestled with for the last five months and had yet to come up with an answer. She was tired of feeling sad and hollow however, and if being with Flynn made her happy, wasn't that better? It was the same argument that went round and round in her head almost daily.

Susan came back into her office. "Harper, it's none of my business but I'm gonna tell you something that you seem to need to hear. Life is for the living. Grab it by the balls and have the best damn time possible. You only get to come this way once. You were right, I was fucking up at work. Now I fuck outside of work and I am so much happier." She grinned. "Do what makes you happy and stop worrying about what the world thinks."

Harper stared at her boss. Was that the real hang up? She was worried what people would think if she were with Flynn?

He was a killer. Didn't that make him a bad man? Not necessarily. Look at the scum he'd killed. It was like someone had lifted a thousand pound weight off her shoulders.

"Susan," she said as she got up from her desk. "Thank you." She hugged the other woman tightly for a moment. "I won't see that specialist, but I am going to New York," she said with a wink. "I'll see you next week." With that, she breezed out of the office.

Five hours later, she landed at LaGuardia Airport. About a week after she'd signed the papers with Flynn, a package had been hand-delivered. It was a USB stick with the rules of the Society on it that disappeared once she closed the file again, and a phone number along with a small silver seagull. She was to call the number and they would tell her where the nearest Society location was, or so the note said before it too disappeared.

Harper caught a cab into the city and placed the call. "I would like a location in Manhattan, please." Butterflies took flight in her stomach.

"Any particular type?"

"I'm not sure. I'm new to this." Crap was she supposed to know what each type was? Where the hell had that been written?

"Okay, Ms. Edwards, you have a few options. There's a—"

"I want to see Flynn O'Connor. I want the location he is at," she blurted out.

There was silence on the other end of the phone. "Hold please." There was nothing but silence for two long minutes. Her stomach was churning. Was she crazy for doing this? The operator clicked back on the call and gave her an address for a hotel in Union Square. "Talk to Gerard at the concierge desk. He is expecting you."

Twenty minutes later, she walked into the hotel and asked for Gerard. He smiled at her. "Ms. Edwards, lovely to see you. Right this way." He took her over to an elevator and ushered her inside. Then he hit a button and stepped out. The door closed and the elevator went down. That was unexpected. Harper's knees jellied. She closed her eyes and said a small prayer.

The doors opened to reveal a young woman smiling at her. "Right this way, please." Harper followed the woman down a hallway and into what looked like a bar area. She led Harper to a booth in the corner. As she slid in the young woman said, "We'll take your bag for you and put it in your room."

"Oh, um okay." Then the woman left the room with Harper's roller bag behind her. *Now what?* Was she supposed to order a drink? That might be good. Something to settle her nerves. She looked around but didn't see a bartender. Getting out of the booth, she made her way over to the actual bar and stood there. Maybe someone would come along.

"Harper," Flynn said.

She turned to find him standing behind her. "Oh, God."

He looked so damn fine in his jeans and white shirt with a black blazer. A day's growth of stubble shaded his jaw, but it was his eyes. She'd forgotten how dark they were. Black, and she was sure they could see into her soul.

"Is there a problem? Do you need help?" he asked. His face was neutral, but his voice held concern.

"Um, no. I...I just wanted to see you." How did she explain? She'd been in such a hurry to get here she hadn't thought this part through.

His expression became guarded. "What can I do for you?"

She stared at him. What did she say? "Um, I…" She didn't know how to start.

Flynn just stayed silent watching her.

There was no starting point. It was all a jumble in her head.

He glanced at his watch. "If you need something from me, now would be a good time to tell me. I have things to do."

"I need you to love me," she blurted out.

Flynn froze. He stared at her. Hard. There was anger in his gaze.

She was losing him. "I… it took me a while to get over what happened, but I've been miserable without you and I just needed to see you again. There's like a big frozen hole in my chest and I can't fill it. You have to fill it for me. I need you to be in my life, Flynn," she stopped speaking and sucked in oxygen.

He still hadn't moved. Not one muscle. Shit. Did he hate her? Was he going to tell her he was over her?

He took her hand, then led her down first one hallway and then another. They finally stopped in front of a door, and he opened it with a key card. It was an upscale hotel room, and her bag was by the bed.

He let go of her hand and turned to face her.

"You have a choice to make. You can stay here and accept me as I am… or you can go. This is the only chance you have to make this choice. If you go, you can never come back to me. If you stay you can never leave. I can't go through that again. Do you understand? It just about killed me to leave you back in Maine and I am still trying to put myself back together. I will never go through that again. Not ever. If you stay you are locked in permanently."

She stared up at him. Her heart pounded. A million

butterflies flitted inside of her. He was telling her this was for life. "Are you asking me if I can do forever with you?"

His expression remained neutral, but a telltale pulse jumped in his jaw. "Yes."

"Abso-fuckin-lutely," she said and then claimed his lips in a scorching kiss.

The End.

SNEAK PEEK: LOCKED OUT

A shadowy adversary with the power to unlock her destiny
just might be the key to her survival.

LOCKED OUT
CHAPTER 1

Larissa Day moved swiftly along the canal. Dense fog had settled in, cloaking Venice in a deep gray cloud. The night air was thick and cold, and she pulled her cloak tighter around her shoulders to ward off shivers. Why had she agreed to come to Venice? It had seemed so easy, so simple when she was home in New York. Now, though, she condemned her decision to travel here with every echoing step.

A splash made her halt, her footsteps falling silent on the ancient cobblestone street. She peered through the darkness, but swirling mist blocked her view. *Ridiculous,* she scolded herself. She was letting the city and the eerie layer of fog get to her.

She resumed walking forward along the canal. The note had said to follow this canal until she came to the pretty bridge. What did that mean? Whose idea of pretty? Nonetheless, she continued. So far, she'd passed only one bridge so far and the structure had been nondescript, not at all her definition of pretty.

She shivered once more in the damp darkness. The streetlights enshrouded in fog, didn't cast much more than a dim glow. She didn't bother pulling out her cell. Signal in Venice seemed to be touch and go. Besides, who would she call? Everyone she knew was a world away.

The idiocy of what she was doing clawed deeper into her soul with every step. A note that promised the truth about her birth with directions to come to Venice had appeared in her mail and she'd hopped on the first plane. Was she honestly that desperate? Her friends all told her not to go. Not by herself at least. Wait until one of them could go with her, they'd urged. But had she listened? No, she'd gone on her own.

They didn't understand. It was the not knowing. Her adoptive parents had been wonderful people and she missed them more than she could stand, but the idea of finally knowing the truth? Finally understanding where she'd come from and who her people were? That was too much of a draw to resist, to even hesitate to come.

It was the fundamental feeling she'd had about herself all her life, that she was somehow special, or maybe different was a better word, than those around her. Her adoptive parents had thought it was just fantasy, but she knew differently. That awareness hadn't gone away as she reached adulthood.

And now, a stranger had promised to tell her the truth. She'd do almost anything to find out about her origins.

Ahead, a bridge emerged from the fog. The bottom section was constructed of stone but the balustrade was done in intricate iron work. The black color made it hard to see in the darkness but as the mist lifted, she knew this was the bridge that the author of the note had meant. It was pretty. Like many bridges in Venice, this one featured love locks people had fastened on the scrolling wrought iron to declare their undying love.

She paused at the bottom of the bridge and took a deep

breath, the mist filling her lungs, and pent-up excitement making her quake. She took a tentative first step and then a second. Her thudding heart made it difficult to draw a deep breath. Would she finally know the truth?

She hurried to the top of the bridge and stood there in the gloom-shrouded night. No sound broke the muted stillness. No people, no wildlife. Not even water moving. Had the letter been a lie? Some kind of bad joke? She glanced at her watch. The note hadn't specified a time, just a day, or rather a night, and a location. Was she to wait for hours?

Time ticked by slowly. Gradually she became aware of a scent. She couldn't quite place the familiar essence. Sound shattered the night, loud and aggressive.

She turned to her right and peered into the fog. What the hell was it? Mist twisted and swirled as the sound grew louder. She took a step forward just as a form emerged from the darkness. Instinctively, she threw herself backward, losing her balance and falling over the iron railing. The canal's icy water surrounded her, flooding her nose and mouth and dragging her down into its grip. She fought to get to the surface but the water would not release its deadly, frigid grip on her. As she sank deeper, the dim light from above faded to black.

A NOTE OF THANKS

YOU READ MY BOOK. You read the whole thing! I cannot thank you enough for sticking with me. If this is the first book of mine you've read, welcome aboard. I certainly hope it won't be the last. If you are already a fan then I can only say, thank you so much for your continued support. Either way, you have made my day, my week, my year. You have transported me from writer to *author*. I feel so special. You have made my dreams come true. Genuinely, truly, you are a fairy god-parent. So thank-you!

Now I'm hoping you love this new-found power of making dreams come true and, like a truly dedicated reader, you'll check out my other series, Callahan Security, Coast Guard Recon, Coast Guard Hawai'i, and the Brotherhood Protectors World. You can find links to these books on my website, www.lorimatthewsbooks.com

If you would like to try your hand at being a superhero, you can always help make me a bestselling author by leaving a review for **Locked In** on Amazon, (My Book) or Review On Goodreads or Review On BookBub. Reviews sell books and they make authors super happy. Did I say thank you already? Just in case I forgot, thank you soooo much.

And now that you are reveling in your superhero status, I would love it if you would stay in touch with me. I love my readers and I love doing giveaways and offering previews and extra content of my upcoming books. Come join the fun. You can follow me here:

Newsletter: Signup Form (constantcontactpages.com)
Website: www.lorimatthewsbooks.com
Facebook: https://www.facebook.com/LoriMatthewsBooks
Facebook: Romantic Thriller Readers (Author Lori Matthews) https://www.facebook.com/groups/ killerromancereaders
Amazon Author Page: https://www.amazon.com/author/ lorimatthews
Goodreads: https://www.goodreads.com/author/show/ 7733959.Lori_Matthews
Bookbub: https://www.bookbub.com/profile/lori-matthews
Instagram: https://www.instagram.com/lorimatthewsbooks/
Twitter: https://twitter.com/_LoriMatthews_

ABOUT LORI MATTHEWS

I grew up in a house filled with books and readers. Some of my fondest memories are of reading in the same room with my mother and sisters, arguing about whose turn it was to make tea. No one wanted to put their book down!

I was introduced to romance because of my mom's habit of leaving books all over the house. One day I picked one up. I still remember the cover. It was a Harlequin by Janet Daily. Little did I know at the time that it would set the stage for my future. I went on to discover mystery novels. Agatha Christie was my favorite. And then suspense with Wilber Smith and Ian Fleming.

I loved the thought of combining my favorite genres, and during high school, I attempted to write my first romantic suspense novel. I wrote the first four chapters and then exams happened and that was the end of that. I desperately hope that book died a quiet death somewhere in a computer recycling facility.

A few years later, (okay, quite a few) after two degrees, a husband and two kids, I attended a workshop in Tuscany that lit that spark for writing again. I have been pounding the keyboard ever since here in New Jersey, where I live with my children—who are thrilled with my writing as it means they get to eat more pizza—and my very supportive husband.

Please visit my webpage at https://lorimatthewsbooks.com to keep up on my news.

Made in the USA
Las Vegas, NV
31 October 2023

80041566R00192